FOR
THE
LAST TIME

Also Available by Heidi Perks

The Other Guest
The Whispers
Three Perfect Liars
Come Back for Me
Her One Mistake
Beneath the Surface

FOR THE THE LAST TIME

A NOVEL

HEIDI PERKS

CROOKED
LANE

NEW YORK

Published in the United States by Crooked Lane Books, an imprint of The Quick Brown Fox & Company LLC.

Crooked Lane Books and its logo are trademarks of The Quick Brown Fox & Company LLC.

Library of Congress Catalog-in-Publication data available upon request.

ISBN (paperback): 978-1-63910-705-6
ISBN (ebook): 978-1-63910-706-3

Cover design by Nicole Lecht

Printed in the United States.

www.crookedlanebooks.com

Crooked Lane Books
34 West 27th St., 10th Floor
New York, NY 10001

First Edition: December 2023

10 9 8 7 6 5 4 3 2 1

For John

my wonderful husband

NOW—AUGUST

Raina Poole has already been working an eleven-hour shift when the red phone in the trauma centre rings. She grabs her pad, ready to take down notes, because when the red phone rings, it means that whatever is coming their way is time sensitive.

The paramedic on the other end of the line says they're blue-lighting a road traffic accident victim. They estimate they'll be at the hospital in seven minutes.

She writes quickly as he speaks: *34 y/o female pedestrian. Accident presumed pedestrian vs. car. Airway unsafe. Ventilated and sedated. Initial BP 60/30, now up to 80–90 but keeping below 100. Working diagnosis massive haemorrhage due to intra-abdominal injury.*

Raina puts the phone down and tannoys out to the resuscitation and emergency departments.

Like every other trauma nurse, Raina is dead on her feet. She's been on them for the entirety of her shift and has clocked up another twenty-three thousand steps. She had been ready to leave, but still the adrenaline hits her as it always does. It's what keeps her going, even at one thirty AM on a Sunday morning.

She races over to the main doors of Emergency in time for
the ambulance to pull up. The doors swing open, and there's
a flurry of activity to lift the stretcher out. Raina glimpses the
woman's face as she's rushed past. She's in a neck collar, intu-
bated just like the paramedic said. She'll be taken for a CT
scan straightaway so the doctors know what they're dealing
with.

Raina holds back for the police officer, who arrives within
minutes. "I'm a nurse in Resus," she tells him as she leads the
way. He'll stay with the patient so he has eyes on her, then will
want to talk to the family when they get here.

"Odd one, this," he tells her as they scurry along the corridor. "Looks like a hit-and-run, but God knows what she was
doing out in the middle of nowhere on foot. Hopefully someone will have some idea."

He waits by the doors to Resus. He can ask his questions
when the family gets here. In these precious moments Raina
knows the woman is a body to be worked on, to be cared for, a
life to be saved. She shouldn't let thoughts of who the patient
is—what family she has waiting for her or whether they even
know yet—catch her off track. But for Raina these thoughts
always come sooner or later.

The CT scanner will take only five minutes. Raina uses
the time to look through the patient notes. The woman's name
is Erin Harding. She's thirty-four years old and lives in Lexington Close, which is on the other side of town and not far
from the sea. Raina knows the area well; she has a friend who
lives near there. She likes it. She would live there herself if her
job paid the kind of money that could pay for a mortgage in
Lexington Close. It's a ten-minute drive to the beach, on the
west side of Keyport. Far enough off the through roads that
you wouldn't get troubled by holidaymakers.

Already Raina has an image in her head of who Erin
Harding is. At thirty-four, you'd be unlikely to live in one
of the three- or four-bed detached houses if you were single.

Erin has a husband and a couple of children, most likely. They have money but aren't super well-off. The houses in Lexington Close are nice, but there are other, richer neighbourhoods in Keyport. This is where you live when you have two cars and two good-enough jobs but you probably both work.

She's already doing what every nurse is told not to do and involving herself too much. But every patient has their own story. This is the part Raina can't forget. In the midst of the drama, she doesn't stop to think, but when she has the time and space, she sees life for just how very fragile it is. It's draining to absorb so much grief and anxiety day in, day out.

The scan shows that Erin Harding has a grade-four splenic injury, which means taking her straight to theatre to take her spleen out. She's already being operated on when the double doors at the far end of the corridor crash open and a man appears, looking well dressed and actually quite together for this time of the morning. But his wild eyes that frantically search Raina out tell her he's someone's family member.

"My wife's been brought in—she was in an accident. Erin—Erin Harding—"

He's out of breath, panting, pressing his hands onto the desk as he leans forward. He's slim but maybe not fit. Also in his midthirties, Raina thinks. His dark jeans and pressed white Hugo Boss top make it look like he carefully selected an outfit. It looks a little out of place, if only for the fact that Raina would expect someone in his position to be arriving in joggers and a thrown-on T-shirt, hair sticking up from getting hauled out of bed in the middle of the night. This guy doesn't have a hair out of place.

"Mr. Harding?" she says as he looks around anxiously. "Your wife is in theatre." She goes around the desk and steers him towards a family room.

"In theatre? What's happened to her? Is she okay?" He stops abruptly in the middle of the ward.

"She's been in a nasty accident," Raina says, veering him out the way of another stretcher being pushed past. "They're having to operate on her now, but I'm going to get a doctor to come and talk to you and update you."

Around them, doors crash open and phones ring as nurses run this way and that. Raina is used to it, but she can see by the way the man's eyes dart around that the constant flurry of urgent activity is alarming to him, as it is for most people who aren't used to emergency wards.

She steers him into the quiet room, then pours water into a plastic cup and hands it to him.

"Is she okay? I mean, is she *going* to be okay?" he asks again.

"As soon as she's out of theatre, we'll know more," Raina tells him.

She wonders how he got the call, if he was asleep or waiting up for his wife. Did he have to find a babysitter to come and sit with the children Raina imagines they have?

"What happened?" he asks her. A light sheen of sweat covers his forehead.

"Your wife was in a road traffic accident. It's believed she's been hit by a car."

He stares at her like he hasn't heard her. His eyes are wide and intense and such a deep chestnut brown. He is very good looking, and she finds herself wondering what he does for a living. She imagines it's something in an office, maybe financial. She can see he would look good in a suit.

"But where?" he says.

"I'm sorry, I don't know where she was found."

"I don't get it," he says, and then, "She's going to live. Isn't she?"

"Mr. Harding." Raina pauses. They are always so desperate for answers. "All I can say is that your wife is receiving the care and treatment she needs right now, and as soon as a doctor is free, he will be right in here to tell you everything."

The husband carries on staring at her. She knows her response isn't good enough for him. He slumps forward in his chair and hangs his head in his hands, one of them still gripping the plastic cup, which is now crushing into the side of his scalp. He doesn't seem to notice the water that's spilt out of it.

"What's your name?" she asks.

"Will."

"Will, can I get you anything else? A hot drink, maybe?" She carefully removes the cup from his grasp and stands it on a table.

"No. Thank you." He sucks in a breath as he leans back in his chair. "I don't get what she was doing out at this time of night," he says.

She looks at him quizzically. Had his wife gone out without him knowing?

Will closes his eyes and shakes his head. "Where was she?" he asks again.

"Were you not at home, then?" Raina asks tentatively.

"No. We're not—I don't live with her anymore," he tells her. "We're separated. I wasn't with her."

"I see."

"I don't even know why everything went so wrong. We'd started seeing a counsellor." He has a need to talk, she thinks. To explain. When he looks up at her, she sees a flash of something in his eyes, but she isn't sure what it is.

Raina thinks there must be a whole raft of thoughts going through his head right now. He still cares enough to come and see his wife. He feels guilty he wasn't with her. He's angry he doesn't know everything about her any longer. Was she the one to leave him?

"They said on the phone it was a hit-and-run."

Raina nods, remembering what the officer told her about how odd the circumstances were. How Erin Harding was alone in the middle of nowhere.

She wonders about this and what happened to their marriage, and who might be looking after the children she imagines they have. There really is so much to everyone's story, so many ways it can all go wrong, that you never see just from looking at them.

CHAPTER

1

Six months earlier
ERIN

WILL WAKES ME up by pressing his lips against my forehead. "Happy Valentine's Day," he murmurs. "I've made you a cup of tea."

"Ooh, thank you," I say, rolling over and opening my eyes. He has placed a mug on the bedside table next to me. In front of it is a white envelope with my name on, and in front of that is a small box that has been wrapped in gold paper and tied with a purple ribbon. "What's this?" I push myself to sit up and pick up the box.

"It's just something little."

"Will?" I question. "We don't do presents for Valentine's." We haven't done for years; I can't even remember if we did in the early days. "I've only got you a card," I say as I reach into the drawer of the table, pull it out, and hand it to my husband, who is now sitting on the side of the bed. I didn't even put much thought into the card—I just grabbed one that looked okay, with a picture of two penguins on it, from the card shop three days ago.

"I don't expect anything. This is just small, like I said. It's nothing. Just—" He shrugs. "Just open it."

I squint at the clock on the dressing table on the other side of the room. "What time is it?" I ask. My vision is getting blurrier. I swear it's becoming harder to see long-distance.

"Six thirty. I have to be in early this morning. The new head is arriving. She wants a quick meeting before assembly." Will is already dressed in a white shirt and grey trousers. His breath smells of toothpaste. "I just wanted to give this to you before Sadie wakes." He taps the box I'm holding.

I tug at the bow until it unravels and then peel away the paper, opening the box to find a silver charm inside attached to a chain. "What is it?" I ask automatically, because I don't wear much jewellery. The most I'll put on are chunky bracelets if I'm going out, but not necklaces with dainty little charms like this. And yet as I pull it out of its box, I see the tiniest of fingerprints pressed into it, the word *Sadie* engraved in italics underneath. "Oh my God, Will." Tears spring into my eyes.

"Do you like it?"

"Like it? I love it," I say as he laughs at me, wiping my tears that are now trickling down my cheeks with his fingertips.

"I know Valentine's is supposed to be about you and me, but—" He doesn't have to say it. It isn't about just us anymore. Since Sadie was born, it has only ever been about the three of us.

He peels back the duvet, and I shuffle over for him to get in beside me. "I thought you had to go to work," I say, leaning my head on his shoulder and turning the charm over in my hands.

"Are you happy, Erin?" he says.

"Happy?" I laugh. "Why wouldn't I be happy? I have a man I love and a daughter I adore. Oh yes, and you too, Coco," I say as my Cavapoo jumps onto the bed between us. "Why do you ask?"

He shrugs. "Just making sure."

I smile, turning the necklace over in my hands. He does this every so often. Will checks in with me, letting me know he's there, especially since Sadie was born. He always wants to make sure that if there's anything wrong, I know I can tell him.

We sit like this for a while more, not talking, just feeling the warmth of each other beside us. When he moves, I reach out for him. "Don't go," I whisper.

"I have to. I'm sorry. I'll get home early, though. I'll make dinner tonight."

"You're making a fuss about a day I don't care about."

"I'm making a fuss of *you*," he says as he stands up and bends down to kiss me. "Here, let me put the necklace on you."

I pass it to him and he unclasps it, moving forward to put it on me, but as he does so, I find myself jerking out of his way.

"What is it?" he asks instantly.

I don't know what it is, this feeling that has suddenly come over me in a quickening of my pulse and a sense of trepidation, and so I brush it off and say, "What do you mean?"

"You flinched. You pulled away."

"I didn't." I shake my head, my hand automatically reaching up to my neck to where his fingers momentarily brushed my skin.

Will is staring at me, the necklace hanging from his hand. "What's the matter?"

"I don't know. I'm fine," I say. I *don't* know. But I don't feel fine, and it scares me, this sudden sensation. It's something I haven't experienced before.

"You don't look fine," he points out.

The feel of his fingers against my neck is already beginning to dissipate, but the memory of them still makes my heart pound and my body burn, and I have no idea where any of this has come from.

I pull the duvet off me and get out of bed, heading into the en suite and grabbing the basin, splashing cold water over my face. The heat radiates off me, making me feel like I'm on fire, but my breaths, which had been catching in my throat, are at least beginning to return to normal. Is this what a panic attack feels like? I wonder. Are they over so quickly?

"Are you feeling all right?" he asks from where he's now standing in the doorway. "You look hot."

"Honestly, I'm fine." I turn off the tap and come out of the bathroom, kissing him on the cheek. "You'd better get to work."

"Yeah. Okay. As long as you're all right, though?"

"I am. Don't worry about me. I don't know what came over me," I tell him. "But I'm fine," I say again. The moment, whatever it was, has already passed like it never happened.

I stay in our bedroom as he pads down the stairs. The cupboard door in the hallway opens and closes and then the front door. I stand by our window, a hand splayed against the frosty glass, as I watch my husband walking to his car.

I frown as he gets inside and closes the door behind him, his image faint behind the windscreen now. I touch my neck again, trying to make sense of a feeling that came from nowhere and went again so quickly. There's a simmering deep in the pit of my stomach, that sensation you get when you think something bad is going to happen, only you don't know what.

In the end, I shake my head along with any thoughts that are in it. I pick up the necklace from where Will left it on the bed, but I don't put it on. Instead I place it carefully on my dresser before going downstairs.

*   *   *

An hour after Will has left for his job at Keyport Secondary, any strange feelings I had earlier are a distant memory, partly because of my daughter's foul mood. I try encouraging Sadie into going for a walk with Coco, despite my own reticence, which I put down to period pains that have worsened since giving birth.

Sadie is crying for reasons I can't fathom and takes all of my attention and patience as she kicks out at me when I try to get her dressed. "Don't want to go," she shouts. "You take Coco."

I sigh. Coco is our family dog, although really she's mine. I was the one who walked in the house with her five years ago, a bundle of soft, brown puppy huddled in my arms.

"Erin?" Will questioned cautiously, eyeing the dog and then me. "What's this? What's going on?"

"I couldn't leave her," I told him, burying my nose in her fur. "A friend of a colleague at work had this litter, and she took me round there at lunchtime. This one was the last one left. Someone was supposed to have her, but they never showed up." My eyes filled at the thought of it. There was something so desperate about her being the last one and no one wanting her that made me all the more certain I needed to take care of her. The moment I picked her up and she looked at me, she was already dependent on me not to let her down. "The place was awful," I went on. "It stunk of God knows what—it was a tip. They had animals everywhere."

"You shouldn't get dogs from places like that. You encourage them to breed for money."

"Maybe, but I couldn't help it. Look at her." I held her up for Will to see what I saw, but he only sighed and reminded me that we had talked about it before and that it wasn't fair to have dogs when we were at work all day.

Will isn't a dog person. I had a dog as a child, a mutt I loved who died of old age when I was thirteen. My dad had apparently found him abandoned and just brought him home, but that was before I was even born. Will, on the other hand, tells me he is a cat person.

But there was no way that little brown puppy was going anywhere, and eventually Will relented.

Now, as Sadie howls at the breakfast table, I bend down and run my hands through Coco's fur, listening to the constant hammering of rain on the windows. "You're not fussed to go out yet, are you, my little baby?" I say to Coco, knowing I'm just giving in to Sadie, but I'm hoping she'll calm down and we can go out later in the morning when the rain might have finally stopped.

Coco looks up at me, licking my hand. "You're my good girl," I whisper to her, like she's my better-behaved child. In a way, that's exactly what she is today, although Sadie isn't usually like this. "Shall we go out later instead?" I purr to Coco as she rolls over in her bed and lets me tickle her tummy. "Shall Mummy let you have a lie-in this morning?" Will doesn't like me calling myself *Mummy* to the dog, and I have found I've begun to do it only when he isn't around to hear.

*   *   *

It is only eleven thirty when I say to Sadie, "Shall I get you some lunch?" How slowly the days sometimes pass when it's just me, Coco, and my three-year-old, when we have no plans and the weather is awful. I make cheese-and-Marmite sandwiches that I cut into strips and put in one section of her plastic plate, then chop carrots into round pieces and halve cherry tomatoes. I slice grapes down the middle and sprinkle on a handful of Pom Bears, finishing the rest of the packet myself.

Sadie doesn't touch any of it. I finally get her out of her chair and we sit in the middle of the living room surrounded by teddy bears as I pretend to feed them and pour cups of tea into the china tea set Will's mother gave her four months ago when she turned three.

The rain keeps drumming on the windowpane. Coco is bugging me now to go out for a walk; a run in the wet garden hasn't done the trick. She is circling my legs and looking at me with eyes that make me melt. She kicks her precious fir cone at my ankles, begging me to throw it for her.

The TV is now on, low in the background, drawing Sadie's attention. It's the only thing that intermittently stops the crying.

"What is it, Sadie?" I say to her, stroking her fine hair off her face, feeling her forehead with the palm of my hand. She rapidly lost interest in the tea party, and now I'm beginning to worry she's sick. With this acknowledgement comes a lurch in my stomach, and now I don't want to put her into the push-chair and force her to go out. I hate the idea that my daughter might be ill. That I will have to hover over her now and take her temperature, watch her for signs of decline. My mind always goes to worst-case scenario. I'm certain I was never so alert to danger before Sadie came along. Coco brought her worries with her, but nothing like this.

"Come on, lie down on the sofa, and I'll put *PAW Patrol* on," I tell her. She does as I say, her hot red face pressed against a cushion as her small body curls up. I put a blanket on her, sit next to her, and rub her tummy until she falls asleep, and then once she has, I fret over what I might be missing.

This isn't Sadie, skipping her lunch and crying. My daughter is a happy girl. Her nursery teachers say so, although I suspect they tell most parents the same.

I never once long for the child-free days Will and I enjoyed before Sadie came along, although sometimes I remember how much easier it was not to have someone else to worry about to the pit of your stomach. Where does that come from? That burning love that's so deep and intense you would die for this person? Because I certainly never expected it.

If anything, I worried before my daughter was born, when I was carrying her inside me, that I wouldn't love her. "What if I don't bond?" I might have said. *Or I don't want her?* I definitely thought. After all, I'd had no experience of motherly love myself to learn from, and they say that kind of disinterest passes from generation to generation.

"Of course you'll bond," Will reassured me. "Look at the way you love the dog."

I didn't know that it would be the same thing. I imagined it probably shouldn't be. Weren't people supposed to love their children more than their pets? And yet there was something in what Will had said, because he was right. I did already love Coco to the pit of my stomach. I had sat with her in the vet's when she was only a year old and wouldn't eat; I had stayed awake all night when the vet operated on a suspected cyst, praying my dog would make it. Then I had bawled with relief when I was told she was going to be all right.

Of course, your own child is different. Children are little humans with their own traits and needs and thoughts. Children answer you back; they don't patter around your feet, wagging their tails when you give them any sign of attention. I can be gone from the room for two minutes or two days, and Coco gives me the same excited greeting. She always will. I could do anything to my dog, and she will always love me.

But with children, you have to be careful. Children you can screw up, like my mother had every chance of doing to me. Children can one day turn their backs on you, and I suppose this was what I was scared of. What if I got it wrong? What if *my* child turned round at eighteen and told me they didn't want anything to do with me, like I had done with my own mother?

Before Sadie was born, Will was always telling me everything would be okay and that I wasn't my mother, the woman he had never met and whom I hadn't seen in years. He was forever saying we were different from my parents, we weren't that couple. Of course we would love *our* child. He said it like it was obvious.

Well, my mother didn't. So what did that make me? Unlovable?

But Will insisted we had *his* family around us, to learn from and to help us. As if that made it better.

I know this is why Will asks me sporadically if I'm happy, though neither of us admits it out loud. I think he worries that one day my childhood will catch up on me. "You're not your mother," he tells me. "We are *not* your family." He's right, but surely he must consider there are genetics at play?

Sadie is calm now she's asleep, her head lolling to one side as her thumb finds its way to her mouth and she gently starts sucking on it. I feel a pang of love so great it's like I'm going to break right here. If anything ever happens to my girl—

No. These thoughts are unhealthy. I am not to go there. Sadie is fine. Nothing is ever going to happen. We have a perfect life, the three of us and Coco. We are happy, safe, healthy. The only things that matter.

I pull myself away from her, careful not to disturb her, but she doesn't move, and so I creep from the living room and into the kitchen, where I make myself a coffee and wander to the patio doors to look out through the rain-smeared glass, where a greyness now blankets the sky.

When my phone rings, it pierces the silence. "Hi, Zoe," I say. "How's it going?"

"Well, work's hectic, but I'm going to need to leave early, because Marlie has a ballet exam tonight. And now Dave has texted to see if I want to go to dinner because it's Valentine's Day. I mean, what the hell?" she says. "He never usually remembers it. Do you think he's having an affair?"

Ever since we met at fourteen, when Zoe joined my school, we've been best friends—although she's more like a sister, our relationship so woven into my life that our families are as close as if we were related. "Surely if he's having an affair, he'd want to go out with her tonight," I point out, knowing Zoe is joking.

Zoe saved me when I was a teenager. I've told her this often enough over the years. She made me realise there was someone I could always depend on, someone who wouldn't let me down. Zoe and then Will are the only people who have ever truly loved me in all the twenty years I've known her and the fourteen years I've been with him.

"Yeah, you're right," she says. "I actually just phoned to see if you could do me a favour. Are you going to the shops this week? Could you pick up a present I ordered for Dave's birthday for me? I just don't know I'll be able to get there."

"Sure. I can go Wednesday," I tell her.

"You're a star," she says. "Thank you. And what about you? Did Will remember Valentine's?"

"He got me a necklace," I say, thinking of the small charm upstairs.

Zoe chuckles. "I already know. He showed me. Isn't it lovely?"

"Yes," I say eventually, pausing, then adding, "Yes, it's gorgeous." But I must seem distracted, and Zoe picks up on it.

"Erin?" she says. "Everything okay? Don't you like it?"

"No. Of course I like it." I close my eyes, trying to stop the sensation that the walls are closing in on me.

"So what is it?"

It's a good question and one I don't think I can answer, because I just don't get it. But when Will attempted to put the chain around my neck, I had a fleeting moment of panic, and now, as I think about it again, I remember how it felt and my stomach flutters in response.

But I don't want to say any of this to Zoe. Instead I tell her, "I think Sadie might be ill, but she's sleeping now."

"The best thing for her if she's coming down with something," Zoe says, a mother of two who professes to have dealt with every childhood illness going. She's so much more relaxed than me when it comes to her children being sick. After a beat, she says, "But everything else is okay?"

"Yes. Why wouldn't it be?" I turn to look at my daughter, who is sleeping soundly on the sofa.

"Because I know you, Erin Harding, and I know when something is up."

I sigh. "I don't know. Something bothered me earlier. I felt—" I cut off, not wanting to say it. I didn't want my husband to touch me. I recoiled at the feel of his fingers on my throat, and yet I don't know why. I love how Will touches me, I crave his hands on me at times.

"But everything's been okay?" she says. "Since last year? Nothing else has happened? That girl's family haven't said any more about Will?"

"No. Nothing more."

"Good," she tells me. "God, when I think back to what you both went through."

"Hmm."

"Erin? You're both okay, aren't you? You and Will?"

"Of course."

"You'd tell me?"

"Yes, I'd tell you—" I break off. I have always told Zoe everything.

I tap my fingers on the work surface, thinking. I've also always trusted my husband with every inch of me; even last year there was not one moment I doubted him. But now I say, "I don't know. I was right, wasn't I, to believe him? Nothing happened, did it?"

"Is that what you're thinking?" she asks in disbelief. "You can't seriously be questioning Will? They withdrew the complaint. The girl was lying, Erin. We all know that."

"I know we do. I know. Just sometimes . . . Oh, it doesn't matter. Forget I said anything. Honestly, I think I'm just worried about Sadie," I tell her, although I don't know that to be the case at all.

NOW—AUGUST

FORTY MINUTES LATER, PC Mike Gray is still waiting by the operating theatre doors when the red-haired nurse who met him when he arrived appears and tells him, "The husband is in the family room, but he hasn't spoken to a doctor yet."

Gray nods, his eyes flicking down to her badge, which reads *Raina*. "Thanks." He looks over her shoulder. "Down that way?"

"He's very shaken," she tells him, frowning.

"Of course. He must be."

"He wants answers we don't have."

"His wife's in a bad way?" Gray asks.

"I don't know—she's not good," Raina says. "She'll need careful monitoring when she comes out of surgery. I guess it depends how long she was lying on the roadside before the ambulance got there. How much blood she lost." She pauses. "You should know her husband told me they're separated. He isn't living with her."

"Oh?" Mike sucks in a breath that makes a noise as it squeezes through the gap in his teeth. His own wife is forever telling him it annoys her. He hadn't even noticed he did it, but now he can't stop noticing and wishes she never said anything. But then everything he does seems to annoy her these days.

"He's clearly very concerned about her, though," the nurse goes on, before giving him a tight smile and heading off.

So the husband is estranged. Regardless, he's going to be asking about the accident, though there's little Mike can tell him. Maybe he should wait for the senior investigating officer to turn up. Lynsey Clayton will likely be here within the next thirty minutes. Clayton is probably already up to speed; she probably even knows more than he does.

All Mike knows is that the woman was on foot on the road that leads away from Harberry Woods. No place for anyone, let alone a lone female, to be at half past midnight on a Sunday. He knows it was called in by an anonymous male who was apparently driving past. Didn't leave his name, didn't hang around for either the ambulance to turn up or the police, who arrived at the scene five minutes later.

While the paramedics were stabilising the victim at the side of the road, Mike Gray did a quick sweep of the area. There was no one in sight, which means the police will need to direct their sights on finding the caller. It's likely the guy hit Erin Harding, then cared enough to call an ambulance for her but not enough to make sure she was okay or hand himself in. Drink, most likely, or drugs—whatever it was, he was probably over the limit. The police will be analysing the call recording anyway, tracking the phone down. People can make stupid mistakes when they panic.

But on top of the fact that this was a hit-and-run, the scene was suspicious, not least because Erin Harding was there on foot, no sign of her car nearby, and the first thing Clayton will be asking is why.

Gray makes his way down the corridor and peers through the small glass window of the room Raina pointed him towards. Will Harding is leaning forward in his chair, elbows on his knees and his hands steepled into the prayer position as they press against his mouth. His eyes are open as they search the ceiling for a God or other higher being. Gray taps lightly on the door as he pushes it open, and Will's gaze springs to him.

"Police Officer Mike Gray." He introduces himself quickly, before Will assumes he's a doctor. "I was at the scene."

Will drops his trembling hands in his lap. "Where was she found?" he asks. "Where was my wife hit?"

"She was on the edge of Harberry Woods," Mike tells him.

"Oh, Christ." Will appears to roll his eyes as his body slumps, an odd reaction that suggests the couple might know this area.

Mike takes a seat next to him, about to ask what he thinks his wife was doing at the woods, when Will asks the same question.

"What the hell was she doing there?" he says.

"You don't know?"

"I don't know what my wife's been doing at all lately," he says. "I don't know what's been going on in her head."

Mike pauses for a moment, waiting for him to continue, but when he doesn't, Mike asks him, "You and your wife are separated?"

Will turns to stare at him, as if wondering how he knows this, before saying, "It's not like that. I'm just . . . not living at the house at the moment. We've been having some problems. We've been trying to sort them out, but . . ." His words fade.

"I understand," Mike says, which seems to be the right thing, because Will inhales a deep breath and carries on talking.

"We started seeing a counsellor early on. It was supposed to help." He shakes his head. "But it didn't. I think it made everything worse."

Gray would love to ask more, but they're interrupted when the door opens and a doctor appears. Will jumps up from his seat as the doctor closes the door behind him, the look on his face so grave that Mike wonders if this hit-and-run has already turned into a murder investigation.

2

Six months earlier
ERIN

As soon as I put the phone down, the doorbell rings. I turn towards the hallway, still clutching my coffee cup, as I wonder who it could be.

A blurred shape moves behind the stained glass, distorted by the bright-red-and-green tulip on the window. I recognise them from the way their shadow sways side to side, shifting weight in agitation from one fluid heavy ankle to the other. She'll be wondering whether we're in and whether she should have called first rather than turning up unannounced. It will be the first thing my mother-in-law says when I open the door: "I should have called first." While I always smile and say, "Really, it's no problem," I'll be thinking, *Yes, you should have.*

Reluctantly, I put down my coffee cup and wander through the hallway, opening the door to Will's mother. "I should have called first; I'm so sorry," she says as she steps inside.

"It's fine," I tell her, opening the door wider and standing aside. She immediately peers over my shoulder, making a song and dance of trying to see into the living room. "Where's my girl?"

My hackles are up, but I try not to let it show. Clive and
Pauline have only one grandchild so far, and they dote on her.
Or Pauline does, anyway, to the extent that some days it feels
like she can't stay away.

"She's not feeling well, I don't think," I say as she brushes
past me, stopping suddenly when she sees Sadie lying on the
sofa. In some ways I should feel lucky to share my worries with
a mother like Pauline, who has been there and done that and
might know what to do, especially when I don't have my own
mother to tell. And yet somehow I never do.

"Oh, the poor child. What's wrong with her?" Her voice is
an exaggerated whisper. She starts walking over to Sadie.

"Don't wake her," I say quickly.

"Of course I won't. I just want to see her," she tuts as she
continues to approach the sofa. "What's wrong with her?" she
repeats.

"I'm not sure. She's just grizzly, and nothing was making
her happy."

Pauline lets out what sounds like a short laugh that suggests she thinks I'm overreacting. She has a habit of making
me feel like a bad mother, though Will always downplays
it. "She isn't doing that, Erin," he'll say to me. "She's just
there to help you." There is an undeniable sense that everyone thinks I must need help when I've had no one to learn
from, and certainly Will's immediate family feel Pauline is
the answer.

Will and his sister had a perfect upbringing, or so the
three of them like to make out. But there is a strange connection between Will and his father that I'm still trying to
fathom. Whether it's that deep down Will loves him and is
slightly scared of him, or that Will loves him and is slightly
in awe of him, I'm not sure, but it's a relationship that Will
certainly does not have with his mother. Will and his mum
adore each other, and while it's unsavoury for me to admit that
it makes me a little jealous, the truth is, it does.

Pauline lays her hand on Sadie's forehead, which wakes her. "Oh, my baby girl," she says as Sadie opens her eyes and stares at her grandmother for a moment.

Then, to both my relief and horror, my daughter suddenly sits bolt upright, a smile spreading over her face, and says, "Gran, we're having a tea party." She leaps off the sofa, tugging Pauline down onto the floor to where the cups and plates are still laid out, and proceeds to pour her a cup of "tea."

"I don't think there's anything wrong with her at all, dear," Pauline says, and I smile back as my insides tighten. She's right: Sadie is fine. I don't like it when Sadie isn't herself, and so if it takes Pauline to make her smile again, then that is good. But I just wish it had been something else. I wish it could have been me she saw when she opened her eyes.

I leave them to it and go to the kitchen to make Pauline a tea—weak, plenty of milk, no sugar. I roll my eyes at Coco, who I'm sure agrees with me when it comes to my mother-in-law, the only maternal figure in my life. I sometimes wonder if Pauline is as jealous of me as I can be of her. Because I'm the woman who came in and swept her son off. "I don't know that I'm ready to lose my boy," she apparently said to Zoe on the morning of our wedding.

As the kettle boils, I turn my attention back to Sadie and watch her and Pauline from the doorway, my eyes resting on my daughter. It makes me break to think that my own mother couldn't love me the same way I love Sadie.

Will was right: I bonded with her the moment she was born. That pure love I felt when my eyes rested on her was like nothing else I'd ever experienced. I often consider what my mother must have thought when she looked at me and whether she could have regretted having a child as much as she made out she did.

I suppose that whatever Pauline's faults are, I at least admire the way she mothered her children. Will has certainly never been starved of love, and I should be grateful for the way she hunches over on the floor, eating an invisible cherry bun.

"Be careful of your hip, Pauline," I mutter.

"Oh, tsch." She waves me away. "I'm okay, aren't I, Sadie?"

*   *   *

Pauline leaves after playing tea parties, complaining that her hip is aching and that she needs to get up off the floor, suggesting that Sadie watch *PAW Patrol* with her on the sofa instead, and then finally telling me to give Will a big kiss from her, as she really should go.

I find Coco padding across the kitchen floor, waiting by her bowl. I should have taken her out when Pauline was here, and yet I didn't think to leave my daughter and mother-in-law together, or maybe I didn't want to. "Shall we go to the park, Sadie?" I say, though there's still no sign of the rain relenting. She ignores me as she carries on sucking her thumb, staring at the screen.

Through the window behind her, I see Will's car pulling into the driveway. He's home earlier than usual, which means he likely has a pile of marking to do if he hasn't done it at school. As he climbs out of the car, I see he's holding a bunch of roses, red and yellow tied with a thick raffia bow that makes me think he bought them from a florist rather than the supermarket. He pulls his coat hood over his head as he runs to the front door, and I open it for him.

"More gifts?" I say.

He grins. "I had to go to the post office on the high street, and I saw these and thought of you." He kisses me on the cheek as he passes them over, dropping his bag in the hallway and opening up his arms for Sadie to run into. "What have you done today?" he asks her.

"I had tea with Gran," she tells him.

"Oh, how lovely." He turns to me. "I didn't know Mum was coming."

"Neither did I," I respond, a little gruffly.

To my irritation, Will laughs as he picks Sadie up and swings her around, making her squeal with delight.

"I don't even know why she came by, actually," I persist.

"Just to see you both, I expect."

"I haven't taken Coco out yet," I add. "I might do that now."

"Or I can? We can go, can't we, Sadie? Let Mummy have some time."

"Are you sure?" I ask. "You've only just got home."

"Of course. I could do with some fresh air anyway."

"If you're really happy to? I might go and do some work." It isn't work, but I've taken to calling it that. All it is, really, is time in the shed at the bottom of the garden that I've turned into a little office so I can sit and create the children's books that have been in my head since I was a child myself. "I won't be long. Maybe just an hour."

"Take as long as you need," he replies as he calls for Sadie to find her boots. "And remember, I'm making dinner."

* * *

I spend an hour and a half writing in the end, working on my imaginary world that may or may not one day get published. That isn't why I do it. In some ways it's a form of therapy for me, a way to confront my own childhood by re-creating the one I wish I had.

When I'm done, I lock the shed door behind me. As I step into the garden, I turn to see Will standing in the open doorway to the kitchen at the back of the house. Already I can tell something is wrong by the way he's looking at me, eyes boring into me, his rigid shape lit up by the glow of the kitchen lights.

"What is it?" I walk across the lawn, my mind racing to Sadie and thinking she must have taken a turn for the worse.

"I don't know where the dog is. The dog has disappeared," he says to me.

I don't answer for a moment, strangled by a ball of bile rising into my throat like it might choke me. Thoughts of Coco blur into something else I can't even put my finger on. The way Will is looking at me, maybe. Or no, it's his words—the words he's used—that cut into me like sharp knives. That make me recoil from him again like I did earlier, stepping back, almost losing my balance.

He's talking to me, saying something I don't hear until I pull myself out of whatever trance I'm in and say, frantically, "What the hell do you mean, Coco's disappeared?" I run the rest of the way to him now, demanding answers. "Where? Where were you?"

"We didn't go out for a walk in the end," he says, holding up his hands like he's trying to rid himself of any blame. "I'm sorry, I just got caught up doing something with Sadie."

"Then what happened?" I'm screaming now, my whole body shaking. His hands are still held up in a silent gesture, asking me to calm down.

"I left the kitchen door open for her to run around, and she's—" Will gawps at me, his brow furrowing.

"How long?" I cry. "How long's she been gone?"

"I don't know. Maybe only ten minutes."

"Maybe?" I yell. "You don't even know? How long *could* it have been? When did you last see her?"

"Erin, calm down. I've only just noticed, and I've been looking for her. She'll be fine."

"How long?"

"I don't know. Maybe an hour. But she won't have gone far. It's not as if she ever wants to walk much."

"Oh my God!" I cry in disbelief. "Did you actually just say that?" How is his world not falling apart like mine is?

"Get your boots on, Sadie!" I shout through the house. "Now!" I turn back to Will. "I'm going out. You'll have to find me when she's ready."

I race through the side gate and onto the driveway and street beyond, calling Coco's name, dipping in and out of neighbours' driveways. With every minute that passes, my heartbeat is more erratic, and my head floods with thoughts that she has been run over, is hurt or dead, that someone has stolen her.

There is no sign of her, and I'm running back towards the house when I see Will seemingly ambling out with Sadie in tow. "Where is she?" I cry, falling against him and beating my hands against his chest. "Where's she gone?"

3

IN THE AFTERMATH of Valentine's Day, I do not fall apart, although it feels like Will is making out I am. But with Coco gone, there is a void in my world that I don't know I could ever fill.

That evening we walked around the streets again, knocking on neighbours' doors. I called the police and then our vet and others in the area too, logging our details and telling them Coco was chipped. They assured us they would call if anyone brought her in.

I posted on various Facebook sites, local ones and lost-dog ones and my own page, uploading a photo of Coco and begging readers to share. I received plenty of comments, but none of them proved useful as I sifted through the pity and the curiosity about whether she was chipped and spayed. No one was helping me find my dog, and I wished people wouldn't waste my time by making me read what they had to say or answer their pointless questions.

The roses Will had come home with died after a few days. One by one, they shrivelled and drooped in the vase as the water level dropped, and they no longer looked pretty. The water began to stink, and yet in some ways the flowers were a reminder of Coco. How I had felt her soft fur against my leg when I put them in the vase, telling her *Daddy* was going to take her for a walk. It was some wild superstition that made me keep them rotting on the windowsill, as if she would never come home once I threw them away.

After five or six days, I found them gone. The vase had been washed out and was upside down on the draining board. I opened the bin to find the dead roses splayed on the top of the rest of the trash.

"Who's done that?" I said.

Will looked at me curiously. "I did, Erin. They're dead. They were smelling."

Of course I couldn't tell him he'd done the wrong thing, so I just took my foot off the bin's pedal and walked away from him.

* * *

The days are passing, and now the weeks are beginning to too, and there has not been one sighting of my baby. She has seemingly disappeared into thin air. I have walked the streets calling her name, stuck posters on lampposts. I have sobbed at times and at others been angry, and I have comforted my daughter, although Sadie, being only three, has handled Coco's disappearance much better than me. At least I have that to be grateful for.

As the shock begins to wane, it gives way to not just grief but other concerns, questions, that start to grow.

After ten days I pick up the phone to call Zoe.

"Hey, any news?" she says when she answers.

"No. Nothing."

"Oh, hon." I know Zoe is upset for me, but she doesn't have dogs, she has a hamster, and she's the first to admit it isn't the same thing. She can't really understand the hole in my world that Coco has left.

"Zoe, I know this is going to sound odd," I say. "But when Will told me she'd disappeared—" I break off, trying to think how to put into words something I can't even understand myself. "I just—"

"What is it?" she asks.

"There was just something about it. It all felt so wrong."

"I don't get what you mean," she says.

I don't either, I think. "It just felt like Will knew more. Than he was telling me." I didn't trust him; that's what it comes down to. That the man I love beyond anything I thought possible might somehow be holding something back from me.

"Knew more about what?" Zoe asks.

I sigh. I can't even put it into words, but I try anyway. "I just wonder if I know everything about him. I mean, how can you ever fully trust someone?"

"This is about last year again?"

"No. It isn't. Or I don't think it is. But maybe."

"Erin, we spoke about this before."

"I know we did." On Valentine's Day, I think, when I'd felt a rush of panic as he touched my neck.

"You *know* Will didn't do anything," she's telling me.

But do I? I trusted him fully before, never questioned him, like Zoe says, so why am I now?

A seed of doubt has planted itself inside me and is taking root, beginning to grow and spread like a tumour, and as it does so, it fills me with questions and an insecurity that I've never before experienced with Will. I'm questioning the man I love, and this in itself scares me. But now it's got its claws into me and won't let go. Because if I pass it off, I find I'm left with a lingering uncertainty: *What if I'm right?*

* * *

Another week later and Pauline appears on my doorstep. "How are you, Erin dear?" she says, unwrapping her coat and taking the liberty of hanging it up herself in my under-stairs cupboard. I make her a cup of tea while Sadie draws at the kitchen table.

Pauline joins me by the kettle, hovering on the other side of me and lowering her voice so Sadie won't hear. "Will is worried about you," she tells me.

"What?" I screw my eyes up at her.

"He tells me you're very down about your dog."

"Of course I'm down about her. I've lost her, Pauline." I can't believe he's saying as much to his mother, but mostly I don't get how he doesn't understand.

A divide has been growing between Will and me since the day Coco disappeared. I can feel it, and I know he must too, but I've been tiptoeing around it because I don't know what to say. How can I tell him my worries when I don't even know what they are? When I tried to explain them to Zoe, even she threw them back at me, so of course my husband will too.

"He tells me things aren't good between you, though, my dear, and I'm worried about you both."

I look up at her sharply. So he's been talking to his mother about this? "That's ridiculous," I mutter.

"Are they okay, then?" she says. "Is he wrong?"

I ignore her as I pour the water into our mugs and finish making us tea. It feels like Will has betrayed me by talking to Pauline, but at the same time I can't deny that things aren't good, and I know it's largely because of me.

"What has he said?" I ask her eventually.

"That you're pulling away from him," she tells me, sipping her tea and watching me carefully over the rim of her mug. "He says you won't talk to him. But he doesn't tell me much more than that."

"So it's all my fault," I say. "Is that he what he thinks?"

"Well, I'm not saying that, dear, but I don't really think Will knows what he's done wrong."

I seethe as I watch her put down her mug and then wander over to the table to sit with Sadie. I won't give her the satisfaction of discussing my marriage with her any further. There's no point in telling her that the reason I don't look at my husband the same way anymore is that every time I do, I find myself wondering what it is he's holding back from me. What it is I can't put my finger on.

I play back the moment he told me "the dog is missing," and each time I do, the words reverberate through my skull, taunting me with a sense that something is feeding my anxiety beyond the fear I feel for Coco. In that moment, I feared my husband too. It is a simmering of disquiet that bubbles inside me and whispers to me that Will is lying to me about something, but I don't know what.

* * *

"What's going on with us?" Will says to me one evening as we pick over a pasta dish I've made us for dinner. "Something has to change, Erin. You barely talk to me anymore."

"That's not true."

He shakes his head and rolls his eyes, and it hits me how quickly our marriage is unravelling, and how if I don't do something to stop it, it might come undone completely.

And I do not want this, because I don't want to lose my husband, but at the same time I can't fathom out how to hold us together. "Maybe we should see someone," I say.

"What?" He laughs, choking on the forkful of penne he's putting into his mouth. "Like a counsellor?"

"Maybe. Is it such a bad idea?" Someone else to listen to us, a stranger who doesn't know us, someone who can give us some perspective. Maybe that's all I need. A little perspective.

"If it's what you want to do," Will says, "then of course." I glimpse the husband I love in that moment, the one who would do anything for me, and for the first time in nearly four weeks I feel a shard of light creeping back and think this is all going to be okay. Whatever I've been feeling about my husband can easily be explained with the right space and time to discuss it.

The following day Will comes home from work and hands me the name of a woman. "How about her?" he asks. "Her name's Maggie Day. She's a couples therapist who works out of the Cliff House."

I know the building, a beautiful Edwardian manor house. I nod and smile at Will. "Thank you," I say. "I'll look at her website."

Within twenty-four hours I've booked us our first appointment. Will and I are seeing Maggie Day next Monday.

NOW—AUGUST

Zoe Sawyer pulls up into the hospital car park, peering out the window as she scours the area, swearing at the person who has parked their BMW on the line and left no room for her to squeeze into the only empty space she can find.

"Bastard!" she says as she carries on driving around until eventually she pulls into a tight spot as far away from the entrance as it seems possible to be. She has to be in the wrong car park; it's so bloody small. The last time she came to this hospital must have been five years ago when her youngest was born and she was in no state to appreciate the layout of the parking spaces. For two thirty AM on a Sunday morning, she can't believe it's this busy.

Grabbing her bag from the passenger seat, Zoe swings herself out the car, locks it, and begins running to the front doors of the hospital.

This is the first chance she's had to get here. An hour has passed since Will phoned to tell her that her best friend was seriously hurt in a hit-and-run, but Zoe couldn't ask any of her neighbours to look after the children, because she doesn't know them well enough, and her mum would have taken longer to arrive than it was supposedly going to take Dave to return from his night shift. By the time Zoe heard his key in the front door, she wondered if she should have called her mum after all.

Zoe feels tears stabbing at her eyes as she pushes through the revolving doors and strides over to the reception desk. She gives Erin's details and is directed down a corridor to her right towards the intensive therapy unit, where Will's latest text told her to come. Zoe thanks the woman as she runs off again, sliding to one side to narrowly miss a trolley coming in the other direction.

She hates the idea of what lies ahead of her, of not knowing what state her friend is going to be in or what she looks like. She needs to tell Erin that she still loves her and still cares about her. Especially when she hasn't shown it over the last few months. She needs to say she's sorry.

Zoe rounds a corner and sees Will talking to a nurse. He looks over his shoulder at her when he clocks her approaching. His body is deflated. In the past few months, Zoe has watched Will suffer from not knowing what to do about Erin. And she's taken his side, despite feeling her own betrayal of her best friend, because she believes him.

Often, lately, Zoe has asked her husband what this says about her, but Dave has always told her that Will's done nothing wrong. That they can't side with Erin over this.

Zoe always imagined she would kill for Erin if her best friend turned up on her doorstep one night and asked her to. Only when it came to it, she couldn't even stand by her when her marriage collapsed.

Now Will holds out one arm towards her as she walks over and takes his hand. "What's happening?" she asks.

"They had to remove her spleen."

"Oh my God, is that serious?"

"She can survive without it, but . . ." Will pauses. "Well, they don't know what other effects there are at the moment. They're keeping her in a coma. Until she's stable." He rubs his hands over his eyes.

"A coma?"

"They don't know how long she was on the side of the road. She lost a lot of blood. They told me they won't know until they wake her up what effects it's had on her brain."

"Oh my God, Will." Zoe's eyes glisten with tears. She can feel the pressure of her own blood pumping through her body.

"What was she doing, out in the middle of the night? Do you know anything?" he asks her.

Zoe shakes her head. He's asking her the question because he has to, but Will knows Zoe hasn't spoken to Erin in weeks, because they had this conversation only two nights ago. Will had called Zoe Friday night to tell her Erin had turned up on his mother's doorstep, screaming at him, and Zoe promised him she would call her friend. Only she put it off for fear of Erin hanging up on her.

The weight of her guilt continues to press into her, furiously crushing her. If anything happens to Erin, she will never forgive herself. Erin must not die without knowing she's still the best friend Zoe could ever have.

"Will," she starts, "do you think she did this—"

She breaks off, unable to finish.

He shakes his head emphatically. "No. No," he says, but his eyes are screwed up, as if he must have been wondering himself. "It was an accident. She was hit. She couldn't have done. No," he says, and then, "could she," though it isn't a question, more a consideration.

"She could have walked out in front of the car," Zoe says in a murmur, looking at him, desperate for him to tell her it isn't possible. She holds a hand up to her throat, which is filled with a knot of tension, coiled up into a hard ball, making it hard to breathe.

"No. No. She wouldn't," he says. He's trying to convince both of them.

Zoe hopes she herself knows, deep down, that Erin "wouldn't." She wouldn't leave her daughter. Ever. But then, with what's happened lately—Will leaving Erin, Sadie—who knows what's possible?

The last time Zoe spoke to her friend, she told Erin she was mad. "You're acting crazy, Erin," she said, and Erin, with glassy eyes, replied, "That's exactly what Will says."

After the call with Will two nights ago, the other reason Zoe put off phoning Erin was because she knew she could no longer reason with her. Erin had made it clear she didn't want to talk to her anymore. But Zoe knew she should have persisted. She shouldn't have given up.

"She was by Harberry Woods," Will tells Zoe.

"What the hell was she doing back there?"

"I don't know." He shakes his head.

Zoe considers the meaning of it and eventually says, "We've abandoned her. Both of us have." Erin can't have had anyone to turn to over the last few months. Anyone apart from that counsellor, Maggie Day, of course. A woman Zoe has never met, but whom Erin decided to share everything with. Did she become a friend to Erin? Zoe doesn't know, because Erin stopped talking to her about their therapy a long time ago.

Will doesn't take his eyes off Zoe, as if he's contemplating the truth and making his mind up about whether he believes he had no choice but to abandon his wife. Surely now, with Erin here in hospital, he believes he should have done things differently.

"Did she have Sadie? Was she looking after her?" Zoe asks him. The idea that her goddaughter might have been left with anyone else is another punch she can't bear.

"No. Sadie's with me. She was—Mum and Dad have her."

Zoe nods.

"All this is killing her, Will," she tells him. "Literally killing her. You know that, right? Whatever's going on, it's—" She stops and waves a hand in the air, gesturing for a word that never comes.

And what if it's too late?

4

Five months earlier
MAGGIE

THE CLIFF HOUSE is falling apart. I can see cracks in the bricks that I am certain weren't there a couple of months ago. I run my fingers across the rough surface, rubble crumbling beneath them, then over the shiny brass plate next to the door that bears my name along with the names of others who work out of the house. *Maggie Day, Couples Therapist.* I still have to pinch myself to believe I've got to where I am, working from this imposing building that takes prime position on the edge of Dorset's Keyport cliffs.

Three years ago I saw the room at the front had come up for rent, and I knew I had to have it. All my stars were aligning, though I don't really believe in all that stuff. I showed Richard, a little apprehensively, because I already knew what he would say, and he didn't let me down.

"Mags, the cost—we'd really be stretching ourselves." He frowned. My husband was worried, but at the same time he knew how much it meant to me, the chance to be working here. He pointed out its location, and questioned the insurance about it being so close to the cliff edge, and threw in words like *subsidence* that I didn't want to consider.

By then I'd been running my practice for six years, having started training two years earlier, and had built it up successfully. I had published my first article, which has since led to more, and I declared to Richard that for someone *Life in Dorset* magazine was calling a leading expert in psychotherapy and psychodynamics, I needed a room more suitable than the tiny one I'd been renting in the centre of Keyport. I needed somewhere that reflected my professionalism, and he couldn't argue that the Cliff House wasn't perfect.

The double doors could do with a good lick of paint, I think now as I push them open. I didn't have any say in the deep grey that was chosen three years ago. My first day here coincided with that of the decorator hired to paint the outside, who arrived in his white van behind me. The job was supposed to take him three weeks but ended up taking double that because the weather was particularly bad that March.

He was afraid he would fall off his ladder. He told me this every morning as he stood with his flask, looking out to sea. "Don't know how much I'm going to be able to do today, Maggie." I always told him to be careful. I had visions of him falling, because I knew as well as he did the wind could whip up wildly on the cliff top. I didn't want him breaking a limb, or worse.

I decide to have a chat later with Craig, who runs his chiropractor business from the back, about getting Cliff House painted again. Craig pays less rent than I do, but then he doesn't have the view of the sea from his windows. Every time I see it, it still takes my breath away.

Over the last three years, as my business has continued to grow, Richard has worried less. He's never questioned my decision—he supports me wholeheartedly—but he'll check my books every so often, just to make sure we're going to be all right.

Richard and I are so different in many ways. I often say that if we'd met a year earlier, we'd never have made it. I was thirty when I stood in front of him in a coffee shop queue near Keyport Harbour. He, it turned out, was forty and also my saviour when I realised I didn't have my purse. He paid for my flat white, adding a muffin to my order.

Only six months before that I had started my therapist training, and only six months before *that* I had been seeing a counsellor myself to help me through a bad breakup. Paul had been a nice guy on the surface, but we couldn't seem to stop hurting each other.

My counsellor helped me realise that the breakup wasn't all my responsibility and helped me let go of the blame I'd been layering onto myself. She only scratched the surface of the rest of the blame and guilt I'd been buried under for the whole of my twenties, but what I did realise was what I wanted to do with my life—help other people before their relationships got to the point of no return, as mine and Paul's had.

Richard and I walked out of that coffee shop together, chatting and eventually swapping numbers. I was relieved he hadn't met the twenties version of Maggie, who used to drink too much and party too often, and had instead met the Maggie who was turning her life around. I can't imagine what life would look like now without him in it.

Two weeks after we met, I told my mentor, Elise, about him, and she looked at me and beamed and said she'd known as soon as I walked through her door that there was something different about me that day.

Elise had been appointed to me at the start of my training, and she acted as a counsellor too, someone to help me dig into my own past as a way of unearthing my demons before I counselled other people. "God help our clients if we take our own issues into their problems," she'd joked early on.

When I left her that day, she said, "Take it carefully, Maggie." Maybe she could see how important Richard was already becoming to me, or maybe she worried that there was still too much I was dealing with, stuff that made my breakup with Paul seem trivial in comparison.

Elise is still in my life, and I see her every month, but now I share with her any obstacles I have with my clients. It isn't about me any longer.

I twist the blinds on the windows so the shutters open, and light pours into the room. I have a new couple this morning. Erin and Will Harding. I know nothing about them yet, and as always, this fills me with a little buzz of anticipation that's either excitement or apprehension, or just a mixture of the two.

*   *   *

I have fifteen minutes before the Hardings arrive. They're taking the first slot of the week, nine AM on a Monday morning, which I was reluctant to give over because I'm not a morning person; my sessions don't normally start until ten AM. But there was something quietly desperate about Erin when she called that made me find a slot to fit them into.

As always with first-time clients, I laid down my rules on the phone:

They must pay for the slot every week, regardless of whether they can make it or not. This is their time and I won't give it to anyone else, which means they have to commit to coming.

I see the two of them together and *never* one of them on their own. This is couples therapy, and if they can't both make it, then we don't go ahead with the session. They are my clients together, and I don't want to ever find myself swayed towards one of the parties. I need to remain impartial.

My rules are my code of ethics. I have never crossed them, and there is nothing that would ever make me. It's important for me to have boundaries, not least because Elise taught me this from the start, but also because I realise I need them for myself too. When I went through my own counselling and my life was all over the place, it became a way for me to keep it together.

While I wait for the Hardings, I make myself a coffee, popping a pod into the machine that sits on a chest tucked into an alcove of my room. I have one espresso shot that I knock back quickly, enjoying the sharp kick.

I've spent a long time setting up my room just the way I want it. I have a reclaimed chair that I fell in love with when Richard and I were on holiday in Cornwall. He hired a van so we could go back the following weekend to pick it up. It's covered in soft blue birds and green vines, and it's where I always sit. It's one of those possessions that makes me remember happy things. I often have a flash of the long, lazy lunch we had after I'd seen it, the two of us sitting in the window of a bar as the rain pattered relentlessly down the pane.

Opposite me and across from a coffee table, I have a two-seater sofa in pale blue, and the back wall is hidden by a white bookcase that catches the attention of the inquisitive clients: the ones that want to run their fingers along the spines of my books, assure themselves that someone this well read in their field of psychology must know what they're talking about. I advertise myself as specialising in psychodynamics, the idea that we are all shaped by our pasts. They mostly come to me knowing this is what we'll dig into, but still they look for reassurance that surely *I* must be able to fix their broken relationships.

My couples don't all come with hope. Or maybe their hopes are differently aligned, because they all want a resolution, after all, an outcome, a solution to their problems. But not all of them hope for me to fix them; some are looking for a way to escape. They need me to tell them they're right and the only way for them to be happy is to leave the person sitting beside them.

I wonder what it is the Hardings are here for. What they need me for. I don't know much about them yet, apart from the basics they completed on their forms.

Will is thirty-six and a history teacher at a local second-ary, which surprises me, as I cannot imagine that nine AM on a Monday morning can be convenient for him or how he's man-aging to escape the first hour of the week. This isn't my place to ask, yet it leaves me wondering what it says about them. That he would move heaven and earth to please her, or that there's something he's desperate to get resolved too?

Erin is thirty-four and had a good job as a medical rep before she gave it up when her daughter was born. A job that would have demanded long hours and structure and is likely a far cry from the life she has now.

I don't ask for backstory over the phone, because I learnt when I was starting out that you can give over too much of your time to a client who hasn't paid you yet.

It sounds so harsh, but I learnt my limits the hard way, occasionally giving clients a bit of extra time on their session if they were midflow on a topic when the big hand hit the ten. Fifty minutes in, I now know, I need to wrap up swiftly. Not doing so led clients to expect more, and I ended up disorgan-ised once my diary began filling up.

Now I can close down the session promptly, but I can never be accused of not throwing myself wholly into my clients. I give them my all, sometimes too much, but I always remember that I am their therapist, not their friend. It's important to realise how much influence I can have and, if I'm not careful, how much harm it could cause.

*   *   *

A black Audi pulls up outside the window, its tyres slowly roll-ing across the gravel.

I peer between the slats of my blinds to get a first impres-sion. He is driving; she sits beside him. I don't see her properly, as she's on the other side of him, not until she steps out of the car and stops to look up at the house.

Erin Harding is wearing a long camel-coloured woollen coat that reaches to her midcalves and beneath that dark jeans and small black pixie boots that will dig into the gravel with each step she takes. Around her neck is a brightly coloured scarf and on top of her head a woollen hat in salmon pink with a pom-pom on top.

Her face looks pained as her eyes trail the old house, and she stares at the windows above me as if she has seen a ghost. I wonder what's going on in her head, whether she's relieved to be here, if a little nervous, or if she's thinking she's made a big mistake.

He, on the other hand, is busying himself with his jacket, taking it off the back seat and pulling it on. I think he asks her if it looks okay as he straightens it and taps his hands against his sides, maybe even if he should bother wearing it, because she flaps a hand in a gesture and he takes it off again. Already I am making my assumptions about them, but I also know they can count for nothing.

I stand back from the window as he locks the car and walks to the door. Erin has turned to face the sea so that she has her back to me now. Her body is immobile. Even when he rings my bell and I press the buzzer to let him in, she doesn't move. I've always believed that the sea can bring out myriad thoughts and that if you look at it long enough, it will hurl the answers back at you.

Erin doesn't get the chance to wait for any answers, though, as through my door I hear him call her, and she spins around and walks across the gravel until she disappears out of my sight, into the porchway that I can't see through my windows. Eventually I hear the heavy oak door close behind them.

I give it a few minutes, refolding the chequered woollen blanket that is draped over the arm of the sofa, tidying away my coffee cup, and filling the jug with water. I put that and two glasses on the coffee table and then open my door and greet them.

"Erin, Will?" I smile and stand aside, gesturing for them to come through.

He nods, and she gives me a small smile. They both look sheepish as they enter the room. I notice this with a lot of my couples, that on their first visit it's as if there is some shame in coming to a therapist.

"Please, take a seat," I say.

"Thanks," Erin murmurs. They sit next to each other, her on the left of him, and this is likely the way they'll always be. People are creatures of habit; they will find their "sides."

Once we're all settled, I say to them, "Perhaps you'd like to tell me what's brought you here today and what you would like out of our sessions?" I turn to Erin, as she was the one who called me.

"Well." She dips her head, fiddling with her hands in her lap before eventually slipping them underneath her so she is sitting on top of them. "It's hard to say, now I'm here. You know, to put it into context. I mean, people come to see you when their marriage is breaking down, don't they?"

"Is that why you're here?" I ask her, helping her out. "Because you feel like your marriage is breaking down?"

"Yes. I suppose it is. Yeah." She takes a deep breath and seems to hold it.

Beside her Will is shaking his head, and so I turn to him. "Do you not agree?" I ask.

"Oh no, I do agree. Only I have no idea why. Because one minute everything was absolutely fine between us." He glances at his wife. "And then the next it wasn't."

"How long has this been?"

"A month," he tells me.

"One month?" I repeat.

"Yes."

"And things were good before that?" I don't believe this can be the case. Four weeks is no time for a couple to be calling in a therapist for help unless something very major has happened between them.

"They were perfect," he says. "Everything has always been perfect." *No marriage is perfect*, I want to tell him, but Will seems to know what I'm thinking, as he adds, "We had ups and downs, but there was nothing wrong. You know when there's something wrong, and I can tell you, there wasn't. I still think there isn't. I still love my wife. Nothing has changed for me," he goes on. "*I* haven't changed."

"I don't think I have changed either," Erin says.

"But you say your marriage is breaking down, though?" I clarify. "Yet only in the last month. And so something must have changed."

"Erin has," Will says. "I don't know how you can say you haven't." He turns to her. "You pull away from me when I try to touch you; you don't speak to me like you used to. Sometimes it feels like you don't want to be in the same room as me. Like that," he adds, clicking his fingers. "Like someone flicked a switch."

I wait for a moment, for one of them to say more, and look to Erin for clarification. "Do you agree with what Will says?" I ask her. "He thinks you've been withdrawing from him."

"Yes. Maybe. I don't know. I suppose I do agree, but I don't want things to keep spiralling the way they are. I do love Will," she says, her eyes glistening. "I just—I don't know. Things don't feel right, and I want them to be." She turns to her husband. "I do *want* them to be right, Will," she repeats.

"So what isn't right?" I ask her.

"It feels like everything," she answers.

I cock my head, trying to fathom what she's getting at, but she doesn't expound. "Okay, maybe you could give me some background to your life together," I say. "Tell me about who you are as a couple."

As Erin speaks, I make notes. They've been together for fourteen years, married for six.

"We first met after Erin finished university," Will tells me. "She moved back to the area and was working in a bar on the harbour."

"That isn't true," she corrects him. "We were at school together."

"Yes. I know that. We went to the same school together, but I didn't know Erin then," he says to me. "I was two years above her."

"I knew you, though," she says. She pauses, and after a beat moves on. "Anyway, we have a daughter called Sadie, who is three." I circle this, noting that the shift from couple to family can play an important role in marital issues. "I look after her now. Full-time."

"You work too," Will says. "My wife is writing a children's book."

"Are you?" I ask, noticing the way her face flushes a deep red.

"It's nothing. It's not work. It's a hobby more than anything." She brushes it off, and so I let the subject lie for now.

"And where is Sadie today?"

"She's with Will's mum," Erin says, straightening her back as she does so. I'm not sure if I can put this down to discomfort or if there's a degree of displeasure in this fact. "She goes to nursery for one and a half days a week but not Mondays."

I nod and gesture for Erin to continue.

"And we have a dog." She stops abruptly. "We had a dog. Coco, she was my Cavapoo. She went missing a month ago, and I don't know what happened to her." Erin blinks back tears and holds a hand up to her mouth.

"I'm so sorry," I say. "I can understand how awful that must be. I have a dog myself," I tell her, thinking of my huge black Lab. I can't bear to think of anything happening to Rocky, let alone him suddenly going missing. "Does this have a bearing on what's happened between the two of you, do you think? You said it's been a month since things have been breaking down. Losing a dog is like losing a family member."

"Erin blames me," Will says as he holds out his hands, palms splayed upwards. "For Coco."

"Erin?" I ask. "What do you think of what Will has just said?"

"I don't know," she says quietly. "Maybe he's right."

Will sighs and sinks into his seat. He appears to be as much in the dark as I am, and I wonder if he genuinely has no idea why things have suddenly changed in his marriage.

"It isn't just that," she goes on. "I don't know if I trust him. I don't feel safe."

"Are you joking?" he says with a laugh. "Why on earth would you not trust me? And why wouldn't you feel safe, for God's sake?"

"I think Will's done something," she says. "Something he isn't telling me about."

"What?" he cries. "This is madness."

"Erin?" I say, glancing from Will, who is either as shocked as he appears to be or is doing a bloody good job of pretending he is, over to her, whose face is blank as she stares straight ahead of her, not even at me. "What do you think he's done?" I ask.

Eventually she turns her head until she reaches my gaze. "I don't know," she says blankly.

* * *

When their session is over, I watch Erin and Will from behind the slats of my blinds as they approach their car. From the outside, they look as flawless as Will told me their marriage was. The way they dress, their shiny car—they are a *perfect* match.

But they've shown me a glimpse of more. They wanted me to see inside their relationship, and yet I can't work out why or what it is I'm supposed to be looking for, because we've only skirted the edges.

Potentially, it is nothing more than that Erin blames her husband for their dog disappearing. But then I question again whether he really has no idea what's happening to their marriage, as he makes out. If so, does that mean she's the one in control? Or is that Will has more of a hand in what's at play here?

I don't know which one of them I should be watching more closely, but what I do know is that there is something oddly unsettling about them.

Before my next couple arrives, I message Elise. *New couple called the Hardings today*, I write. *I don't know what it is about them—but I don't trust either one of them.*

NOW—AUGUST

Pauline Harding puts down the phone to her son. It's 2:40 AM. She hasn't slept a wink since Will got to the hospital, and she knows she won't get any sleep for the rest of the night, however much he tells her to.

She creeps across the landing to the spare room at the front of the house and opens the door a crack more. A shard of light splinters the darkness of the room so that she can just make out Sadie's little body curled up in the double bed of their spare room, oblivious to her parents' plight. As she should be.

Pauline tiptoes in a little farther so she can look over her, her eyes trailing to the two-day-old bruise on her granddaughter's arm, her thoughts skipping back to Friday when she'd rushed Sadie back to theirs, and then to later in the evening, when Erin had turned up on her doorstep, screaming.

Pauline wants to reach out and touch the bruise, but Sadie was complaining about how tender it was. Her heart is breaking. How the hell did it all come to this? Everything her poor son has been through, and now little Sadie.

Slowly she creeps back out the doorway and goes downstairs, where she switches on the television for company. She has no idea how her husband was able to get up and make them both tea when they heard the news about Erin, then forty minutes later be back in bed snoring. Yet that is Clive. He cares, but somehow sleep always finds him.

Will didn't tell her what she should say to Sadie about her mother, and so Pauline has decided that when her granddaughter wakes up, she won't say anything about Erin until they know more.

She shakes her head as she flicks through the channels. What was Erin thinking? Walking through the woods on her own in the middle of the night. Though the way Erin has been acting lately, she supposes nothing surprises her. There is too much history with that girl. It was bound to come out sooner or later in one way or another.

Back when Will met Erin, Pauline took her in and made her feel like part of a family, something Erin had never had. She felt sorry for her after hearing the stories Will had shared. But she also worried that someone with two parents who had shown such little affection must be plagued by issues. How did you move on from that kind of neglect? She worried even more when Erin fell pregnant with Sadie, although this time Will refused to agree with her.

But then again, Erin has held down a successful career, and until these last few months has been nothing but a doting mother and wife, as far as Pauline has seen. Her son was happy. Or so she was led to believe.

She wishes she knew what went wrong. She wishes her son knew too, but they are both in the dark. All she does know is that two nights previously, Erin showed up on her doorstep with wild-eyed crazy accusations, which of course no one would ever believe, and then the following night was found wandering the woods on her own.

Pauline thinks she's right to start taking things into her own hands. She shouldn't have been so quick to trust Erin in the first place. But that's another thing about her, Pauline thinks: she's just far too kind to everyone.

CHAPTER

5

Five months earlier
MAGGIE

I HAVE BEEN DREAMING of Lily again. Always the same dream that she is still alive but I haven't seen her in years. In my sleep I haven't *bothered* to see her, which means that in many ways waking is a relief.

This morning I woke drenched in sweat. I had been putting it down to early menopause, and yet today the nightmare was etched into the forefront of my brain. I could see my sister's body lying at the edge of the lake.

"Maggie?" Richard said softly as he rolled over his eyes wide, to find me sitting in bed, hugging my knees to my chest. "Another one?"

I nodded. I didn't want to tell him about it, and he never pried. "It's nothing more than a dream," he said. Except it wasn't. It was memories.

At the start of my counselling training, when I was undergoing my own therapy, Elise was keen to dig into the guilt that kept me company like a shadow. She thought it curious that I hadn't brought up the fact that my sister was dead when I went through counselling to get over Paul. I told her I didn't think it had anything to do with my breakup, and she looked at me as if to say, *Of course you know it has, Maggie.*

Looking back now, I don't know how I could never have realised that my sister's murder was impacting every choice I made. In truth, I don't believe I didn't; I just chose not to acknowledge it. Elise taught me how much every part of our past affects our present, and so something as significant as this was going to have a bearing, whether I wanted to see it or not.

She proposed to me that I might have buried some of the memories of the night my sister was killed. I told her it was an interesting idea, and it was, because I looked into it after that—the notion that we can protect ourselves by repressing memories. It wasn't me, though. My problem was the opposite. If anything, I remembered too much.

Lily is the reason I swam through my twenties in a haze of grief and guilt. Lily, my little sister, who was only fourteen when she was murdered. I was nineteen, had left home by then, and was convincing myself I wanted a career on the shop floor. I hadn't long been made a department manager in Keyport's one and only department store, which was a grander title than the job entailed in an old fashioned shop, but I thought I was happy. And maybe I was, in my own small world, where I was making enough money for the rent in my shared house and the drinks in the clubs, where I would meet my latest boyfriend. I was certainly happier than I was going to be for the next ten years.

As was to be expected, it was Lily that Elise wanted to dig into most when we began my counselling and training—how her death had affected me and how I might take it through with me if I didn't process it. "Tell me what happened," she said.

"I don't know what happened," I told her. "Well, that's not wholly true. I know that my sister was found dead on the edge of the lake on a Friday morning by a jogger. I know that a man called Kieran Blake killed her. But I don't know why," I went on. "I don't know what possessed him to take the life of my sister, who was the sweetest and kindest person I knew." I broke down then, of course. Reliving it was always going to be painful, but at the start of my counselling, ten years had passed, and it was something I had to finally confront.

"I don't know why he did it," I told Elise, "because he has still never admitted he did."

He hadn't admitted it back then, but this changed five years ago. One day I was called out of the blue by a detective inspector called Jack Lawson, who told me he'd been working on the case when Lily was killed. I hadn't remembered his name. Those days had been a blur of officers coming and going, relaying the "good news" that they'd arrested a man for Lily's murder, then charged him, and finally that he was going to pay for what he did. But five years ago Jack called me to say that Kieran Blake had finally confessed to killing my sister— eighteen years after her murder.

"I want to see him," I demanded. I needed to know why. I had to hear what Lily had gone through in those final hours so that I could piece together a story I only had the start of. But Kieran Blake refused, as he has ever since. And so I'm left with nothing more than the nightmares.

*　*　*

It's seven thirty when I go downstairs, and Richard is dressed, waiting by the door in his boots and coat. "Let's take Rocky to the beach, and then I'll make breakfast," he says.

"I have a nine o'clock, remember?" The Hardings, back for their second appointment.

"Oh yes." He smiles thinly. "The couple who are making you get up and work early."

"Hmm," I murmur. With them it isn't just that they're making me work early, it's that I'm having to think hard about what I need to do to get more out of them. I want to dig into their backgrounds, but right now I still can't fathom what their problems are.

My area of expertise always draws me to my clients' pasts. I work from the idea that we are all shaped by our childhoods and relationships and experiences, that it all determines our actions and reactions. My own interest was piqued by the very fact that I can now see how shaped I am by my own. One tragic event that pulled my family apart—leaving me with only a mother who lives 120 miles away, who I have rare contact with.

Richard is my family now. He and my dog, I think, as I pull my own boots on and grab my coat and we leave through the front door. I wave to Hattie across the road as she throws her yoga mat in the back of the car. "I hope I'm as fit as she is when I'm in my sixties," I say.

Richard grins, and we head to the end of the road and then dip off to the left towards the path through the fields that leads down to the beach. I worried over us buying our house when we found it five years ago, because it's in an older neighbourhood, ours being the only bungalow where they've built a bedroom into the roof. I was thirty-seven at the time, and it felt like I was settling too early, and yet at the same time I couldn't think of anything I'd rather be doing.

We talked about its location, how close we'd be to the sea, and how we didn't need to think about school catchments when we didn't plan for children. I had wanted them once. In fact, I'd wanted a big family of four children or even more. But then, after Lily, I couldn't see myself being a mother. Not when I'd been responsible for her. Not when it was my fault she was dead.

"Your dreams have come back again, Mags," Richard says. The sea has come into view in front of us, and Rocky pulls at his lead. I lean forward and unclip him and tell him to "Go on, boy." A few flashes of the Hardings' little Cavapoo have come into my head over the last week, and I think how broken my life would be without Rocky. It wasn't hard to see how much Erin is suffering.

"I guess," I say.

"Have you spoken about them to anyone? To Elise?" he asks.

"No."

"I wonder if you should."

I shrug. Richard reaches for my hand and takes it in his own. This is all he will say—he won't add more if I don't want to talk about it, and usually I don't—but today I say, "It's her birthday at the end of the week. She would have been thirty-seven."

"I know," he replies.

I turn to him, surprised. "Do you?"

"Yes. I know when your sister's birthday is."

I shake my head. "But I never mention it."

"It doesn't mean I don't know these things, Mags," he tells me. "It doesn't mean I don't remember days that are important to you."

I stop and turn my whole body towards him now, trying to think if I know when his dad's birthday was and unable to come up with a date. It makes me love Richard even more, if it's possible.

"I guess every year I wonder if you might want to do something, or you might just want to talk about Lily and—" He breaks off.

"And I never do," I finish. "It's not that I don't want to."

"I know. And I know you have Elise."

"No. She's not the same as you."

"I hope not," he laughs.

"I mean, if I wanted to talk to anyone about my sister, it would be you."

"That's nice to hear," he says, though a frown appears on his face.

"What?"

"Only I guess I was hoping you were speaking to someone."

"What is there to say?" We pick up our steps again, making it onto the stony beach, where Rocky is running in crazy circles by the edge of the sea. The water makes him excited, though the mad dog will never actually venture into it. "Nothing has changed in the twelve years I've known you. Apart from Kieran Blake admitting he killed her, of course," I add dryly.

"But you have dreams, Mags, that wake you up and you're shaking and sweating. Maybe the problem *is* that nothing has changed," he points out.

"I don't know what you mean," I tell him, though of course I do. I, more than anyone, know that Lily is still very much alive inside me. I may have spoken to Richard about her. And I may have opened up to Elise about the guilt I'd felt all those years, and the part I'd played in the night she died. But that doesn't mean I've stopped seeing her face in my dreams, or hearing her voice when I stand on the edge of the cliff outside the Cliff House. I rented the room there because it made me feel close to her, after all.

The cliffs were Lily's favourite place. We used to play hide-and-seek on the grounds of the grand house when I was about ten and she was five. Lily once told me she wanted to live there when she was older.

I never told Richard any of this; he was already too worried about the practical aspects of me signing a contract to rent a room in the Cliff House. But then in some ways I wouldn't be surprised if he knew there was more to my wanting to work there that involved Lily.

Richard squeezes my hand, and I tell him I can't be long today because I need to leave the house by eight thirty. It's only a five-minute drive to the Cliff House, but I want to make sure I'm there before the Hardings arrive.

We have only touched the surface of their marriage, and I find I'm apprehensive about seeing them later, if only because I have no idea how the relationship between the three of us is going to pan out. I want to help them. It's not just my job; it's the reason I do what I do. I want to know I've made a difference to their lives for the better. But how can I when I'm unable to shake the feeling they're holding something back from me on purpose?

6

MAGGIE

B Y THE TIME I've made myself a coffee, I hear the crunch of tyres on the driveway outside and look out to see the Hardings' Black Audi pull up.

Today Erin is wearing her hair in a ponytail. It's brown and flicked with the odd highlight, but I can't tell if it's natural or not. I noticed last week how her skin still has that pressed look of youth, as if it's been ironed flat, something I can only wish for. She wears a smudge of makeup, brown eyeshadow on her lids and a bit of colour on her cheeks, but nothing more. She is naturally pretty, someone who seems able to take little effort to get out the house and yet still look good, but I also think this is how she'd look if she were on a night out. She doesn't appear to be a woman who would thicken her eyes with dark makeup. She wouldn't attract the "townie" lads like I used to.

I can easily see how Will and Erin are attracted to each other. He is handsome, with dark hair long enough to give him the look of having just rolled out of bed, though really it's likely been especially styled. Everything about Will looks thought through, from the crisp white shirt he's wearing again today to the navy V-neck jumper over the top, the dark-navy slim-leg jeans, and the brown boots that don't have a scuff on them.

His Audi is the same, clean and polished like it has just been through a car wash. Nothing like my Land Rover with its wheel trims caked in mud. I doubt there are empty water bottles in the passenger footwell of Will's car, and I don't even have children to blame my mess on.

Erin is getting out of the car and walking to a spot at the edge of the cliffs, closer and closer until I almost tap on my window to pull her back. Will is looking over at her himself from his position behind the steering wheel, and now he's swinging his car door open and calling out to her as he climbs out the car.

As Erin pulls herself away, I do too, and when the buzzer goes, I press it to let them into the communal hallway, downing my espresso. "Come through," I say, opening the door and standing aside to let them both into the room.

As I suspected, they take the same sides of the sofa they took last session. "How has your week been?"

Will glances at his wife, who purses her lips into what I think is intended as a smile but doesn't quite come across as one. "Much the same," he says, "But possibly worse. She still won't talk to me about what the problem is."

"If I try to talk to Will, he shuts me down," she says.

He lets out a laugh, rolling his eyes. I don't know if this means he's infuriated with her or if he doesn't agree with what she's said.

"How long have you felt like that, Erin?" I ask. "That Will shuts you down?"

"Only recently," she admits. "In the last few weeks."

"Erin, what do you want to get out of your sessions with me?" I ask, leaning towards her.

She frowns. "I want to make everything better again," she says. "I want it to go back to how it was."

"That's all I want," Will mutters beside her.

"But I want to know what's going on," she adds.

"What's going on?" I repeat. "What do you mean by that?"

When she doesn't respond straightaway, Will says, "Yes, Erin, I want to know too."

"You know what's going on," she says, so quietly I can barely hear her.

Will laughs loudly in disbelief, flinging himself back into the sofa, holding up his hands in surrender.

"Can you tell me what that is?" I say, but she just shakes her head again, and so after a beat I steer the conversation away from the repetition. "Erin, maybe you can try and explain to me how you *feel* instead," I suggest.

"I feel like I don't trust him," she says eventually. "But like I said before, I don't know why." Her gaze drifts, and she looks around the room before her focus eventually settles on the top of the bookcase, where I know without looking that it's a photo that has caught her attention. She can't see it clearly from where she sits, because it's facing towards my chair, but it's one of me and Lily not long before she died. I angle it so that my clients can't see it properly. It saves questions.

But Erin is shifting forward, trying to make out the figures in the picture. "Have you always felt like this? Erin?" I ask her, pulling her attention back to me.

She shakes her head, adamant. "No. I've never felt like this before."

"Or had times when you didn't trust Will without understanding why?"

She thinks about this and then eventually says again, "No. I haven't."

"So from what you're telling me, you have always trusted your husband in the past," I say, "but in the last few weeks, something has happened to make you feel differently." It has to be the dog, I think. What else has happened recently? "Have I got that right?"

"I don't know whether that's really true," Will says.

"What do you mean by that?" I ask, but it's Erin who answers.

"He means he doesn't think I can trust anyone." There's a flash of something on her face, either anger or hurt.

I nod. We're getting somewhere. Will believes his wife has issues with trust, which he knows will have stemmed from somewhere, and most likely this will be her childhood or a previous partner. Someone has let her down.

"That's not *you* talking, though," she goes on. "You didn't ever think that. Your mother has put that idea into your head."

When Will doesn't answer, I ask her, "Do you think there's any truth in what Will says? Do you find it hard to trust other people?"

"Will's suggesting it's because of my parents. I haven't seen them since I was eighteen. And yet I feel like I'm constantly having to justify it, because people can't believe I can move on from them. But to be fair, I think I did a pretty good job of not letting them overshadow our relationship," she adds, directing this at Will. "I have done a pretty good job of not letting any of it overshadow my life at all, and so I don't know how you can bring it up now." Her eyes fill with tears, and I notice the way she inhales a deep breath, as if to steady herself. "This isn't about them," she says.

She holds his gaze for a moment before shaking her head as she turns away from him. Whatever the issue is here, he has hit a note and I can't let it go. "I would like to know a bit more about your relationship with your parents," I say. "If that's okay with you, Erin?"

"It's not important," she snaps. "Like I say, they haven't been in my life for sixteen years, so they don't affect me anymore."

"You might not think they do directly," I tell her. "And whatever reason you have to not trust Will, it might have nothing to do with them."

"But it could?" she jumps in. "That's what you're saying? That this is all my fault."

"No. What I'm saying is that it could affect the way you react to situations."

"Isn't that the same thing? Anyway, I didn't want to get into all this. This isn't why I'm here," she says. "I'm here because my dog went missing five weeks ago, and I can be pretty certain *that* has nothing to do with my parents."

"Oh, Erin." Will sighs, closing his eyes, an interesting reaction to her finally talking. "I refuse to believe this started with the dog."

"She's not just 'the dog,'" Erin spits, tears escaping and running down her cheeks. "She was Coco. She was like a child to me."

"That's ridiculous," he says, staring at her.

"No. It isn't. You know how much I love her." She looks at me. "I still walk every day," she tells me. "Every morning I go round to the park with Sadie so I can look for her. I mean, how does it even happen?" she says. I don't know if she's asking me or her husband; her gaze is snapping between the two of us. "How does a dog just vanish?" she questions, settling on Will like she's waiting for him to give her the answer.

"Do you *know* how it might have happened?" I ask, when he doesn't respond.

"No. I don't," she says firmly, very much making a point as she slowly takes her eyes off him. "The garden is fenced off; we have electric gates and a Ring doorbell with a camera. We would have seen anyone coming in to steal her, and she isn't the kind of dog to run out. She's lazy and loves being at home." Erin chokes out a sob, and I pluck a tissue from the box on the coffee table, passing it to her.

"Erin blames me," Will says blankly. "That's all this comes down to."

"What do you *actually* blame Will for?" I ask her, wondering if it's as simple as the fact that Coco went missing while on his watch. Because if it is, then maybe my job is nothing more than helping her find a way to forgive him.

But when Erin opens her mouth to speak and the words don't come, Will eventually answers for her. "My wife believes I killed Coco," he says.

NOW—AUGUST

DETECTIVE INSPECTOR LYNSEY Clayton arrives at the hospital to find a small gathering outside ITU, which is a pretty perfect start for her, she thinks, having the nearest and dearest all rounded up like sheep into one place.

It's three AM. She got the call half an hour ago to tell her there had been a hit-and-run out near Harberry Woods, the scene quite rightly arousing suspicion with the officer, Mike Gray, who had attended it. A thirty-four-year-old woman on her own and on foot at one AM on a Sunday morning, in an unlit road that ran alongside the woods. The "wrong" side of the woods to boot.

This wasn't someone going out for a middle-of-the-night jog. The woman was wearing jeans, a sweatshirt, and soft slip-on beige shoes that still had a price sticker on the bottom of one of them—£49.99, if that makes any difference, which it does insofar as Lynsey thinks that's a hell of a lot of money to spend on shoes, and loafers at that. She didn't even pay that much for her own wedding shoes.

With Erin Harding still unconscious, ventilated and being monitored around the clock, this is already being treated as attempted murder, as all hit-and-runs are. But add to that the questionable circumstances, and Lynsey's got some questions of her own to ask.

She spoke to Gray on her way in, asking for an update. "Was it an accident?" she posed, wanting his take.

"Can't be sure, of course. Looks like she'd been hit front on. She was heading south, facing the car, straight patch of road. Unlit area, but where she lay it wasn't hidden by trees, so if I had to guess, they should have seen her unless they were driving incredibly fast or under the influence."

"And the person who called it in?"

"Nothing as yet. Pay-as-you-go phone."

"Hmm," she muttered. "So what the hell was she doing in an area like that on her own at one AM on a Sunday morning?"

This is the million-dollar question, and what's interesting to Lynsey right now is that on paper it doesn't stack up. Female, thirty-four years old, wife and mother. There's nothing that suggests Erin Harding should be the target of a callous attack, so for now Lynsey should be working on the assumption that it was an accident. And yet her gut won't let her.

Erin Harding was on foot, on the east side of the Harberry Woods and walking away from them. Before Lynsey got in her car, she pulled up a map of the Harberry area. The small town is a half hour's drive north of Keyport, in northwest Dorset and not that far from the Somerset border. The town of Harberry, however, lies to the west of the woods, the opposite side to where Erin was found. The woods themselves cover a large, sprawling area and can be entered from various points.

Lynsey wanted to see where Erin could have been heading, but her map confirmed what she already knew—there's nothing on that road within easy walking distance. The nearest house is a mile away from where she was heading.

And where had she been coming from? Lynsey can only guess it was either from the woods, for whatever reason, or from the Harberry estate, a loose term for the cluster of homes that sprouted up in the early seventies. If the latter, what the hell would Erin be doing there? Was she walking to or from something?

Gray has confirmed that the road is dark, no streetlights, and can be pretty unsafe at the best of times. But to walk it? Erin Harding had to be either out of her mind or desperate.

Lynsey can proudly admit that her gut isn't often wrong, and so she's going to be working on the assumption that Erin might have known the driver. That they might have been somebody she was with. Erin had to have got where she was somehow, and there was no sign of her car nearby. Was it an argument that got out of hand? Did Erin try to escape their car?

Lynsey thrives on the puzzle of questions that are hers to untangle at the start of a new case. From them she can build the picture, and while she might not get the answers immediately, she's in the right place—the hospital, where her best hopes are in talking to the family. It's a shame, though, because if there's one place Lynsey can't stand, it's hospitals. They unnerve her. It's something about the smell, the harshness of the cleaning fluids mixed with the scent of despair and grief.

Now she is here, she hopes the husband can give her something, because he's as good as anyplace to start. Gray confirmed not only that Will Harding had arrived at the hospital at one thirty AM but also that the couple are separated.

She wonders if he's the man ahead of her, outside one of the side rooms talking to another woman. The nurse who was with them when Lynsey rounded the corner has now disappeared and left just the two of them, and for a moment Lynsey holds back and watches while they're unaware of her eyes on them.

William Harding, who prefers to be called Will. She doesn't have a clue if he's a suspect or not, but she'll be treating him like one until she knows more. At the very least, she hopes he can shed some light on what his wife was doing at Harberry Woods on her own at night.

While she talks to him, her colleague can hopefully be getting her some intel on the car that hit Erin, because at this stage she doesn't have a bloody clue who was driving what.

Will has his hands on the shoulder of the other woman, who in turn is sobbing. When they pull apart, Lynsey moves forward and flashes her badge, getting Will's attention. "Will Harding? I'm DI Clayton."

Will nods and rubs a hand over his face with an expression that she tries to read. Undoubtedly he's exhausted as well as worried. His eyes are wide, flicking over her, likely assessing what comes next, but it's always interesting to watch the initial reactions.

"I was wondering if we could have a chat?" Her eyes trail to the woman beside him, and she wonders what conversation she just walked in on. "You're here for Mrs. Harding too?"

"I'm her best friend. Zoe Sawyer."

Lynsey nods and makes a mental note of Zoe's name. She'll be an interesting one to talk to next.

"Maybe we could take a seat somewhere?" she says, turning back to Will, which is a joke, because there's nothing but a run of plastic chairs to sit on in the corridor. He nods and follows her to the seats as Zoe makes herself scarce with the excuse of getting a coffee.

"I'm sorry about what's happened to your wife," Lynsey says.

"Yeah. It's . . ." He drifts off, but she can see tears pooling in her eyes. Whatever's gone on, he does look genuinely upset, but then she's seen all sorts, and some can be bloody good actors.

"Can you tell me what she was doing in Harberry Woods last night?"

Will closes his eyes. "I wish I knew."

"Where was your wife supposed to be?"

"I would have thought at home." He looks at her. "Things haven't been good between us recently," he admits. "I'm not there at the moment."

"You're separated?" she asks, though she already knows this.

"No. I don't know, I suppose . . ." He trails off.

"But you're not living together?" *So you are clearly separated*, she thinks.

"We just had to have a bit of time apart. I moved in with my parents, and so it means I don't have a clue what she was doing last night. It's as much a mystery to me as it is to you."

Lynsey waits for him to add more, but he doesn't. She isn't sure how relevant this separation is, but it's possible that it is. The woman has been hit by a car, and the husband is estranged. At the very least, this wasn't a happy marriage.

"I didn't want it," he says eventually, looking across at her. "It wasn't something I wanted. Not to live with my wife."

"It was Erin's choice you move out?"

"Well, no. I suppose in the end it was mine." He shakes his head. "But it wasn't my fault."

No, she thinks. *It never is.*

"We were totally happy until a few months back."

She's intrigued he's so keen to talk. "So what happened?" Lynsey asks.

Will gives a slight shrug. "Everything went downhill quickly."

"And you don't know why?"

He doesn't answer her but says, "I know the counselling didn't fix it. It only made things worse."

"How long did you have counselling for?"

"I don't know. Three months probably in total."

"I thought therapists were supposed to make everything better," Lynsey says grimly. She herself has never seen the point in them. The idea of airing her innermost thoughts in public sends a chill down her spine.

"Yeah, well . . ." He trails off.

"What is it?" she asks. Because she's certain there's more to their therapy sessions than Will is telling her. "What happened?"

"My wife started making things up," he tells her plainly. "I knew she was lying, but our therapist, Maggie, didn't."

Over Will's shoulder Lynsey sees the friend, Zoe, appear with two paper cups, which she plants on the table beside Will's seat. "Can I get you one?" she asks. "There's a machine round the corner."

Lynsey grimaces. "I'll get something from the café in a bit, thank you," she says as she turns back to the husband.

"By the end Maggie Day seemed more interested in Erin than she was in the two of us," he continues.

Maggie Day. Lynsey will be looking into her as soon as she finishes here.

"I wish we never went in the first place." He stops, staring up at the ceiling. "You know, I think my wife carried on seeing her? On her own?" He shakes his head. "Which is funny, because Erin was the one who wanted us to stop going. Plus Maggie made it explicitly clear at the outset that was something she would never do. It was against her *code of ethics*," he says, making the gesture of quotation marks. "She was especially professional in explaining she would never break them." Will turns to Lynsey. "She got too involved," he says, seeming to stare straight through her. "Too involved with Erin and her stories."

CHAPTER

7

Four months earlier
MAGGIE

WHERE DO YOU go when your client accuses their husband of killing their dog? Funnily enough, it's not
something I've had to deal with before. Of course, Erin didn't
say as much outright, but neither did she deny it. She just
looked at me, eyes wide with what appeared to be fear.

I'd expected her to laugh off the allegation and tell her
husband it was a ludicrous suggestion. I'd wanted to laugh
myself. Will had to be joking. Only it seemed he wasn't.

"Do you have children?" Erin asks me today. It's their
third visit and she's standing by the bookcase, her gaze trailing
my books until settling on my photo again.

I usher her towards the sofa. Maybe I should remove the
picture of Lily and me if I don't want anyone looking at it. It
isn't as if I need to see it when I could draw it from memory.
Lily's face as she beams at the camera, mouth wide and teeth
on show. She was always the more photogenic of the two of us.
She's wearing the gold necklace our dad gave her on her thirteenth birthday, just over a year before she was killed. It was
so delicate and so unique, with a leaf that curled at its edges,
dented with little pockmarks.

Lily hadn't once taken it off since her birthday and I know she had it on the night she died, and yet it was the one thing no one has ever been able to find. Despite months of searching, tipping the house upside down, scouring the edge of the lake where Lily lay, we have never seen the necklace again.

Erin moves towards the sofa, and I give a glimmer of a shake of my head to tell her I don't talk about my own life.

"Oh sorry, I shouldn't—" She cuts off quickly.

"It's fine, don't worry." I have been asked enough times in the past about various aspects of my life, and mostly people are well-meaning. A lot of the time I don't mind telling clients I don't have children of my own, but I don't have any inclination to share my personal life with the Hardings.

"Some days I can't remember what life was like before Sadie came along," Erin muses as she takes her place on the sofa next to Will, who is already sitting down. "It's as if she's always been here."

Will nods in agreement. "She's just a part of us," he says.

"Coco was too," Erin goes on. "I still can't believe she's gone."

Now Will looks awkward. "There's been loads of reports of people dognapping in our area," he tells me. "You see plenty of it on some of the local Facebook groups. It's horrible. But it's likely what happened. I think someone has taken her." I notice how he doesn't glance at his wife as he says this, but I can also tell he wants to, to see how she reacts.

I could tell him it's hard to tell what Erin is thinking when she isn't responding in any way.

"It is truly awful," I say. "Have you spoken to the police?" The way she sits there rooted to the spot, I can almost believe Erin had something to do with Coco's disappearance herself.

"Yes, of course," Will says. "But there's little they can do."

"I'm so sorry," I tell them, but I direct my words at Erin, hoping for something back.

She glances away, looking over my shoulder, and it hits me that she might be trying not to cry. "I don't think Will wanted her," she says suddenly. "He didn't want the dog."

"What?" he cries, turning to her. His face is a picture of shock. "What are you on about? I loved it, you know I did."

"Why did you say that in the past tense?" she asks him. "You said you loved her. Like you know she's gone for good."

"I didn't mean anything by it. Don't look into it, Erin."

She turns away from him and back to me. I can see there's more on her mind, and so I lean towards her to let her know I am listening. "I think we have to address what Will said last week," I say. "That you think he killed Coco."

"I never said that."

"But I know you're thinking it," he says. "Like I could even be capable of it."

"You were so clinical when she disappeared," Erin says to him. "So functional."

"I knew how much you were hurting," he cries. "I was trying to make it easier for you. I *thought* we would find her. And I wasn't clinical. I was just trying to be practical."

Erin turns back to me. "The other day I walked in the house and saw Will holding her lead. He was just swinging it." She moves her own arm back and forward. She seems to have gone a shade paler.

"Erin?" Will lets out a laugh. "Seriously, what the hell are you talking about?"

"Erin?" I prompt her myself. "Can you explain what you mean?"

She closes her eyes as she tells me. "That was all. He was just swinging Coco's lead. Back and forth. I don't know why." She shakes her head. "I don't know," she repeats. "It frightened me, though."

"This is crap," Will snaps. "It didn't even happen. And when was it supposed to be?" he demands.

"A week ago, maybe. I don't know; I can't remember."
She squeezes her eyes tighter, as if trying to will the memory
back. Her hands are shaking now, and when she opens her eyes
again, they're filled with tears.

"This is bollocks, Erin. I've got no idea why you're saying
all this. I never touched the lead. I don't even know where it is."

"Of course you do. It's still hanging up on the rack. Where
else would it be?"

Will shakes his head. "None of this is true," he says, staring at her, his mouth agape in horror. "I haven't picked the lead
up since she went missing. Why would I?"

"Erin?" I say. *Is it true?*

Her eyes flicker. Something has passed behind them—
a memory or a thought, I'm not sure which—but something
tells me she isn't convinced by her own story. As Erin frowns,
her head gives the minutest of shakes. There are words on her
lips that she is refusing to speak, and eventually she turns her
gaze away from both of us and back out to the window, her
eyes shining with tears as they catch the light.

Will is looking at me now. He still seems surprised, with
his eyes raised and his hands splayed as if to say, *See. I told you
she isn't even here most of the time.*

I wonder if this has happened before, but I have to choose
my words carefully. I can't make it seem like I'm taking a side,
but it's hard to believe Erin. I go in softly, speaking to him. "Is
this the first time Erin thinks you have done something that
you believe you haven't, Will?"

He nods, glancing at his wife. "I always make sure you
know how much I love you," he says.

"I know," she says in a whisper, as if she truly believes this.
"I do know that."

It's the first time I feel the weight of the crack in their marriage, and my heart breaks a little to see it. In this moment the
Hardings are nothing more than a couple crying out for my
help to save them from unravelling further, and I know I need

to delve deeper to what lies at the core. But, where I'm usually excited at the prospect of what I'll find, with Erin and Will, I realise I'm a little uneasy about what might be lurking there.

*   *   *

"I want to talk about your childhood today, Erin," I say to her. "I know last week when we spoke, you felt it wasn't relevant, but I want to talk about both of your pasts in turn."

"Fine," she replies.

"Tell me about your parents, your family growing up," I say.

Erin inhales a tight breath as she starts, rolling her shoulders forward and pressing her hands between her thighs. "When I was young, it was my dad I always wanted to be with. He showed me more attention than my mother ever did. I knew he was a good man because he always had such a nice smile and he used to tickle me under the chin and tell me how well I did things. My mother, on the other hand, didn't have any time for me. She never asked me how my day at school was or reminded me to brush my teeth at night. She never came to anything at school if she didn't have to, only the things she thought she should be seen at.

"She bought me things I didn't want from the money Dad worked so hard to earn, but she always bought herself more. Dad started working more, because she was always demanding more, and so by the time I was ten or eleven, he was barely in the house. It was just me and her."

"That must have been hard," I say. *And it must be hard to let yourself get close to anyone else now*, I think.

Erin shrugs. "I knew no different. Just that my mum never wanted me and my dad allowed her to reject me. He was weak. I realised that when I was in my teens. He did everything she wanted, and he never stood up to her. He idolised her for some reason, but she was just with him for the money. Or the prospect that one day he might make some."

"That kind of rejection is very hard to deal with," I say.

"Yeah. But I felt it more from him by the end. She wasn't capable of loving anyone but herself—but my dad could have. I know because, like I say, I saw it in those early years from him."

"Do you have any siblings?"

"Sam," she says. "He was my half brother, my dad's son, and he was five years older than me. He lived with his mum not that far away from us, but whenever I wanted to see him I had to go over there, because my mother made sure he knew he wasn't welcome at ours.

"Even when he was a teenager and our age gap felt widest, he always made time for me. We used to play cards, and he built me dens. He told me he knew what my mother was like and I could always tell him anything. I used to tell him that I hated her, because at that age I couldn't think what else he might mean, and Sam used to smile and say, 'Yeah. I can understand that.'

"Then when I was ten and he was fifteen, his mum got sick and I wasn't allowed to go over. Sam used to come out and meet me sometimes, but often he just started crying and I never knew what to do. She died within the year, and that's when everything got worse, because by then he was sixteen and he had to move in with us. I was super excited when I heard the news, but the day he moved in, even at eleven, I knew it was going to be awful. My mother could barely look at him, and every time Sam was out of the room, she'd tell my dad that Sam had broken something or spoken to her rudely, and I knew she wasn't ever telling the truth.

"But then as the weeks went on, it was that Sam was smoking or drinking or skipping school or coming home late. And then one day he was no longer there. I came back from school, and all his stuff was gone. Dad told me he was going to live with his mum's brother and that it was much better all round. Only I knew what he really meant was that it was much better for my mother.

"And that was it. I never saw him again. So that's my childhood," she says bluntly.

"Erin, I'm so sorry to hear about Sam," I tell her.

"You know, out of everything, that is the one thing I would never forgive my dad for. I might hate my mum for it, but it was also expected. But my dad—" She breaks off and shakes her head. "He made that choice . . ." As Erin's words fizzle out, I am certain this must have damaged her much more than she wants to admit.

* * *

I'm glad I have my monthly call with Elise this afternoon, because I need to run past her what I've gleaned from my first three sessions with the Hardings.

"Will Harding told me last week that his wife thinks he killed their dog," I tell her, after giving a brief background.

"Jesus! And she's backing it up?"

"Not outright, but she doesn't deny it. In our session this morning, she described how he was swinging the dog lead around after the dog went missing. I felt she was insinuating he was taunting her."

I hear Elise suck in a breath. I haven't come to her with something like this before, and I don't know if she's dealt with anything remotely similar. "Do you think he could have done?" she asks me.

I think before I answer, because I need to get this right, though this isn't the first time I've considered the question. *Do I think it possible?*

"From the limited time I have spent with him, no," I say. And I should know. I have looked at a killer's eyes. You see a darkness in them, like I saw in Kieran Blake. You see the coldness of their heart, the emptiness that emanates from their pupils. I don't see that in Will Harding.

What he portrays is a man who loves his wife and is confused by what she's accusing him of. Apart from this accusation, I'd be saying he has no idea how they came to the point of needing couples therapy. But am I seeing the truth?

"We spoke about Erin's past today," I go on. "She recognises she was rejected by her parents as a child." We both understand how much of a bearing this can have on any relationship Erin has if she hasn't dealt with it.

"And Will's?"

"We ran out of time. I want to cover that in our next sesssion."

"So what do you think is going on?" Elise asks me.

"Well, Erin is adamant he's to blame and that she doesn't trust him, and he is adamant she's lying."

"Okay. So let's start by questioning *why* they're saying what they are. Why would Erin tell you her husband killed their dog if he didn't? Why blame her husband for something so awful if he hasn't done it?"

"Because she believes he did," I answer. "That's what I keep coming back to. And he insinuates she's crazy."

"Which he's going to do if he says she's lying. But if she thinks he *did* do it, then something must have given Erin cause to think her husband is capable of harming her dog," Elise points out.

"Or at the very least, knowing what happened to it but not telling her," I add.

"Or maybe she *doesn't* believe he did it?" she tests.

"And so she's blaming him for some other reason?"

"Maybe."

"So Will has done something else that she can't forgive him for."

"Which could be a number of things," Elise says. "Maggie, I understand why you've bought this issue to me, but you have to remember you are their therapist, not a detective. You're just there to listen and help them work through whatever it is they bring to the table. And whatever conclusions you draw, they're going to be purely your own assumptions for now," she says. "Not necessarily the truth."

"Especially if one of them doesn't want me knowing the truth," I murmur.

"Just be careful, Maggie."

"What do you mean?" I ask, although I already think I know there's something off about the Hardings and their contradictions.

"Take a step back from them, distance yourself a little more," she says.

But how can I if one of them needs my help?

8

Four months earlier
ERIN

EASTER HAS FALLEN early this year, which means there's a damp spring chill in the air when Sadie wakes at six AM, consumed by excitement to see if the Easter bunnies have been. I take her through the motions—gathering the little pink bucket I bought the year she was born, when she was far too young to be finding her own eggs—and hold her hand as she slips on her shoes to go outside.

It doesn't pass me by how different I feel to last year as she guides me around the garden, yelping with delight when she finds a shiny foiled egg beneath a bush. I remember the delight I shared with her before, the feeling that bubbled inside me as if I were the child myself, and yet this year I am numb.

I bend down, helping her count her eggs as Will calls from the doorway, where he's standing in his pyjamas, a mug of coffee in his hand. "How many have you found?"

"Twelve," I murmur as Sadie shrieks the number back to him excitedly.

Sadie releases my hand as she runs to him, and he steps out onto the decking to peer in her bucket. "Oh wow, the bunnies have been very generous to you." He reaches out to ruffle her hair, and I notice the way his gaze flicks to me, guarded, his smile reaching no farther than his lips.

*   *   *

For the most part we are making a good pretence that everything is normal. We're at an impasse, neither of us budging—me holding on to the belief that my husband is somehow deceiving me, him insisting it's all in my head. Only one of is right.

But for the sake of Sadie, we carry on. "Breakfast?" Will asks. "I'm making pancakes."

"They smell good," I say, "don't they, Sadie? Shall we cut up some berries to go with them?"

Together Sadie and I get berries from the fridge, a chopping board and knife, and I slowly halve the fruit for her to pop into a bowl. She chatters away, and Will and I respond, and on the outside nothing has changed. Or at least I hope this is the way she sees it. I don't want my daughter to have any idea that as we stand here making breakfast together, my stomach is churning and my heart fluttering. That I don't enjoy any of these happy moments with her, because my head is filled with questions I can't make sense of. That I feel like something awful might happen but couldn't say what.

I find myself watching Will intently nowadays, looking for another reason to mistrust him and to pull him up on a lie. I search for clarity, an explanation, because while he continues to tell me it's all in my head and he had nothing to do with Coco, I can't help but replay the way I felt that day.

At times I wonder if I'm imagining a darkness behind his eyes and the distance I can feel growing between us. I search for moments before Coco's disappearance that I might have overlooked, the signs that my marriage was already beginning to turn down a darker path, because I can't understand how this could all be imagined.

There were days when Will worked later than I'd expected him to, though he always returned with an excuse.

I didn't know the passcode for his phone, but at the same time I'd never thought to ask him for it. Would he give it to me if I asked him now? I wonder, as he makes Sadie giggle with a funny story. Would it sound out of turn if I suddenly did so?

"What's the code for your phone?" I say, which to him is apropos of nothing.

"What?" He screws up his face.

"Don't most married couples know their other halves' passwords?"

"Isn't Mummy being silly?" he says, smiling at our daughter with one eye on me as he piles pancakes onto a plate and takes them to the table. "But I can tell you it." He reels off six numbers that I slot into my memory, and yet what is the point of it when his phone sits in his back pocket? "Sadie, are you going to have some of your chocolate egg with breakfast?" he asks, and she claps her hands and starts unwrapping one.

I look for things, but I don't find them, and so the next moment I tell myself that maybe I was wrong. Whatever I felt on Valentine's Day, it wasn't real. My husband is still the same person I married and I have no reason to mistrust him, and so we can try to move on and get back to normal.

After all, the only thing that has changed for certain is that Coco is still missing. And what if it's nothing more than grief making me feel this way? I'm blaming Will because he was looking after her. So what happens if she one day reappears and an explanation is given? How amazing that would feel. To be able to concede I was wrong.

Of course, I question myself about this constantly. I could be wrong about Will. I *must* be wrong about him, for how is it even possible that the man sitting across the table from me, the man I have loved for fourteen years, now induces fear in me rather than security? It makes no sense.

But then I remember the feel of his hands around me when he tried to put on the necklace, and it all comes flashing back. That was the moment everything changed; it didn't even start with Coco. It began that morning.

* * *

I take a shower after breakfast and start preparing the lunch, because Zoe and her family are coming. Sadie wants to help me, always by my side, and so I ask her to wash the carrots and give her a big sieve that keeps her happy for a while.

At eleven thirty, when the lamb is in the oven, Zoe's lot arrive. Sadie is swept up in the excitement of having two older children to play with and follow around.

"Happy Easter," my best friend says, kissing me on the cheek and thrusting a chilled bottle of Sancerre into my hand. She has arrived with a stack of Easter eggs, which she piles on the table. "Shall I hide these in the garden?"

"No," I laugh. The kids are already outside with bubble wands. Zoe's youngest, Jacob, is using his as a sword as her seven-year-old, Marlie, entertains Sadie with bubbles. "I think they're fine playing."

"In that case, is it too early?" She doesn't wait for an answer as she reaches into my cupboard for wineglasses and pours us both some wine.

"I guess not," I say. "Just don't let me forget the lunch."

"God, no way. I'm not allowing you to ruin my favourite roast."

We have been doing this for years, for as long as the four of us have all been a group, since Zoe met Dave at work three years after I got together with Will. It's one of our many traditions, Easter lunch, along with Boxing Day sleepovers and New Year's Eve parties. Ever since we met at school, Zoe has been the sister I never had, the sibling I craved after Sam left, and we've both always been so grateful that our husbands became best friends too.

Right now the men are chatting at the end of the garden, beers in hand, as Will points out something in the fence that he wants Dave to have a look at. I can sense Zoe looking at me. "What's the matter, Erin?" she asks. "Something's clearly on your mind."

"Everyone seems to have forgotten Coco," I say.

"I haven't forgotten."

I shrug. "I know, it's just . . ."

"It's hard. It must be awful. I can't imagine."

No, Zoe can't, because she can't conceive how broken my heart is.

"Does Sadie ask about her?"

"She stopped a couple of weeks back."

"Well, that's good. And to be expected, you know that, right? She's three. Time moves on quicker for her."

"I wish it could for me." I take a large sip of my wine and then put the glass down. I know if I carry on, I will mess up the lunch.

"It is weird, though, isn't it?" Zoe says. "That there hasn't been one sighting of her. What does Will say about it? What does he think must have happened?"

At this I feel myself stiffen, and Zoe must notice it too, because she says, "Erin?"

"It is weird." I ignore her. "And Will can't offer me anything more than I know myself. The gate was locked. I know, because I did it."

I stop myself then and think back to that day. I had checked the gate that morning, I know I had, because the rain and winds had been high in the night and some of the fencing was wobbly. As soon as Will left for school, I had done a circuit of the garden, and I remember in particular checking the latch. "So there's no way she could have got out down the side," I say. "What *is* Will doing by the fence?" I add out loud as I watch my husband pulling at a loose piece of panel.

Zoe looks out to the garden, but she doesn't answer me. She doesn't realise the way I examine every single thing Will does these days.

"And you didn't notice anyone around?" she goes on.

"No one." Our cameras didn't pick anyone up, but neither did they catch anyone leaving the house, because they don't cover every patch of our garden and driveway. There are blind spots, a fault in the decisions Will made when he installed them himself, and we have never done anything to rectify it.

Zoe sighs. "I'm sorry, Erin," she says as she fills our glasses up with another slug of wine, picking mine up and pressing it back into my hand.

"Zoe?" I say, turning to her.

"Yes?"

"What happened last year—did you and Dave ever question Will's innocence? Did you ever wonder if he might have done something, just hadn't wanted to say it to me?"

"No!" she exclaims. "Of course not."

"Not once?" I persist. "Because I wouldn't blame you if you had."

"Erin," she laughs, "I'm telling you the truth. We didn't. We know Will; he would never hurt anyone. And besides, that other teacher, Rebekah, was with him. She said the girl made it all up."

"I know," I say.

"So why are you asking me this again? Didn't you believe him?"

"No, I did," I say, and I had. I never once doubted my husband when a fifteen-year-old told her parents he had called her out in class on how she looked, said his comments had been inappropriate. I believed him because this was Will, even before the child retracted it and was made to apologise, and his colleague, Rebekah Hasler, confirmed she had been in his class when it was supposed to have happened.

"Look, this is going to sound odd to you, but I need to say it and I need you to just hear me out," I tell her.

"Of course."

My hand trembles against my glass, my stomach turning over with that awful trepidation you get before making a confession. I have no idea how my theory will be received, and once it's out, I can't unsay it. "I think Will had something to do with Coco."

Zoe frowns at me. "What do you mean?"

"I mean, what if he knows what happened to her?"

"You think he's covering it up? Because he doesn't want to hurt you? No," she says. "He wouldn't do that. He knows how much you're breaking over it, and anyone knows it's better to know than be left guessing."

I shake my head, turning back to look at him. They have moved away from whatever he was showing Dave. "I had this feeling," I go on. "The moment he told me she had vanished, I went cold."

"Of course you did—"

"It was more than that," I interrupt, before she can minimalise my feelings. "I just—I *knew* he had something to do with it. I don't know what it is, call it some sixth sense or something, but I'm telling you, Zoe, he did."

"He did what?" she says. "What do you mean?"

"I think he was responsible."

Zoe parts her mouth, glancing outside to our husbands herself now. Her face drops in surprise. "How could you think—" She turns back to me questioningly. "You really believe that?"

When I don't reply, she goes on. "Okay," she says, and I think for a moment she believes me, but then she places a hand on my arm. "Okay, Erin, I can see you really believe this, so don't get me wrong, I'm hearing you. Whatever it is you felt, it's real, I get that."

I frown and pull away from her. I don't know what I expected, but she doesn't believe me at all.

"But this is Will," she goes on, grabbing my arm again and making me turn back. She gestures to outside the window. "Will wouldn't harm your dog. He'd never do anything to hurt you or Sadie, you must know that."

"I do," I say, "or I always did. And anyway, I can see you don't believe me."

"I do believe you felt something, but—" She pauses. "I don't know, it must be the shock of hearing the news. Whatever you felt in that moment has got mixed up with some other feeling. I mean, don't you think that makes more sense?" she says. "Don't you think you're overlaying the anxieties of Coco disappearing and how it made you feel in that moment onto thinking Will's the one who did it? I mean, he was the one who told you, right?"

"Yes."

"So you could be blaming him because he was the messenger." She seems pleased with her observation and analysis, like she's come to a logical conclusion and surely now I must agree with her. "Erin?" she prompts me when I don't respond.

"I know how I felt," I say in a whisper, tears pricking at my eyes. If Zoe doesn't believe me, then I know without a doubt no one else will. Not Maggie. Not anyone.

Only before this happened, I would have been saying the same thing myself—there is no way on earth my husband would do anything to hurt me or Sadie. And so what has happened to change that?

"And why would he do it, anyway?" Zoe continues. The hand holding her glass waves about as she speaks. "I mean, even if he did it by accident . . ." She drifts on, realising what she has just suggested, before shaking her head and picking up again. "No! Will could never live with the lies." As if she knows my husband better than I do.

"Right," I say.

"Erin, don't clam up on me."

"What's the point when you're not listening?" I open the oven door, prodding at the lamb until its juices flow out. I wish I had never said anything.

"I am listening," she begs. "It's just . . ." She trails off.

"We're having counselling," I tell her, closing the door back up. I don't know why I didn't say anything to her before, maybe because it all happened so quickly. "I thought you should know, before Will tells Dave."

"Counselling?" Zoe puts her glass down heavily beside the sink as I stand back up. "Since when?"

"We had three sessions before the holidays started. We've missed a week."

She screws up her face and looks over her shoulder and out into the garden again. "But what for?"

"Because we're falling apart, Zoe," I say, closing my eyes, willing the tears not to start again.

"No." She comes over to me and takes hold of my arms. "No, you can't be. This is because of Coco?" she asks, incredulous. "Because of what you've just been telling me?"

I shrug and look away, picking up a tea towel and mindlessly wiping it around a serving dish that doesn't need cleaning. I shouldn't have told her. What if she tells Dave and they laugh about it, and he talks to Will and my husband confides he's worried I'm going mad? They will both believe *him*.

"I just—" She stops, not knowing what to say to me, and I wish I had never brought it up.

"No, you're right," I tell her. "Of course you're right. It's probably just the emotion of losing Coco, like you say. Counselling's not just about that. It's about us, families, everything."

"Oh. *Your* family?" she says.

I don't bite but Zoe knows my childhood well enough, and I can't believe she has insinuated that it has to be my side that brings the problems. She knows better than to do that. I ignore her and just say, "Please don't say anything to Dave."

"Of course I won't." Zoe nods and gives me a smile, but it's an uneasy one. She knows I'm not happy and that there's plenty I'm not confiding in her like I normally would. But she also has to understand there's nowhere else for us to go if she doesn't believe me, or even want to try to.

As our conversation drops and I continue making lunch for everyone, I feel betrayed by my best friend. It's a betrayal that sits heavily inside me and makes me question how we move on from here.

But whatever Zoe says to try to convince me, I feel it deep in my gut. My husband is lying to me. I just don't know why.

NOW—AUGUST

CORINNE PASHLEY ARRIVES at the hospital, where her daughter is in a coma, at seven o'clock in the morning. She knows the exact time because Mick is fussing over the parking ticket, asking her how long he thinks they'll be there for.

"I don't know, Mick," she mutters. "However long it takes."

He tells her to go ahead, that he'll be with her in a moment, as he fumbles in his pocket for change, holding a handful of coins and starting to pick through them.

Corinne tuts and rolls her eyes. She should have come on her own. The old fool is slowing her down these days. She knows he didn't want to come to the hospital; she saw the panic in his eyes when he relayed the message that their daughter, Erin, had been in an accident and that she was in a coma, though she knew his fear likely only mirrored her own. Neither of them knew what to do when they hadn't seen Erin in too many years to count.

Mick had woken her up at five AM to tell her. "Erin's unconscious in hospital," he said.

"What?" She screwed her eyes up at him. "What are you talking about?"

"Erin. I had a call—"

"How did they get our number?"

"It was a friend," he told her. "One of her friends called me."

"My God," she said. It must be serious. "I didn't hear the phone ring."

"What do we do?"

"How did one of her friends have our number?"

"I don't know!" he cried, like he was exasperated with her. "What does that matter? I want to know what we do now."

"How am I supposed to know that, Michael?"

"Well, do we go to the hospital?" he said. "We should, shouldn't we? We need to make sure she's okay."

She turned over and looked at the clock. "It's five AM!" Corinne exclaimed. "We can't go yet. Perhaps when it's visiting hours."

"Does it matter whether it's visiting hours or not if it's an emergency? Do you still have to wait?"

"I don't know! But now you've woken me, I need the toilet." She pushed him out the way as she left the bedroom and wandered down the landing to the bathroom.

When she came out, Mick was hovering outside, waiting for her. "I think we should go later," she said. "Seven o'clock. We'll go at seven." And eventually her husband agreed. That way at least they'd have time for some tea and toast first.

Now they're here and Corinne is inside, she weaves her way through the maze of hospital corridors. She's wearing heels from New Look that were £19 in the sale, and they clip-clop on the shiny surface and occasionally slip, and maybe they weren't the best choice, but she likes to make a good impression when she meets new people, especially doctors.

As soon as she turns the corridor to ITU, she comes face-to-face with a man she can only assume, by the look of confusion and then recognition on his face when he sees her, is her son-in-law, for he says, rather too loudly, "What the hell are you doing here?" He puffs his chest out like he's getting ready for a fight. She assumes he must recognise her from photos.

"William?" she questions. "Well, she is my daughter. We have every right to be here." Corinne has never been one to be told what she can and can't do. "Now where is there a doctor we can speak to?" She brushes past him, looking over her shoulder, wondering if Mick will be with her anytime soon or if he's taken himself back to the car and is going to wait there till she's out.

She wouldn't put it past him. For someone who was so anxious they come to the hospital to see how Erin is, he's now anxious to be away from it. She often wonders what she's still doing with the man. She should have got out twenty years ago when she still had her looks.

William steps in front of her. "I can tell you what's happening. Erin's been in an accident. She lost a hell of a lot of blood, and she's had her spleen removed. And she's now in ITU and she can't have visitors."

"Whyever not?"

William laughs at her. "Because she's in intensive care," he almost shouts at her. "And so why don't you give me your number, and I will call you if there's anything you need to know."

"No. Thank you. I will speak to a doctor myself."

"Is this all just for show?" he says.

She raises her eyes at him as a door to a side room opens to her left, and in that moment she catches sight of a woman on a bed. Corinne takes a step forward. "Is that Erin?" She barely recognises her. She tells herself it's because of her daughter's ghostly white complexion and the tubes inserted into her nose, trailing over her body, and the bruising down the side of her face that puffs it out and distorts it, and the hair scraped back from her forehead. She tells herself all this, but she also knows it isn't the truth. She doesn't recognise Erin because she hasn't seen her in years, and even without all those things, she can see how much she has changed.

Corinne inhales deeply and turns away. Her legs are shaking, and she's afraid they might buckle any moment. William is staring at her.

"She's a strong girl," she says to him.

"How would you know?" he spits back.

She knows. She has seen her defiance.

"Mr. Harding?" a voice from behind them calls out. They both turn to see a young woman standing in front of them. "My name's Etta Banks. I'm a family liaison officer." She turns to Corinne and smiles, holding out a hand. "Are you family?"

"Yes," Corinne says. "I'm her mother."

Beside her Will laughs again. "You haven't been her mother for the last sixteen years. And you were barely one before that."

Corinne feels her face burning bright red. "And what do you know about that, William?" she says.

He is turning to the FLO, who is watching them both with surprised interest. "Well." She smiles at them awkwardly. "I am here to help"—she pauses—"the family." She looks from Will to Corinne and back again.

"You're not a doctor, though?" Corinne asks. She knows deep down that she can't really call herself family when she hasn't had anything to do with her daughter for so long. Not that it was her choice. It was Erin who left home at eighteen and made it clear she didn't want either her or Mick in her life anymore. As she said, she has seen her daughter's defiance.

"No. I'm not a doctor. I'm a police officer," she says. "But my role right now is to support you."

"A police officer?" Corinne repeats. "Why do we need a police officer supporting us?"

"Because Erin was in a hit-and-run," Will tells her, like he thinks she doesn't already know this. "And because they want to know what happened. But like I said, Corinne, I can call you. If you need to know anything."

He wants her gone. And to be honest, she doesn't particularly want to hang around herself when she can't see her daughter and there are police officers lingering. But what would it say about her if she went? "I'll get myself a cup of tea, and then I'll be back," she says.

As she begins to walk away, she feels an unexpected swell of emotion. Corinne is not and has never been maternal, and there's no getting away from the fact that Erin was an unplanned mistake. Corinne had gotten pregnant and not known what to do, and because she and Mick were married, they just carried on through, until one day she was holding a baby in her arms and realising this wasn't what she wanted— not one bit.

Mick already had a son, whom she didn't take to, with his ex, who lived too close for her liking. And then he was telling her how happy he was about having another, and she actually believed he was. But for someone who was happy, he certainly let her deal with Erin on a daily basis while he went out to work to make the money he never brought in. They should have swapped roles and they might have both done a better job.

Corinne remembers the first time she was left alone with Erin when Mick had gone back to work. She stared at her daughter's tiny body and wondered at how fragile she was, and the panic struck as she took in how responsible she was for something she hadn't even wanted.

Seeing her here, today, reminds her of that fragility. Only Corinne no longer has any responsibility. She gave up that right a long time ago.

Corinne stops. What she really wants to do is say to William that the reason she knows Erin is strong is because she has become a wife and a mother to a child Corinne is sure she adores. And so she has broken through a long line of bad mothers. She has learnt how to do this despite not being shown, which is something Corinne was never able to do herself.

But she doesn't say anything. Instead she listens to that annoyingly smiley woman, Etta, say to William that she hears he and Erin are recently separated, and she turns around sharply and takes a step towards him again. They were separated? Her daughter's husband leaves her, and the next minute she's in a hit-and-run?

"Did you say it's support you're here for?" Corinne asks Etta.

"I'm sorry?" Etta looks over at her.

"You said you were here for support," Corinne repeats. "But they have nurses for that. And you're a police officer. So I just wondered, is the reason that you're here, with Erin's family"—she gestures towards Will—"for some other reason?" She sees it all the time on TV, the family liaison officers keeping a watchful eye. Yes, she surmises she knows very well what Etta Banks is doing here, and it's because they suspect foul play. They think Will might have had something to do with it.

CHAPTER

9

Four months earlier
MAGGIE

I HAVEN'T SEEN THE Hardings over the Easter holidays but as soon as they settle, I tell them I think a good place to start today would be to learn more about Will's background.

"Sure," he replies casually. "But I don't think there's much to say about my family. I had a pretty normal upbringing. It was Mum and Dad, me, and my younger sister, Jenna. Dad was in the navy, so I didn't see so much of him growing up. We travelled about for his work when we were younger, till I was ten and he retired, and that's when they settled in Dorset. My mum stayed at home to bring me and Jenna up." He pauses. "I'm not sure what else to tell you."

"What was your relationship like with your parents?" I ask. There is no such thing as normal. I always thought my family life was "normal" until after Lily died, driving a knife straight through whatever relationship I had with my parents and cutting us in two.

It wasn't until Elise made me look back at it that I began to realise how much they'd always doted on Lily so much more than me. She was my mum's rainbow baby, as we'd call her now. After Mum suffered a miscarriage, for a time she didn't think she'd be able to have more children. I assume this is why she treated Lily like a precious stone, mollycoddling her, worrying over her as much as she did.

Some days I wonder whether, if my parents had been different towards her, my sister could still be alive. But then I live with all the what-ifs. What if they hadn't gone abroad and let me persuade them I could look after Lily? What if I hadn't failed in doing that?

So I don't believe there's any such thing as normal, but Will is continuing, telling me, "It was all good. My mum was always there for us. She still is if we ever need her." He looks at Erin as if to convey the *us* includes her now, but she doesn't react. She's sitting upright, watching Will as he tells his story. "She's just nice, isn't she?" he asks his wife, who still doesn't respond. "I mean, everyone loves my mum; they always have. When I was young, all my mates used to. Jenna's friends too. They would always be at our house, watching films or getting ready to go out. Mum's great." He carries on gushing. "She's the one out of my parents I'd turn to if I ever needed to. Mum has been good to us. She's always there."

"She is always *there*," Erin chimes in, but the look on her face suggests she has surprised herself by saying anything, and maybe she didn't mean to.

"What's that supposed to mean?" Will glares at her.

"It doesn't mean anything," she says, trying to brush him off.

"Yes it does. You don't like the fact that my mum is involved in our lives. You're jealous of my family. You always have been."

"Jealous?" she says.

"Yes," he replies eventually. "I think you are. My parents are still together and they're both around for us, and sadly, I think that sometimes you begrudge it." His breathing is heavier; he's on a ride that I'm not sure he wants to be on, but at the same time he doesn't know how to get off. "Like our wedding. You hated that they paid so much money towards it, and yet it was the only way we could afford what we really wanted, and so we took it. And you didn't like that you had to be grateful for it."

"No. I didn't like the fact they were buying slots for guests we didn't even know," she says. "I said I thought they had a stake in our wedding because they were spending so much money on it. That's how it felt. Your dad mentioned people he worked with who he wanted to invite, and we hadn't even met them, but you just went along with it."

"I didn't really see what the problem was," he says. "And yes, maybe I did think they could have a handful of their friends if they wanted when they were giving us so much money for the day."

"I wanted you to stand up to them," she says.

"You sound so ungrateful, Erin," he replies, ignoring her comment.

"Do I?" she says. "I don't mean to." She doesn't look remotely bothered that she does. "I *am* grateful. I just some-times think their help comes with caveats."

"My mum comes over every Monday morning to look after Sadie so we can come here," he says. "Did you know she's had to cancel an appointment this morning so she can do it for us?"

"What appointment?"

"She says it's nothing important, but I don't know that's true. The fact is, she does it without a fuss, so tell me what caveats she's imposing on us for looking after her grandchild?"

"Really?" Erin says in a way that means, *You really want me to go there?*

Will looks at her, astounded. "Yes. Really," he says through gritted teeth.

"They bought us our house so we would live near to them," she snaps.

"What?" Will shakes his head, incredulous.

"So that she could be as involved as she wants to be. Which is a hell of a lot."

"What are you saying? That my parents helped pay for our deposit, just so, what—they could control us?"

She turns back to stare at him. "Those are your words," she mutters.

Will's hands ball into fists; his eyes flare as he gapes back at her. His whole posture changes, and while I want to see how he responds, I fear he might get up and walk out.

"Will?" I say softly. "How does this make you feel?"

"Angry," he snaps. "I can't believe she's saying all this. Why are you? Why are you trying to hurt me, Erin?"

"Hurt you?" she cries, tears springing into her eyes. "You're hurting me!"

"How? How the hell am I doing that?"

"I don't know!" she says. "I don't know," she adds, quieter this time, her eyes filled with what looks like both panic and desperation. She flings her head back on the sofa and stares at the ceiling. Eventually she says, "I don't see how any of this is helping."

"I am trying to help you," I say. "But often we have to take a step back first to move forward. And it's interesting that both of you have focused on your mothers. They seem to be focal points in your childhoods. Will, you say your father was away a lot when you were growing up, and Erin, you mentioned your dad wasn't at home much either. But it's your mothers who your narratives seem to centre around. They feel like very strong characters."

"And what does that matter?" Erin asks.

"Maybe it doesn't. Maybe it's the relationship with your dad that we shouldn't dismiss."

"I told you my dad was weak," she replies. "He let her control him. She controlled everything. She said she wanted Sam gone, and bam." Erin clicks her fingers. "He's sent off to live with some uncle on a farm like he was an unwanted pet."

"You told me in our last session that it was his behaviour that hurt you more?"

"Because *she* couldn't love me," Erin said. "But he chose not to. There was this time when I was ten and I woke up to find my mum calling me from downstairs, her voice all sickly sweet, telling me she'd see me later. I got to the top of the stairs and looked down to find her all dressed up and smiling and could hear a car engine revving outside. When I asked her where she was going, she said, 'We're out for the day, darling, remember?' She had never told me. I asked who was going to take me to school, and she laughed and said, 'Oh come on, Erin, you take the bus to school.' I remember her rolling her eyes at someone who must have been standing in the living room, but I couldn't see."

"You never told me this," Will says when she pauses.

Erin glances at him but then carries on with the story. "I would have had to get two buses into school on my own, and I'd never done anything like that before. I was at primary school!" she says. "I called Sam, because he always would have helped me, but his mum told me he'd already left. So I hung up and spent the day in my pyjamas watching television and eating cornflakes for lunch. When the school rang, I pretended to be my mum and said I wasn't well. No one ever found out. Mum didn't even ask if I'd made it in okay when she got home, just told me what a wonderful day out she had.

"But I wasn't ever really bothered about what she did, because even by then I didn't expect any more from her. It was my dad—" Erin breaks off. "It's that he let her. When Mum walked out the door that morning, I looked out my bedroom window and saw the car I'd heard was his rusty red Ford Focus. He didn't stop her. And before that I always thought he would be the one to save me. But he didn't. In the end, he chose her over me and Sam."

Erin shuffles forward to the front of her seat, lengthening her back. "But you know what? I didn't carry any of this through to my other relationships, if that's what this is about. I'm well aware of my upbringing, but it has nothing to do with whatever's happening in my marriage."

* * *

That night, Richard suggests we go for dinner at the pub on the harbour. The evenings are getting lighter, the days feel a little longer. I love this time of year, when it feels like summer isn't far off. We leave the house at five thirty so we can take Rocky for a walk before we eat.

"You look tired," Richard says.

"I am. I don't like Mondays. The early start kills me," I joke.

"Mags, it's nine AM. It's hardly early."

"I know, but still."

"How was work today?" he asks.

"Okay. I don't feel like I'm moving forward much with my new couple," I tell him. "I don't really know how to help them at the moment."

This is as far as any conversation about work will go with Richard. I would never tell him anything about my clients, and neither would he ask. He knows how professional I am when it comes to my work, and he wouldn't want me to be any other way.

"You'll work it out," he says, as my mobile begins to ring from deep inside my handbag.

"Hmm," I mutter, fishing around for my phone and eventually getting my hands on it.

I glance at the screen, not recognising the number that flashes on it, and for a moment my thumb hovers over it as I decide whether or not to answer, but in the end I do.

"Maggie Day?" a voice on the other end of the line says.

"Yes."

"My name is Detective Inspector Jack Lawson. You might not remember, but I spoke to you a few years back about Kieran Blake. I worked on your sister's case many years ago."

"I remember," I say, glancing at Richard, my stomach twisting as I wonder what the detective is calling me about. Our last conversation is as clear as if it was yesterday, when he told me that Kieran had finally admitted to killing Lily.

Richard frowns, likely hearing some of the conversation as he bears left into a side road by the harbour, pulls into a space, and turns off the engine.

"Well, I don't know how you'll feel about this, but Kieran Blake has asked to see you. It might not be something you want, and of course it's for you to consider—"

"He wants to see me?" I say, my breath jarring in my throat.

"Yes, but like I say—"

"Do you know why? I mean, why now? Why has he suddenly changed his mind after all this time?"

"I can hazard a guess that it has something to do with his parole coming up this year. But I don't know that for sure."

"Parole?" I exclaim, the word sticking in my throat. "He can't seriously think he's getting out?"

The detective is silent for a moment. When he replies, he says, "I can't answer what's going to happen, and a date hasn't even been set yet, so please don't worry yourself over that."

"Of course I'm going to worry," I laugh, incredulous. "What are his chances of being released?"

"I really can't say. He's admitted to murder, but he'll be hoping his good behaviour will go in his favour. But if I were a betting man? I would tell you not to worry."

"Yes, you've already said that," I reply. "But I still don't get why this means he's suddenly changed his mind. Does he think seeing me will help him, is that what it is?"

"There may be an element of him thinking that," Jack says. "But it would be misplaced."

"Then I can't see him," I say firmly. "Not if there's the smallest chance. I'm not doing anything that might help him get out of prison."

"That's absolutely fine," he tells me. "It's your choice. I'm just passing on his request. But Maggie, if you ever change your mind, you have my number."

"I do. Thanks." I hang up the phone.

"Is that what I think it is?" Richard says. "He's asked to see you?" He reaches over and takes hold of my hand, squeezing it inside his own.

"Yes. But he wants to do it because his parole's coming up this year. He'll be thinking it could help him, like somehow by seeing me, he's proving he's a changed man or something. I can't risk it," I say.

"But this is what you wanted, Maggie," Richard tells me. "The chance to hear him tell you what happened. It's what's been hanging over you all these years."

"I know, but—" I break off, flinging my head back against the seat rest, turning away so I'm looking out the window at the glimpse of sea over the harbour wall. "What if he gets out?"

"He won't. That's not going to happen."

"But he might!"

"Mags, you don't even know when his parole is yet. Anything can happen, and that's out of your control. All you can do is decide whether or not you want to see him."

"And you think I should," I say.

"I think it's what you've wanted for so long. So yes, I think you need to."

"God." I close my eyes, shaking my head. The thought that I could be sitting in front of that man, looking into his eyes, hearing him tell me what he did to my sister. *Why* he did it. Richard is right, it's what I've always wanted, and yet now I know it's possible, I don't know that I can do it.

NOW—AUGUST

It's 7:20 AM, but already DI Lynsey Clayton is on her third coffee of the morning. Two before she left the house and now one from the cafeteria, which she has to admit is actually rather good. She has the stirrings of a headache, though, which she can put down to either the caffeine she's consumed or the three glasses of Rioja she had last night. She asked the nurse, whose name is Raina, if she had any paracetamol, but was given a frown and a brusque no.

Lynsey scans the café and spots Zoe Sawyer, best friend of Erin, sitting in the near corner nursing a mug of tea, and so she makes her way over and gestures to the spare seat opposite, sitting down before Zoe can refuse.

"How are you doing?" Lynsey asks, letting her gaze run over the bedraggled woman in front of her. Zoe's eyes are swollen and red and make her look like she might break down any minute. Lynsey's hoping the best friend might be able to give her more background.

"Okay. I just wish we knew more. It's this waiting, not knowing if Erin's going to be okay or not."

Lynsey nods. She's thought of this, of course she has, how uncertain Erin Harding's future is and how awful it is for everyone around her, but she can't pretend that her focus hasn't been on who and what put her here in the first place.

"She's in the best place," she says, a platitude, but she doesn't know what else she can give that might help. And so she moves on. "How long have you two known each other?"

"Since we were fourteen. My family moved, and I joined Erin's school. We've been best friends for twenty years."

"A long time," Lynsey muses. "Is it okay if I ask you some questions? It could really help work out what happened to Erin."

"Of course."

"As her best friend, you must know better than anyone what's been going on with Erin lately. Maybe even more so than her husband?" she adds, hoping to get on her good side.

"I'm not so sure I do," Zoe says, her voice small and barely audible.

Lynsey grimaces. She was hoping Zoe would be able to shed a whole heap of light on the situation, especially with Erin's marriage breaking down, but she's also sure there's a lot the friend knows that she doesn't even realise is going to be helpful.

"Did Erin tell you where she was going last night?"

Zoe shakes her head. "We haven't spoken in—I don't know—two or three weeks. Maybe more."

"What did you know about Erin's marriage?" Lynsey asks.

Zoe sighs. "I know it started going wrong about six months ago. Their dog disappeared, and Erin thought Will had something to do with it."

"Had something to do with it?" she repeats.

"He didn't. And it came back two days ago Will told me."

"So it was missing for six months but then reappears two days ago?" She doesn't like coincidences, and she isn't sure if this is one or not.

Zoe nods. "I don't know any of the details. I think it might have been dognappers that abandoned her."

"Why did she think her husband had something to do with it?"

"I really have no idea," Zoe says. "She mentioned it to me on Easter Day and said she was worried about her dog, and about Will, and that he—" She breaks off. "She was just saying she had this feeling he was responsible."

"Like he might have killed it?"

"No." Zoe looks horrified. "God. I don't—" She stops abruptly and Lynsey considers that this is exactly what her friend thought, and Zoe knows it. "It was all totally out of the blue," Zoe goes on. "It made no sense. I told her there was no way Will would have done anything like whatever it was she was thinking. If he knew what had happened to their dog, he would have told her. Will's too honest. I told my husband, Dave, what she'd said, because I just wanted his opinion, you know? I wasn't betraying her or anything."

Lynsey nods, encouraging her to go on. She isn't too interested in how guilty this woman clearly feels.

"Dave laughed it off and said that if anyone was going to bury a dog, it would more likely be him. He just meant that there's no way Will would do it. That's all," Zoe confirms, her cheeks flashing a vibrant red.

"So she did say she thought her husband had killed the dog?" Lynsey confirms.

"She didn't say it outright. That was just the way Dave and I are—we were mucking about. We kind of laughed about it at the time. I really didn't think it was anything serious. I thought that whatever Erin was thinking was because she was upset. She was heartbroken over Coco."

"But the dog came back," Lynsey states.

"Exactly."

"So was that a one-off?" Lynsey asks. "Erin thought her husband might have done something to the dog, and then . . ." She trails off, wanting Zoe to fill in the gaps.

"No, there were other things too. She started accusing Will of things he hadn't done, and he had no idea what she was talking about."

"How do you know he hadn't done them?"

Zoe looks taken aback. "Well, I just know. The things Erin was saying . . . I mean, it came from nowhere, like I said. And who suddenly accuses their husband of doing something awful to their dog? And she stopped talking to me about all of it, and so I believed Will when he was worried, because I was worried too. Erin wasn't herself."

"Has this happened before?" Lynsey asks. "Her worrying over something she says her husband has done?"

"No. Never. They had problems last year, but she didn't think he was lying. Not at the time," Zoe adds.

"So her reaction to the dog disappearing, that was out of character for Erin?"

"Yes. They had an amazing relationship. Erin was so happy."

"Why didn't you believe her?" Lynsey asks.

"Because it didn't make any sense. Will wouldn't have done it."

"But you don't know that," she points out again.

"No, but—" Zoe breaks off, not finishing her sentence. Lynsey wonders how much she's now considering the possibility that he could have.

"They started counselling," Lynsey continues. "So she must have wanted to fix whatever the problem was."

"You think I'm a bad friend," she states. "You don't have to tell me that. I know I wasn't there for her."

Lynsey resists the urge to sigh out loud. Why does everyone think it's all about them? It doesn't matter if Zoe was a bad friend or not; Lynsey just needs to figure out if there's anything she's missing with regards to the husband.

She's done some brief Googling on Maggie Day and knows she works out of that crumbling property on the cliffs. They have a home address for her, and someone is on their way to pay her a visit to see what she knows, but Lynsey also gets how unaccommodating therapists can be when it comes to client confidentiality. "Will thinks Erin carried on seeing her when their sessions stopped," Lynsey says.

Zoe nods again. "She did. I saw them together two weeks ago at the harbour."

Lynsey cocks her head, curious as to what a therapist would be doing out with a client at the harbour.

"They were just talking. I wanted to go over to speak to Erin, but she turned and saw me and just seemed to stare right through me, so in the end I didn't."

"Doesn't that seem odd to you? To meet up with your therapist outside? Could they have bumped into each other?"

"I don't know. They might have, although their conversation was quite animated."

"You think they have a friendship, Erin and Maggie?"

Zoe looks up sharply. Lynsey senses a hint of jealousy at the suggestion, and when Zoe answers, all she says is, "According to Will, whatever their counselling was digging into, it wasn't helping Erin, it was making her worse."

"According to Will, of course," Lynsey points out, as Zoe's cheeks flush bright red again and she drops her gaze to the mug of tea she's cradling between her hands. Lynsey wonders why Zoe so readily believes everything Will tells her, even over and above her best friend.

"Tell me a bit about Erin," Lynsey says, more than anything to make sure she doesn't lose Zoe. She fears Zoe might start closing up on her if she feels backed into a corner.

"She's an amazing friend," Zoe says with a shrug, and Lynsey wonders if that would be the first thing that came into her mind if Erin wasn't lying in a coma nearby. "She's a great mum. She's good fun. She has this infectious laugh. I've always been able to tell her anything—" Zoe breaks off.

"Go on," Lynsey urges.

"She's loyal, she's bloody clever. And talented," she adds. "You know she's writing a children's book? I'm the only one who's seen it. It's brilliant. I told her she should get it published. I don't know why she hasn't tried yet."

"What's it about?"

"This family who live in the woods." Zoe stops and lets out a laugh. "I mean, I know where it originated from; she admitted to me that she had this imaginary family when she was younger. Erin was always creating stories, even back then. She was always great at making things up—" She stops, as if realising what she has just said.

"Erin was found at the edge of Harberry Woods," Lynsey says, changing the subject with this lead-in.

"I know." Zoe looks up again.

"Can you think of any reason why she might have gone there?"

"Not one," Zoe says. "Because until last night, Erin hadn't been anywhere near those woods in years. She hated the place."

"Oh?"

"She grew up there," Zoe says. "You didn't know that? They are the woods I'm talking about. The ones in her stories."

Lynsey parts her lips to answer, but she doesn't want to admit that she actually didn't, and now she wonders why Will Harding didn't tell her that his wife was hit by a car near her old childhood home, which she hadn't been back to in years. At the same time she berates herself for not having found out.

"She hasn't had anything to do with Harberry or the woods, not since she left home at eighteen. She doesn't have anything to do with her parents."

"Why would she go back there again?" Lynsey says, though she isn't expecting an answer. She's just as much asking herself the question. What the hell would draw you back to your childhood home if it was a place you hated? A place you made up an imaginary world to escape from?

Lynsey know she's right to think this isn't an accident. Erin Harding could not have been involved in a random hit-and-run; there are too many coincidences, and like she always says, she doesn't believe in coincidences. One thing she knows is she has to speak to Maggie Day. The therapist could be the one holding the answers.

10

Four months earlier
MAGGIE

ERIN LOOKS STRAINED. Her hands are tightly clenched into fists, and her shoulders are tight. She is rigid on her side of the sofa, while Will won't stop shuffling about.

"How has your week been?" I ask them both, as I always do. My own week has passed, and still I haven't picked up the phone to DI Jack Lawson. I've almost done it in the times when I've plucked up some courage. When I've thought it possible for me to sit in front of my sister's killer and demand he tell me what happened. But then I crumble, plaguing myself with those what-ifs again. What if he doesn't tell me? What if he uses our meeting, as I fear, for nothing but his own advantage? What if I get there and can't do it?

"It isn't good," Erin replies. Her words come out in a whisper. Beside her, Will exhales an exaggerated breath. They are both on their sides of the sofa, but they feel farther apart today than they have been. Both of them are facing me head on, their bodies symmetrical, both feet placed firmly on the floor. Neither is relaxed.

"Can you tell me how it hasn't been good?" I ask.

"She's getting worse." Will sounds frustrated. He's been showing signs of getting increasingly so over the last couple of sessions, but there's also an expression of annoyance etched into his face now. His words are tinged with anger. He shrugs. "She's continuing to accuse me of things that aren't happening. I don't know what to do. It feels like I'm losing my wife."

I feel like I'm losing both of them, if I'm honest. I can't profess I've ever trusted either of them fully, but in those early sessions I saw a need in them to make things right. I believed they loved each other.

But today it feels like their marriage is rapidly spiralling, and I still don't know what I can do to help stop it.

"I'm missing work to be here," Will goes on, "but we're not making any progress. I don't see the bloody point anymore," he mutters.

Fifth visit in and he wants to quit. This sometimes happens, but I can usually see why. It's when one of them doesn't like the direction our sessions are going in, when they might have to accept something they don't want to. But I always manage to lead them on the path they need to go.

This isn't the case with the Hardings. Will doesn't see the point, and I don't either when at least one of them isn't being honest with me, but I'm not prepared to give up.

"How do you feel about what Will's said, Erin?" I ask.

"No one believes me. It's always him they believe." Her hands are clenching together tighter, the whites of her knuckles straining through the skin, making me want to reach out and prise them apart.

"Because I've done nothing wrong, Erin!" Will exclaims. In contrast, his hands are still, held loosely together and his fingers steepled. "You keep making stuff up. That's why no one else believes you. So tell Maggie what I'm supposed to have done. And not something that's just in your head. Don't tell her you think I've killed our dog. Tell her something concrete that makes me this bad guy you suddenly make me out to be."

When she doesn't answer, I prompt her. "Erin?"

But as Erin looks away from me, she appears to be going into a trance. "Okay then," she murmurs. "Last Thursday night I was outside while Will was giving Sadie her bath, and I noticed there was something wrong with the back of his car."

"No! Not this again." He laughs, shaking his head at her. "I said not something you've made up." But I hold up a hand to stop him. I want Erin to talk.

"It was dented," she goes on. "One of the taillights had been bashed in. I thought he'd either had an accident or someone had gone into him that he hadn't told me about. So I went to ask him, and he said there was nothing wrong with the car. He told me to leave him alone so he could carry on bathing Sadie."

"Because you were getting into a state and it was beginning to upset her," he says, exasperated. "I thought it was best you didn't start yelling in front of our daughter, especially when you weren't making any sense in the first place." He turns to me and adds more calmly, "I said we'd talk when I'd finished."

"And did you?" I ask.

"When I was putting Sadie to bed, Will told me he'd looked at the car and there was nothing wrong with it. He told me I'd made it up," Erin says flatly.

"Because there *was* nothing wrong with it," he says. "Not even a scratch."

"Erin?" I say. "Is this true? Did you go back and look at the car?"

"No. Because Sadie wouldn't settle. She kept getting out of bed and saying her stomach hurt, and so I ended up lying with her in my bed. And then by the time she got to sleep, it was pitch-black, and I thought I'd go out in the morning. Only Will had left for work before I woke up."

"Because I had a meeting," he snaps. "Don't make out I went early on purpose."

"But when you next saw the car—" I say to her.

"There was nothing. There wasn't a mark on it. He had got it fixed."

"No, Erin. I had not got it fixed, because there had been nothing wrong with it in the first place," Will says, his voice rising in desperation.

"There had," she tells me, leaning forward. "I promise you there had, because I saw it with my own eyes, and yet he's telling me there wasn't. He's trying to make out I'm going mad." Her eyes are wide with fear as the words spill out of her mouth. "And I'm not," she begs. "I am not crazy."

*　*　*

By the end of the day, I feel agitated. When I've cleared up the room and written my notes, I don't go home straightaway like I usually would but walk along the cliff edge until I come to a spot where I sit on the grass and look out to the sea crashing below me.

The Hardings are playing a game of *he said, she said* with me. One tells me one thing, the other says the opposite. I'm frustrated that I don't know what's going on, but also because I don't feel like I'm doing my job. That there's something about this couple that I am missing.

I pull out my phone and dial the only person I can talk to about it: Elise.

"You sound exasperated," she says when I update her.

"I am. And I don't like that I do. But she thinks he's lying and he says he isn't, and we're just going round in circles."

"A sure sign of gaslighting," Elise says. "Have you thought of that? That this is what he could be doing?"

"Of course, but it doesn't make sense. Not this far into their marriage and out of nowhere. There'd have been red flags before, and she's adamant everything was fine until February. And when she talks about her childhood, she's articulate and understanding of what she's been through. She seems certain she hasn't carried it through to her adult life in a negatively impactful way."

"I agree," Elise says. "You're still trying to solve this mystery, like we spoke about before." She pauses. "You sound like you're getting too involved."

"I just want to do my job," I tell her. "They've sought me out to help, for whatever reason. It's what I need to do. But I don't know how I can.

"Something else happened last week," I go on. "Kieran Blake wants to see me."

"Oh, Maggie." I can hear her surprise. "Will you go?"

"I think I have to," I say. "I don't think I have a choice. I need to hear what he has to tell me." I know, deep down, this is something I will do.

I realise how much Kieran, Lily, and the Hardings are battling for my headspace right now. Maybe Elise is right and I should take a step back from Erin and Will. Perhaps I should let them go, if I can't help them as I want to be able to. It's not as if I believe either of them is in any danger. But then I don't know that I can give up on them.

NOW—AUGUST

DETECTIVE CONSTABLE MARGATE pulls up outside the house on Grange Lane. It's more of a cottage, a quaint sort of place. Maggie Day is supposedly in her early forties, but it's the kind of home he could see his parents living in, though it does have the added benefit of the path behind leading down to the sea. Set back from the road, there's an empty driveway to the left that leads to a garage and a front garden filled with bushes and pots of plants.

As he stands on the pavement, he looks up and down the lane and checks his watch. Seven twenty AM, likely the reason there's not a peep on the road. It's funny, but despite the urgency of this house call, he still feels apprehensive about knocking on the Days' door so early on a Sunday morning. All the curtains in the house are closed; they're most likely still asleep. His wife often asks him how he's such a good police officer when he hates to put anyone out.

Despite this, he walks up the path to the front door, locating the knocker in place of a bell and giving it a loud rap. From inside, he hears the sound of a dog barking and the scampering of paws approaching the door. By instinct, he takes a step back and waits for it to open.

Nothing. He peers up to the windows above, but there's no movement of curtains, and with the dog still barking away, he's sure the household would have woken up. Eventually he steps forward and raps the knocker again, following that with banging his fist for extra luck. Still nothing.

Margate screws up his eyes, looking for a side gate. He'll have a peek around the back, but he's pretty certain that no one is in, or if they are, that they don't want to answer the door to him for some reason.

He unclicks a gate attached to the side of the garage and tentatively walks through to the back garden, a long lawn with a stone-paved patio set against the back of the house, with a long wooden table and six chairs neatly tucked underneath. There are bifold doors that he can see through, and so Margate cups his hand to the glass and peers through, jumping back when a large dog suddenly bounds up to the other side.

"Jesus," he says, now clocking it's a Labrador, wagging its tail, barking at him. There's still no sign of any other movement, and so he returns to the front again and back to the pavement, where he stands for a moment, staring back at the house and wondering what to do next.

To his right, a car alarm beeps once, and he turns to find a woman that he'd place in her early sixties, dressed in leggings and pushing a yoga mat onto the passenger seat of her Mini. She is staring back at him.

"I'm looking for Maggie Day," he tells her. "Do you happen to know if she's away?" The barking starts up again, and he imagines the dog has found its way back to the front door.

"No. She's not away. Her husband is, but Maggie's there. I saw her yesterday." She frowns, looking back at the house. "Have you tried knocking?"

"Yes," he says bluntly. "I have."

"Only the dog's in. I can hear it."

"Yes," he says again. The woman is a genius.

"Maggie should be in, then. I mean, she'd never go away overnight and leave Rocky. And she doesn't ever get up this early on a Sunday!" She laughs as she climbs into her car.

As she drives away and Margate turns back to the house, his mobile starts ringing with a call from DI Clayton. "Any news on Maggie Day?" she asks as he picks it up.

"No, ma'am. She's not at home."

"Have you tried her mobile?"

"No," he says. "Just about to."

"Okay, well, get hold of her. I'm hoping she might have some answers," she tells him. "I think she and Erin might have struck up a friendship of sorts in the last couple of months."

Margate puts the phone down and taps out the number he was sent for the therapist. He waits as it rings and rings and then leaves a message when the answerphone kicks in. The dog has finally stopped barking, at least, and Margate wonders if he shouldn't have just one last check round the back again. If there's one thing Clayton is, it's persistent, and if he can't give her an emphatic answer, she'll hound him.

As he goes back through the side gate, he tries the mobile number again. Only this time as he approaches the back, he hears a faint ringing through the glass doors. Pressing his face up to the glass again and preparing himself for the onslaught of a dog, he catches sight of a mobile on the kitchen table.

Can't get hold of her, he texts his boss. *Phone in kitchen. Neighbour says it's strange the dog is here and she's not. Maggie Day definitely not away this weekend but doesn't appear to be at home either.*

He waits for Clayton's response to come through, all the while thinking that he's going to have to find her somehow.

11

Three months earlier
MAGGIE

KIERAN BLAKE WAS known to my family before he killed my sister, inasmuch as he was known to everyone who lived in our town. He was a name to us, nothing more, though some people had been on the receiving end of his criminal activity in the past: he had broken into their home; their brother or son had been in a fight with him. During his teenage years he had been in and out of juvenile detention for theft, actual bodily harm, and grievous bodily harm.

When he killed my sister, Kieran was thirty. He had been keeping his head down for the past few years, but when he was linked to Lily, his name was dragged up again—an ugly reminder.

The day the police told us, we were asked to sit down in the living room. My parents squished themselves together on the sofa, holding hands, while I stood alone by the fireplace.

"We've arrested a man in connection with Lily's murder," they told us.

"Who?" I demanded.

"A man called Kieran Blake."

"No!" my dad cried out, although I wasn't sure why. In some ways, as long as they had the killer, did it matter whether he was some two-bit criminal we barely knew, or someone closer to Lily, or an out-of-town stranger? Perhaps it was the finality of the case that made him cry out.

The police went on to tell us they were certain they had the right man, and only two days later they charged him.

I wanted to know everything. Why had he done it? How had my sister come to be with him that night? Kieran was more than double her age; there was nothing that would put the two of them together. I barrelled questions at the officers in our home, and I couldn't understand why my parents had retreated into silence.

The police couldn't answer on Kieran's behalf, because he was maintaining his innocence in the early hours of his arrest. But he had been seen with her at midnight the night she was killed, they'd been walking together, towards the lake, and the witness described the young girl as being upset.

"Why didn't they do anything, then?" I yelled.

"They regret not stopping, of course. But it wasn't until they heard what happened to Lily that they thought more of it," the police told us.

It wasn't just Kieran Blake I hated for taking her life. I hated the witnesses for not stopping her murder when they had the chance. I hated my parents at the time, for my mother's reaction to me when she landed back from their holiday in the Algarve, the way she looked at me when she walked in the door, the things she said. Most of all, I hated myself for what I had allowed to happen when I was supposed to be looking after Lily.

Within forty-eight hours, Kieran admitted he had been with her. He changed his story: he was walking her back because she was upset when she left her boyfriend's house, a boyfriend we didn't even know existed, although as the days passed, we soon found out there was a lot about my sister we did not know. Kieran said he'd simply been trying to keep her safe.

The jury, along with the rest of the town, didn't believe him. There was too much circumstantial evidence, and the fact that he had lied at the outset did not help his story. The only person to stand by him was his mother, who died ten years into his prison sentence.

I keep this close as I prepare to visit Kieran today. The fact that there is no one left on his side.

*   *   *

I have seen pictures of Kieran since he was sent to prison—photos accompanying occasional news reports on his search for justice in the early years. But they weren't enough to prepare me for seeing him in the flesh. Now there is not one trace of the thirty-year-old that stood in court and denied killing my sister. The man in front of me has aged far beyond his years.

Kieran Blake is a fifty-three-year-old who looks at least ten years older. His eyes are hooded, his expression sad, his skin pallid. Prison has drained the life from him.

My legs shake as I find my seat and sit down onto it. Richard is waiting for me outside. He asked me if I wanted him to accompany me, but I told him this was something I needed to do on my own.

"Thank you for coming." Kieran's voice is flat, and he can barely look at me as his speaks. Only intermittently do his eyes catch mine, and then they dart over my head. Beneath the table his legs judder up and down, and his hands fumble over each other on the table in front of us.

In contrast, I don't move once I am sat. My body feels frozen, and I can barely breathe. I try not to think of those hands around my sister's neck, but the image comes at me regardless.

I turn away, heat blazing through me. I have to remember why I'm here. It's for answers. I just need to know what happened to my sister. I need to understand why he took her life, and then I can leave.

Eventually I turn back to him. It's hard not to see Kieran's younger face flashing before me. The face of a man who stood in court and continued to deny what he had done. It's hard not to remember the rage that burned inside me back then. I try to temper it now.

It was Amira, my best friend at the time, who held me together and sat next to me in court all those years ago, holding my hands in her own, whispering in my ear that it was going to be okay, while my parents sat in the row in front. A wedge was already dividing us, but what I didn't know then was that it would continue to slice us in two and that we would never find a way to come back from it.

The rage keeps igniting inside me again now, making my skin itch. I find myself listening for Lily's voice again, something I haven't done for years. Right now I need her to guide me. I need to feel her close so I can get through this.

"Why did you want to see me?" I say eventually, my words high-pitched and thin.

Kieran blows a breath of air through his mouth. Dark-grey stubbly hairs line his pale lips. I want to close my eyes to blot out the sight of him, but at the same time I can't pull away. I need to look him in the eyes when he speaks to me.

"Why did you want to see me?" I repeat, stronger this time.

"There are some things I want to tell you," he says, but he doesn't go on as his eyes continue to flick over me, and I wonder if he's already changing his mind.

"I've wanted to speak to you for years, but you never would," I say. "Why now?"

"There's—" He lifts his head up and cocks it to one side, as if thinking about whether or not to give me the answer. "I just want to tell you this," he says instead.

I nod. Whatever his reason, I don't want him to change his mind. "Okay."

"I want you to know the truth," Kieran says, his brows arching together. He reminds me of my uncle, a man who constantly looked down. With him it was because of the drink, but they resemble each other in the way they both look permanently beaten.

I can no longer feel myself breathing. "What happened?"

"The actual truth," he says. "Not what everyone else believes it to be."

I screw my eyes up, frowning. I don't like where this is heading.

"I did see your sister that night like, I said," he starts. "She had come to visit her boyfriend, my neighbour, but he wasn't in."

I know this much from what we pieced together in the days following Lily's death. My sister had been seeing a boy called Tony, who was three years older than her. A seventeen-year-old who swore he didn't know her age, though I swore he was lying.

He lived in the mobile home next to Kieran's. The homes angled at ninety degrees, meaning it was easy for each of them to see what was going on inside.

Lily had kept her relationship with Tony quiet from me and our parents for four months. She had been telling them she was in after-school clubs, or at her friend Cassie's house, and no one even considered checking, because Lily had always been so honest.

Only by then she and Cassie were no longer friends. As soon as Lily started hanging out with Tony, their friendship had begun cracking. Cassie had wisely withdrawn herself when Lily wouldn't listen to her saying that Tony was no good. This was something we didn't know either.

"I could see she was upset when she came out of his home, really broken up, you know?" Kieran says.

I don't answer him, just keep watching. His eyes dip away from mine again. It's the same story Kieran eventually told the police.

"I knew Tony wasn't there and I didn't know what happened, but I asked her if she was okay. She said to leave her alone, but I said it was the middle of the night and I'd walk her back. I tried talking to her, telling her Tony wasn't any good, just like his old man. He was a waster," Kieran goes on. "I know I wasn't much better for a time," he adds, "but I was trying to sort myself out then. I was straight. I had been for a while.

"Anyway, she didn't want to listen to me. I walked with her for a bit, and she got angry and kept shouting at me to go away." Kieran looks up at me and holds my gaze this time. This is what he'd always said. In court, he had stood there and said he walked away at this point, that he didn't do anything to my sister. But then five years ago he admitted he did and that he and Lily had struggled and that he had killed her by accident.

"I left her there," he tells me now. He shakes her head. "I didn't kill her, I didn't even touch her."

"No!" I say, "That's not the truth."

"What I was saying to her about Tony wasn't making a scrap of difference, and I realised I was making her more angry, so by the time we got to the lake, I just let her go and I turned back."

"You didn't," I say. "Why are you telling me this?"

"It's the truth," Kieran says. "I didn't kill your sister."

I pull back in my seat, shaking my head, my mouth agape. This isn't what I came for; I wanted to know *why* he had killed her. I wanted to know what happened in those final moments. I did not want to hear him retract his story. "You promised me the truth!" I hiss. "You admitted you killed her, and you brought me here to tell me the *truth*."

Kieran dips his eyes slowly. He is leaning to one side quite badly, like his body has been contorted that way. He looks to be in pain as he shakes his head, but I don't care. I want him to suffer. No amount of physical agony could ever make up for what he did. "I didn't do it," he says again.

"Then why would you say you did?" I cry, my voice rising so that an officer at the edge of the room looks over in our direction.

"It was a coward's way out," he replies.

"A coward's way out? You admitted to murdering a fourteen-year-old girl."

"Yes. But I didn't do it. And I want you to know that."

"You brought me in here today to tell me all this crap?" I say, slamming my hands down on the table in front of me. "After all these years of refusing to speak to me? Why are you doing this to me?" I feel tears springing into my eyes at the realisation that I am leaving with nothing.

"I couldn't face you before," he is saying. "Even before I changed my story, you believed I killed her. Everyone believed I did. There was nothing I could say that made anyone hear me. I am innocent," he says, leaning towards me. "I did nothing to her, and I've spent twenty-three years paying for someone else's crime."

I lean back, staring at him, trying to take in what he's telling me. Trying to ignore the tiniest part of me that could believe his words. "No," I say. "You admitted it."

Kieran nods. "I did."

"So why would you ever do that if you're innocent?"

He looks away from me. "The reason I wanted to see you is because I've got a parole hearing coming up," he tells me. "I wanted you to see me, to hear me tell you it wasn't me. Before I get out."

"You're not going to get out," I say, desperately hoping this is true. "Not when you admitted to killing my sister. You might tell me a different story, but you can't take that back now."

"I can't," he says. "But I never wanted to plead guilty to something I didn't do."

"Then why did you?"

When he turns back to look at me, a realisation dawns on me. "You thought that was your way out of here, didn't you?" I say. "You had this all planned. Five years ago, you knew you'd be getting parole, and you thought that if you pleaded guilty, you had a better chance of getting out? You couldn't just suddenly announce it when your parole came up. You had this all thought through. You thought you could get out on good behaviour."

Kieran closes his eyes. That's exactly what he has done.

I get up, the chair screeching beneath me as it scratches across the floor, my heart thumping in anger.

I hear Lily's voice over the ringing in my ears. Did it ever go away, or did I just silence her? I shouldn't have done that. I should have always listened to my sister instead of letting Elise help me "move on."

"Where is my sister's necklace?" I say.

"I don't know." Kieran shakes his head. "I promise you. I didn't hurt her."

"No one found it. So please, will you just tell me where it is? Do that one thing for me."

"I can't. I don't have any idea where it is. I didn't do it. I'm telling you the truth; they got the wrong man."

I feel like a blade is piercing my chest, sucking the life out of me. "Tell me where her necklace is," I scream as he calls for a guard and one comes over, taking me by the arm, asking me if I'm okay as he gently leads me out the room while Kieran disappears in the other direction.

Richard is waiting for me. He looks worried as he sees me, opening his arms for me to fall into, but I don't break down like either of us expected I might. I just lean against his chest and let him wrap his arms around my shaking body.

*   *   *

That evening Richard tells me he'll make dinner. He's stopped off to buy a chicken to roast on the way home, and he's busy shoving it into the oven and laying out chips on a baking tray.

"He just wanted to clear his name," I tell him again. "He played the system so he can walk out of prison. But why the hell is he telling me he isn't guilty? Why not just keep his head down and wait for his hearing? Why did he feel the need to drag me in and put me through seeing him just to mess with my head?"

"I don't know," Richard says. "It doesn't make any sense."

"I think I need to call my mum," I tell him.

"Oh?" He is surprised, because my mum and I no longer talk often and *never* about Lily. When we do speak, our conversations are functional: she asks what I've been up to and tells me about her neighbours and the women at church.

"I need to tell her what's happened. I can't have her hearing about his parole from somewhere else."

"Of course you should call her," he says. "It's the right thing. Will you tell her you've seen him?"

"I don't know. I can't even imagine having any part of this conversation with her."

"Then leave it for now. You don't have to do it today."

"No. I think I do," I say. "I want to get it out the way." I know I'll only keep putting it off otherwise.

Richard smiles. "Dinner won't be ready till half six."

I look at the clock; it's five PM. I wonder what my mum will be doing right now. Almost certainly she will be at home in the terraced house in St. Albans that she moved into with my father only two years before he died.

Moving so many miles away was their way of coping. It was my mum's belief that if they ran away, she could escape the memories that draped over every part of our lives. It was no different to her covering herself with a blanket and hiding from the world. No different to her closing down and letting me be the one to deluge the police with questions, because she couldn't bear it.

My dad agreed with her plans, because that was what he did. Always he was the one in the middle of us, trying to be the go-between, not sure whom to side with but wanting to be there for both of us. Dad was pulling himself in two different directions, but all the time he was suffering too, and no one was there for him. We were a family of three by then, who all needed someone to look out for us, only we weren't doing a very good job of being there for each other.

I pick up the phone and dial my mum's number, staring at my reflection in the mirror and seeing a flash of Lily in my face. She is still there, living beneath the surface of everything

I do. She is there in my dreams, in my questions, my conversations. For the most part it's where she stays, hidden and buried, but always with me. Lily is a shadow of light, of grief and of guilt that follows me everywhere. I don't know what would happen if I opened the lid and let her out again.

"Hello, love," my mum says as she answers the phone. "Are you okay? I can't recall how many weeks or even months it's been since we last spoke."

"I'm fine, Mum."

"Oh good," she goes on. "It's good to hear from you. How's Richard? How's work and your lovely dog?"

"All good, Mum," I say, and I can hear her breathing out a sigh of relief that my unexpected call isn't because of an emergency. I picture her settling into her chair, making herself comfortable, happy to listen to whatever it is I have to tell her now, however trivial and however short our conversation turns out to be.

This is the relationship we have these days. I love her, and I know she loves me, but there is too much hurt. Too many things were said after Lily that we can't take back.

"Mum, there's something I need to tell you. It's about Kieran Blake."

"Oh?" Such a small word, but I can hear the crack in it.

I close my eyes. "He's up for parole this year."

"Ohhhh." She breathes out the word this time, like she has breathed out every part of her soul with it. "When?"

"I don't know when yet." I squeeze my eyes tighter. I need to tell her I've seen him; I can't keep this from her, because it could come out in some news report. "I saw him today," I say. "He asked to see me. I went thinking he was going to give me answers."

Mum is silent for a moment before she says, "And did he?"

"He said he didn't kill her. He only admitted he did because of his parole. Mum?" I prompt, when she doesn't respond. "Did you hear me?"

"I heard you."

"I don't believe him, but—" I break off, not really knowing what to say next. Maybe because of that tiniest part of me that questions whether this is true.

"Oh dear Lord," she cries. "Why has all this come up again?"

Already I fear I have done the wrong thing in calling her. I don't know how she's going to cope with this. It was always going to come up one day, only neither of us wanted to believe it.

"I don't think we should worry," I tell her, parroting what I was told but didn't believe. "He's admitted what he did. The detective I spoke to said he didn't think he'd get parole. He's guilty," I say adamantly. "They won't let him out."

"Yes. Yes," she murmurs. "But what if he isn't?"

NOW—AUGUST

AT SEVEN THIRTY AM Richard Day pulls into the drive to
see the door of the white Escort parked opposite (which
made it all the more difficult for him to turn into his house)
opening and a man climbing out. He glances over as he
walks round to the boot and opens it to get his suitcase out,
slamming it shut and pressing the lock key on his car remote.

The man is looking straight at him, and as much as Richard thinks he can't be here to see him, he has the disturbing
sense that he is. And right now, whatever this man's reasons
for waiting outside Richard's house, it's the last thing Richard
wants. He hasn't slept the entire night. His flight was delayed
by a totally unreasonable five hours due to engine trouble, and
therefore his plan to surprise Maggie by coming home early
has gone out the window.

He texted her last night from the airport in the end to say
he was coming home, but now it means he's missed any chance
of sleep, because he's never been one for resting in the day.

Richard ignores the man in the hope he'll just disappear in
another direction and makes his way to the front door, where
he slips his key into the lock. But then a voice calls out, "Mr.
Day?" and so Richard sighs and turns around.

"Yes," he says. The man isn't carrying a package, which means it isn't a delivery. Through his tiredness, he can't work out who he might be, but he also doesn't particularly think about it. He certainly isn't worried, but then there's little Richard worries about. He is one of life's optimists, as Maggie tells him. He just gets on with things.

He supposes it's because he's learnt to. His parents both died when he was in his twenties. He misses them both greatly, but now the only person he has to worry about is Maggie. And he actually thinks there's a lot to be said for not worrying about too many people. He sees his small circle of friends frantically anxious over their children. One of them is being bullied; one of them is on drugs; Christ, one of them has even been targeted for drug trafficking. Richard is glad he doesn't have any of that to deal with. He's relieved he never had children.

That's not to say he didn't want them once. Or to be more accurate, he probably assumed he would have them, like most people probably do. But then Maggie exploded into his life and told him that children weren't part of her life plan, and he accepted that he was happy not to have them either. Because one thing he knew from the moment he met his wife was that he could not live without her.

He still feels the same now, twelve years on. Some nights when they're curled up in bed together and he feels her melt into him, she murmurs to him that he saved her. He always laughs at her. He didn't save her; she saved him. From a life of solitude. Which he happens to believe that, if it weren't for meeting Maggie, he would probably have been quite content with. Him and the dog. But after Maggie, there was no way he could conceive of it.

So the reason he isn't concerned when the man approaching him introduces himself as DC Margate is because his wife will be safely tucked up inside in bed, and there is nothing else that could concern him.

"How can I help you?" Richard says.

"I wonder if I could come in and have a word with you?"

Richard frowns. "What's this about?"

"It's about a hit-and-run that occurred in the early hours of this morning."

Richard cocks his head. Only now is his heart beginning to hammer. "A hit-and-run?"

"A woman named Erin Harding."

"Oh." He lets out a breath. Not Maggie, then. And not anyone else he knows. It must have happened around here and they're going door-to-door. "I'm afraid I'm not going to be of any use. I've literally just got back from a business trip; I only landed in the country three hours ago."

"It's really your wife we want to speak to. We believe Mrs. Harding was a client of hers."

"Oh, I see. Well then, you better come in. Maggie's asleep; I texted her when I landed, but she has her phone on silent at night, so . . ." He opens the door, and the police officer follows him in as Rocky bounds up to him, wagging his tail furiously. Richard ruffles the fur on his dog's head.

"I did knock," the officer is telling him, "and tried calling."

"Oh?"

That's strange, but Rocky is here, so Maggie must be sound asleep. Maybe she has her earplugs in, as she sometimes does. "I'll go and check on her," he says. "You can wait in here if you like." He gestures to one of the armchairs that sits by the fireplace in their living room.

Richard leaves his case in the hallway and makes his way up the stairs. He thinks about how well Maggie might know this Erin Harding and whether she's going to be upset. It isn't a name he's heard, because his wife never discloses details of her clients.

He opens the door to their bedroom, expecting to find her lying in bed, but the bed is made and there's no sign of her in the room or in the en suite. He pulls his phone out of his pocket and checks the messages he sent her. There are two grey ticks beside the one from ten thirty last night, which suggests she hasn't read it, and neither has she seen the one this morning.

He frowns as he presses the redial number and tries calling her, but her phone rings and rings before going to voice mail. So he pulls up the handy little tracker that locates her phone. That's strange; it shows she's at home.

He grips the phone in his hand, trying to think. She must have gone out and left her phone at home, but Rocky is here, and it's far too early for Maggie to be up and out on a Sunday morning, especially if it's not walking the dog. Could she have gone somewhere overnight? No, because where would she have gone? And now he wishes he'd called her from the airport, but he assumed at the time she must be asleep and didn't even look to see whether she had read the text.

Richard makes his way down the stairs and finds DC Margate standing by the armchair he was supposed to be sitting in. "Her mobile is in there." Margate gestures. "It's been ringing."

Rocky is by his side as Richard walks into the kitchen. "Where's your mum gone, Rockster?" he murmurs, locating the phone on the table.

"Do you have any idea where she might be?" DC Margate appears in the doorway.

"No, I don't," Richard says, confused, and a little on edge at the whole situation.

"Can you open your wife's phone?"

"Open it?"

"Yes," Margate says. "Maybe see if there's any clues on there as to where she is."

Richard frowns. He doesn't know what the urgency is to find Maggie, but at the same time he wants to know why his wife isn't home. "I don't ever do this," he says, though he has always known her passcode—080706—because it's easy enough to remember.

He taps out the digits, but the phone screen shakes in denial. He must have got it wrong, and so he does it again, but still it refuses him entry. One more time. Slower and more carefully, but the passcode won't allow him in.

He knows Margate is staring at him. Maggie must have changed her code recently, and yet it feels impossible. She has always had the same one. For years.

"Your wife's car wasn't on the drive," Margate states.

"No. It's often in the garage. There were a few break-ins down the road lately." His stomach does funny little somersaults as he looks up at the officer and realises he's expecting him to check. Richard grabs the keys for the internal garage door out of the top drawer that's filled with anything and everything.

But when he opens the door, he's confronted with an empty space where Maggie's Land Rover usually sits. "It's gone," he says.

The DC nods, almost like he already knew this would be the case, and now Richard understands why the man wanted to talk to him when he first saw him and not Maggie. He was waiting for him because he already knew Maggie wasn't here. They're already trying to find her.

"You definitely haven't heard the name Erin Harding?" Margate asks him.

"No. Like I said, my wife doesn't discuss her clients with me."

"We believe the Hardings first saw your wife in March."

Richard thinks back. Maggie had a new couple, the ones she started seeing at nine o'clock on a Monday. The ones she briefly mentioned she didn't know how to move forward with because she couldn't understand what was going on. She tells him so little about her work that even those small details stood out at the time. But what he knows is that she wouldn't have given up; she'd have continued to give them her all, like she always does.

And now all of a sudden Richard is filled with a piercing dread that has come from nowhere and that he hasn't experienced in over twenty years. He's scared. He's frightened for himself and his wife, and he just wants her back home so he knows she's okay.

CHAPTER

12

Three months earlier
ERIN

WILL TELLS ME I'm mad. What other explanation is there?

"I am running out of patience now, Erin," he says. "I've tried, I really have, but you can't keep doing this to me." He looks at me like he no longer knows me.

What right does he have to do this, when it's *me* who no longer knows *him*?

I haven't touched my writing since Valentine's Day. I don't want to immerse myself in a fantasy world when I'm beginning to live one.

And still my heart breaks that there's no news of Coco.

Will has packed her dishes away by now, putting them in a Tesco carrier bag and then storing them in the garage along with her bedding. "We can't keep it all out, Erin," he's told me. "Sadie's going to start questioning where she is again."

All the time I have been questioning myself. Maybe I did just have some kind of panic attack Valentine's Day morning, and of course I could be wrong about Coco. But after last night, I find myself looking at my husband and thinking, *I*

*know what you're doing to me, Will. You want to make me believe
I'm crazy.*

"I'm off to work," he says, and I simply nod. He frowns
and shakes his head, then calls out to Sadie, who comes running into the hallway to say goodbye. As he leaves, I go to the
living room and watch the Audi pull out of the driveway.

His car is his prize possession. Will is particular about
many things, but his car is on another level. Whenever we go
to the beach, he worries over Sadie bringing sand into the back
of it, making her sit in the boot as he wipes her feet with a
towel, draping another over the seat before she climbs in. In his
boot he keeps a big black box for us to throw in wellies, muddy
shoes, or anything that has the remotest bit of dirt on it.

We've laughed about it in the past. I never cared and just
went along with it, and he would smile and thank me and tell
me he knew how annoying it must be. He couldn't help it, it was
just one of those things, he likes everything to be neat and tidy.

We haven't seen Maggie this week because of the bank
holiday. Our last session I'd told her about how I'd noticed the
taillight had been smashed in. But it was funny – I'd stopped
dead in my tracks, a shard of fear driving through me so hard
and fast it left me breathless. I don't know what came over me,
but there it was. One minute I was immersed in thoughts of
Coco, remembering the day Will had told me she was missing, and the next I noticed the state of the car, and everything
began caving in around me.

I know the two things don't relate, but in that moment
they somehow did, if for no other reason than that the feeling
coursing through me was exactly the same as when my husband had told me Coco was missing. And the same as when he
had tried to put the necklace on me earlier that day.

I'd paused and put a hand on the car to steady myself.
Eventually the world began to right itself and my eyes started
to refocus. The spinning subsided and I went back inside, up
the stairs to the bathroom, where Will was bathing Sadie.

"What happened to the car?" I'd said to him. The anxiety I'd felt moments earlier had dissipated, and I just wanted to know why he hadn't told me it was smashed.

When he eventually checked it and came back up the stairs he'd stood in the doorway, his eyes trailing over me, eventually coming back to meet mine as he regarded me like I was losing my mind. "There's nothing wrong with the car," he said.

"Yes there is—I saw it, I—"

He held up a hand to stop me. "There's nothing wrong with it, Erin." Then he turned to Sadie and said, "I'll see you in the morning, my sweet pea." He held his daughter, looking at me strangely over the top of her head, and then went downstairs.

I should have followed him down and made him come out with me, but Sadie wouldn't be left alone complaining her tummy hurt.

But I couldn't sleep. And as Will lay next to me, softly snoring, I couldn't shake the image of the way he had looked at me earlier, insinuating I'd been making everything up.

I didn't tell Maggie or Will that at half past midnight I crept out of bed, taking my phone with me for photographic evidence. I hated that he was making me doubt myself, telling me and everyone else I was making up stories. Will was so sincerely in denial and I couldn't fathom why. All I knew was that I was beginning to mistrust everything he told me. My husband was becoming a stranger, and it was tearing my heart in two.

I padded downstairs, out the front door, and across the driveway in my slippers. Prowling around the car like a burglar, I stopped short when I saw the taillight. I ran my hand across its smooth and unbroken surface.

There was nothing wrong. My heart was in my mouth. I knew what I had seen. I wasn't mistaken. The light had definitely been smashed; in my head I still see it as clear as day. I can picture it now. And yet within hours he had somehow got it fixed.

I didn't tell Maggie because either I *am* losing my mind and I've imagined the whole thing, or my husband is doing this to me. And yet it's not me that anyone believes.

* * *

A week later Zoe messages me to suggest meeting for coffee. It's now been over a month since I last saw her on Easter Sunday. I've never known so much time to go by without us arranging to get together. It doesn't pass me by that while my life is unravelling, she hasn't been here when I need her most. But then maybe it's me who's been shutting her out.

We've swapped texts; she has continued to ask if there's any news on Coco, and I've continued to tell her there's nothing. But other than that, we've been pulling away from each other, and I've tolerated any grief over the distance only because my mind is primarily on my marriage. For the most part I haven't stopped to address the fact that my best friend hasn't been here.

Now I'm sitting in a coffee shop with two slices of cake and two lattes, waiting for her, and I feel nervous, which in turn feels ridiculous. I've known Zoe twenty years, and yet I'm filled with trepidation at the thought of seeing her, anticipating that it might be awkward.

As I wait, I consider why this is and if it's because Zoe has kept away from me for a reason. Is it because she thinks my accusations of Will are unhinged, like he says they are? Did he tell her and Dave I accused him of covering up the fact that his car taillight was smashed while rolling his eyes and telling them it wasn't?

After I had gone out to the car, I didn't go back to our bed. I crept back inside and took myself to the spare room, where another sleepless night addled my brain until I too wondered if I had really seen what I thought I had.

The door to the coffee shop chimes, and I look up to see Zoe entering. "Hey," she says breezily, although I see in her face she is also apprehensive as she sits down. She places a hand on my arm as she throws her bag onto the seat next to her. "It's good to see you." She takes a deep breath. "I've missed you."

"I've missed you too." I smile and place a hand on top of hers. "I've bought us cake."

"Come here." She pulls her hand away and opens her arms, and I lean in to hug her, feeling her press tightly against me.

Eventually she says, "Coffee and walnut, my favourite. How did you know?" She laughs as she picks up her fork with one hand and pierces it into the cake. "How have you been?" She looks up at me earnestly.

"Oh, you know." I wave a hand through the air. "Tell me about you first."

"Okay, well, I had a run-in with that mother from Marlie's school yesterday." She raises her eyes and tell me the story, making me laugh, and our conversation snakes between Sadie and Zoe's children, other friends, and Zoe's holiday plans for the summer. We don't stop chatting, but I can't help feeling the heavy weight of emptiness between us. Like we're skimming the surface of our friendship.

The longer we chat, the heavier it feels, until the need to say something becomes too much. "I feel like things aren't the same between us," I say.

"Oh, Erin, don't say that." She shakes her head. "I don't want it to be like that; I just felt I wasn't helping you when we last spoke, and I didn't know what to do."

I pull a face. "Not helping me? I just wanted you to be on my side, nothing more. I wanted you to listen to me and not make out I was crazy."

"I don't think that," she says. "I never would. I know how hard things are for you with Coco missing, and I understand how you feel about Will, I really do."

"I wanted you to believe me, Zoe."

"But you suggested you thought Will had killed your dog," she says. "I *can't* believe it."

"Okay, well, maybe he didn't. Maybe my mind just ran away with me, but there is *something* going on," I tell her.

Zoe nods. "Okay. Then talk to me about it. Are you still going to counselling? Is it helping?"

"Will told me this week he doesn't think there's any point. I don't think we'll keep going much longer."

Zoe makes an *uh-huh* noise, and it crosses my mind that she probably already knows this and that Will has spoken to Dave about it.

"But it isn't that," I say. "There's other things. Did he tell you about the taillight on his car?"

Zoe shakes her head, but her expression is blank, and I can't work out if she knows or not.

"Well, it was broken. I saw it, and yet Will denies it, and he went and got it fixed in the middle of the night, just so I couldn't prove it."

"Okay."

I glance at her, and she just nods at me to continue. I desperately want to tell Zoe what I found two days ago, but at the same time I don't like the way she's looking at me. I need to tell her how, when I was reaching for my bags in the car, I saw a flash of gold jewellery in the passenger footwell.

I froze when I saw it. Though I could feel my whole body shaking, I couldn't move. My arms were laden with the grocery shopping I had piled on the passenger seat, and I thought I was going to drop the bags, but Sadie had started tugging at my skirt and snapped me out of it. Eventually I pulled back and got out of the car, following her to the house, where Will was waiting to help take the bags off me.

"Who does that necklace belong to?" I said as I followed him into the kitchen. My hands were shaking, I realised, as I let go of the last bag and put it on the counter.

"What are you talking about?"

"There was a gold necklace in your car."

"It's probably one of Sadie's."

I shook my head, but already Will was walking out to the car on the pretence of getting the rest of the shopping. By the time I had followed him, he was shuffling about in the footwell, grabbing loose apples that had fallen out.

"It was down there," I said, pointing to the empty space.

"Well, as you can clearly see, it isn't," he said as he brushed past me and went back into the house.

I had played it wrong. I realised that quick enough. I should have picked it up when I saw it, or I should have gone back for it before saying anything to Will, but as on all the other occasions, I had stopped short, feeling a dizzying sense of everything caving in on me. And now I have no proof.

I announce to Zoe, "I think he could be having an affair."

"An affair?" Zoe laughs. "Will? You're kidding."

"I'm really not."

Zoe shakes her head. "I mean, I don't think Will would ever, but . . ." She trails off, biting her lip as she considers how to finish her sentence.

My husband has to be seeing another woman. Only he's making it impossible for me to ask him when he denies anything I say to him.

"I just can't see it," she finally says.

The truth is, it's the one thing I've never believed my husband capable of either. And over the last two days I've been trying to find more signs, anything I might have missed in the lead-up to the day Coco went missing and everything changed, but that morning he'd been so attentive, so caring. Was it all a clever act?

It's the only explanation I have. Will has met someone else, and now he's doing whatever he can to get out of our marriage. Maybe he wants to make it seem like my fault and my decision so he can appease his own guilt and keep our friends on his side.

And the more I think about it, the more I wonder if this is the root cause of everything that's been happening for the last few months. Why else would someone change so rapidly?

It's funny that in some ways, since this idea has dawned on me, I feel a light shining down on me, bringing with it some relief. I couldn't make sense of the speed of our disentangling marriage before, but of course this must be the reason.

There is another woman Will wants to be with, but he can't bring himself to tell me. So instead he plays the long game. He suggests counselling and willingly gives up an hour of his week to come along to couples therapy with me, to show me and everyone else he's doing everything he can. But deep down he has no intention of staying with me. And all the while he's slowly making me feel like I'm going mad until I can't put up with him anymore.

And it's working. After all, I've already moved out of our bedroom and into the guest room. What will come next: he moves out of our home?

I can't believe I didn't figure this out before. But now I have, it has to be the reason, only Zoe shakes me out of my thoughts when she suddenly says, "I don't believe it, Erin. I just don't. Not of Will."

Sadly, I don't think I actually expected my best friend to believe me any longer, and so it shouldn't surprise me that she reacts this way, and yet it does.

"But what if he is?" I say, holding my ground. "Why would it be so unthinkable? Plenty of people have affairs."

"But Will—"

"Why not Will?" I demand, angrier now at her refusal to believe it.

"Because your marriage was always perfect," she says. "There was nothing wrong with it. Will loves you; I know he does."

I shake my head, my impatience with Zoe increasing. Every time I talk to her, she shoots me down.

"Erin, Will is standing by your side through all this," she goes on, and I look up at her sharply.

"What do you mean by that?"

"Nothing." She shakes her head emphatically.

"Yes. You do. The way you said it, you think this is all my fault."

"No. I'm just saying—" Zoe breaks off. "I don't want to see you two split up. And I worry that if you keep blaming him for all these things, then—"

"Oh my God," I cry. "All these things?" She makes it sound so menial. "You do think this is all my fault. That I'm driving him away."

"No. I'm not saying that," she insists. But of course she is. That's exactly what my best friend is saying. And I'm so hurt by her right now that I pick my bag up and walk out the coffee shop, and I don't know how we're ever going to come back from this, but I can't think about it. It isn't important. All I can think of is what my husband is doing to my family, and what he might be capable of.

13

ERIN

THE FOLLOWING MONDAY Maggie starts our next session as she always does, asking how our week has been. "Fine," I tell her, though my voice cracks as I say it, the word coming out in a whisper. Everything is anything but fine, and all three of us know it. Why I still default to that one word, I don't know.

She's staring back at me as if searching for something. It crosses my mind that Maggie, just like Zoe, doesn't believe a word I've been telling her.

After all, she's a therapist; she's used to stories from both sides. Now she's probably wondering if I'm trying to portray my husband in a bad light. It makes me all the more nervous at the thought of telling her about the necklace in Will's car and my theory that my husband is cheating on me. But I want to bring it up today. I need to see my husband's reaction when there's someone else to watch it.

"How have you been sleeping, Erin?" she asks me.

I regard her curiously, wondering what she's getting at. Does she think I'm driving myself slowly mad too? I haven't been sleeping well, and right now I can feel myself blinking rapidly, trying to work through the exhaustion. She must see this.

"Not well?" Maggie persists.

"No, I'm sleeping fine actually." That word again, but I don't want to admit otherwise.

She screws her face up, like she doesn't believe this either, and so I make up a story and say, "Apart from last night. Sadie had me up."

"Did she?" Will asks.

Shut up. Don't make this harder for me. "Yes." I continue with the lie. "You can't have heard her."

"No," he says. "I didn't, which is unusual." We both know the spare room where I'm sleeping is farther away from Sadie's and it's more likely he'd have heard her than me. I catch a look passing between him and Maggie, as if they have some secret code between them, and all of a sudden I wonder if I made a wrong decision in coming here with my husband so he could convince the woman *I* should be convincing. I hoped Maggie Day would see it from my side. That she would help me figure out what's going on, when instead she seems to be siding with my husband.

"Erin doesn't want to sleep in the same room as me anymore," Will says flatly, like he's resigned to this thing he never wanted.

"So you aren't sharing a bed?" Maggie confirms.

Will is biting the corner of his thumbnail. "She tells me she *can't* anymore," he replies, with an emphasis on the word *can't*. "Because she's scared of me." He frowns and shrugs, like it's some sort of a joke. "That's what you said five nights ago, wasn't it?" he says to me. "You're scared of me. But why?"

Why? Because I know you did something to my dog. Because you lied to me about your car. Because you're lying about the necklace I found last week in the footwell of the Audi.

Maggie is asking me, "Why did you tell Will you're scared of him, Erin?" I try to listen for any trace of mocking in her voice, but I admit I don't find it.

I need to tell her what happened. I can't walk out of her room today without doing so when I've been building myself up to it over the weekend. When I've convinced myself I must be right about Will and there's another woman. I won't let my husband silence me by making out *I'm* the one who is untrustworthy.

"Because I am," I say, so softly that I imagine she can barely hear me. I feel tears pinching at my eyelids, a sharp sting. How has this happened to us? How have we got here? This wasn't our life before three months ago. *How dare you do this to us, Will.*

We talk more, round and round in circles, until Maggie leans forward over her coffee table. "What are you scared of?" She holds my gaze as she waits for an answer. She makes it feel like she and I are the only ones in the room right now.

"I found a necklace in his car," I tell her.

"Erin, not this again. There's no necklace in my car," Will interrupts through gritted teeth and with an exasperated sigh. He makes his words sound so tired, like he's completely bored of the whole thing, but Maggie is holding up a hand to him.

I keep watching her. I pretend he's no longer here and it's just me and her. "There was. And Will is lying about it. I saw it in the footwell."

"And this scares you?" She clearly doesn't understand how.

"I don't know why it does, but . . ." I can feel my hands shaking in my lap, a sheen of sweat glistening on my hairline and threatening to drip as it all comes back to me again, like I'm back in Will's car. It's the same feeling of panic I had the morning of Valentine's, then when Coco went missing, and when I saw the taillight of his car. My body is heating rapidly.

"Erin, do you want a glass of water?" Maggie is saying, though her words are hazy. "Will, can you pour her a glass?" She gestures to the jug that is right in front of us.

My husband starts pouring it so fast that it sloshes over the edge, and then he tries to press the glass into my hands and steer it up to my mouth, but just the feel of his hands on me makes me push him away so hard that he releases his grip, and the glass falls onto the table, smashing into pieces.

"Don't worry about, it," Maggie says as Will leaps off the sofa. I don't move. I can't. I just find myself holding on to my wrist where Will held me. He didn't hurt me, and yet somehow it feels like he did. I catch Maggie's eyes dropping down to my wrist, and I pull it away. There's nothing for her to see.

"Let's take a minute," she says. "I'm just going to clean this up so no one gets hurt."

"I'm so sorry," Will is saying to her, apologising for me.

"It really isn't a problem. They're only cheap."

Maggie is smiling, and then she leaves the room and returns almost immediately with a dustpan and brush, which thankfully gives Will no time to say anything to me other than "What the hell's going on, Erin?"

As Maggie starts sweeping up the broken glass, he says, "None of this is helping."

Maggie tells us to be careful where we put our feet for now, because she won't be able to get it all off the carpet until after we've left. "What isn't helping?" she asks him.

"This talking. It's not what we need. Erin needs more than that. She needs *help*."

"What do you mean by help?" Maggie says, before I can. I know what he means. He's suggesting I need to see a doctor because I'm losing my mind.

"Everything she's saying to you isn't true," he says. "So there has to be something else going on, doesn't there?"

"He thinks I'm mad," I butt in. It isn't for him to take control. "He tells me I'm going crazy, and maybe I am, but only because of what he's doing."

When Maggie has cleaned up most of the glass from the coffee table, she puts the dustpan to one side and sits back down again. "What do *you* think he's doing, Erin?"

"He's messing with my head."

"Erin!" Will cries. "You see what I mean?" he's begging of Maggie. "Why does she even think I'm doing that?"

I catch Maggie nodding at him, seemingly agreeing with him, but then she turns to me and says, "Erin, can you tell me about the necklace you say you found in Will's car?"

"It was lying in the footwell," I say. "I just saw it there."

"And it isn't yours?"

"No. I don't know who it belongs to."

"But you don't like the thought of this necklace," she says, which sounds like an odd thing to mention until I realise that she doesn't believe me either. That she thinks it's somehow metaphoric. "Why is that, Erin? What do you think the necklace means?"

"Means?" I say. *It means my husband is having an affair*, I think, and yet what I say is, "It means I'm in danger."

Already I know this is the wrong thing to say.

Beside me Will is shaking his head and looking up at the ceiling like he's plain desperate. And I know how odd it sounds and that I shouldn't have said it, but I couldn't help myself. It came from somewhere deep inside me. It's the truth. I saw the necklace and I felt it. I knew it. I had seen it somewhere before, and I knew I was in danger, only I can't articulate why.

"I'm so sorry," Maggie says as she glances at the clock. I look too, and I know what's coming. Not once has she strayed over our allotted time. We always finish at ten to ten. "I'm afraid our session is coming to an end."

She does look sorry, to be fair. She's looking at me like she knows she's throwing me to the wolves. Will is nodding, getting up and grabbing his jacket from the arm of the sofa. He can't get out quick enough.

"There is no necklace," he says to both of us. "There never has been. I honestly don't know why she's making it up."

"I'm not making anything up, Will," I spit out as I stand too.

"What was it supposed to look like, then?" he says as he walks to the door and I follow him. "Describe it to me. I mean, for all we know it was one of Sadie's," he adds with a chuckle as he glances back at Maggie. "She has plenty of fake jewellery that she uses for dressing up."

"It wasn't Sadie's," I say. "It was gold and delicate. It has a leaf with little pockmarks in it." I hold my hand to the front of my neck, adding, "That curl at the edges."

Will leaves the room and I step out too, but not before I clock the look on Maggie's face. She looks like she's seen a ghost.

NOW—AUGUST

Pauline Harding told her son she would be at the hospital as soon as she could get there to support him. She didn't want to leave Sadie with Clive, who (though she hasn't admitted it to anyone but Will) has been rather forgetful lately, and so she's asked her daughter, Jenna, to come and pick Sadie up.

When Jenna comes, Pauline frets over what to wear and how she's going to be of any help to poor Will, and Jenna has to tell her to just get on with it because she isn't any use to anyone while she's dithering in the kitchen and attempting to make them both a cup of tea that neither of them wants.

Really, she isn't hesitating just because of what lies ahead at the hospital; she's reluctant to let her granddaughter go. Pauline has been keeping Sadie safe and telling her a few white lies about where her daddy is right now, because there's no way she can tell her the truth. Not after all the things the little one has had to go through lately, the way her mother has been acting.

"What about the dog?" she says to Jenna. "Can you take Coco too? I think Sadie would like that." Sadie has been stuck to the dog's side ever since Pauline sent Clive out to pick it up from Will's house this morning. "You can have her for a few hours, can't you?"

"What am I going to do with a dog, Mum? I don't know the first thing about looking after dogs."

"Coco's easy; you know she is. Just, I don't know, take her out for a walk or something."

Jenna sighs. "Why can't Dad do it?"

"Because like I said, Sadie will want to be with her. You're doing this for her, not for me."

"Fine. I know."

Pauline kneels down in front of her granddaughter, pulling together her pink knitted cardigan, the one she's made her over the last few weeks. She pushes one of the tiny shiny pink buttons through its hole and takes hold of Sadie's arms. "Gran won't be long," she says. "I just have to pop out for a little while, and you're going to have so much fun with Auntie Jenna, aren't you?"

"Yes."

"Good girl." Pauline smiles, still holding on to the cardigan. She really must get going to the hospital, but she doesn't want to let go of her granddaughter. In truth, she loves the fact that Will is staying with her and she's gotten to have Sadie for two nights. They have never been so close. And now there's no doubt they will have to stay longer.

"Mum?" Jenna says. "I'm going now."

Pauline watches her daughter take hold of Sadie's hand and drag her little girl away. Jenna is looking at her curiously. Her lips are parted as if she wants to say something, but Pauline doesn't actually want to hear what her daughter has to say right now.

And yet here it comes; she's getting it anyway. "You know all this won't last, don't you?"

"What do you mean, dear?"

"Living here with Will. Having Sadie staying. You know at some point he's going to move out."

"Of course I know that, darling."

"Don't get too used to it," Jenna continues. "That's all I'm saying."

"I don't know what you're talking about. I'm just looking after my granddaughter and my son when they need me."

"They need to be back in their family home," Jenna mutters. "And I don't think you're helping."

Pauline sighs. "That's a horrible thing to say. You know all I want is for the three of them to get back together."

"Do you?"

"Jenna! Of course I do."

"Well, then you have to suggest to Will he moves back there while Erin is in hospital. It's the best thing for Sadie to be among all her things, in her own home."

"Oh well, I don't know about that," Pauline says. "I mean, Sadie is going to need someone to look after her when Will's at the hospital, and I can cook for them both when they're here and—"

"Mum!" Her daughter interrupts her. "You can carry on helping, but stop taking over. Anyway, this could be just the thing that gets them back together, God willing. Erin's accident will give them both a wake-up call."

"Right. Of course," Pauline says, hesitating. "Yes. Just, well, we have to hope, of course, everything is okay. When they wake her up."

"Mum! Don't say things like that."

"We have to think about it, Jenna. The doctors have told Will that he has to be prepared." Will told her how they'd said they didn't know how much blood Erin might have lost, how it might have affected her brain. Who knows what any of it could mean?

She follows her two girls to the door.

"Erin is going to be fine," Jenna says. "And she'll need Sadie back with her."

It isn't Pauline's place to say anything, because Jenna doesn't know the whole story; she has no clue how much poor Will has been suffering lately. Of course she hopes Erin will pull through okay, but she doesn't think for one minute there's going to be any swift making up to be done. Especially not after what happened two nights ago. After that showdown from Erin when she turned up on her doorstep making accusations against her son.

The thing no one seems to understand is that Pauline Harding would do anything for her children. And right now that means keeping her son and her granddaughter safe.

In fact, she's already had the first meeting with the lawyer this week. The ball is rolling for Will to get custody of Sadie. Pauline thinks it's the best thing all round. Erin's accident is incredibly unfortunate, but it doesn't change anything. She's going to make sure Sadie is in the best place. And that's right here, in Pauline's home.

14

Three months earlier
MAGGIE

THERE ARE SHARDS all over the carpet from where Will dropped a glass and it shattered on the coffee table moments before the Hardings left. I should be hoovering it up—I have another couple arriving in half an hour—but I don't do any of it. Instead I watch the Hardings' Audi roll out of the drive as they leave the Cliff House. I want to make sure they go.

Clutched in my hand is the photo of Lily and me that I picked up as soon as they left my room. I don't need to look at it to know. The necklace she's wearing. The one that Erin so perfectly described. The tiny delicate gold leaf with little pockmarks on it that curl at the edges. It's Lily's.

"Just go," I mutter at them as they slowly disappear, and once they're gone, I still don't move. The picture burns the skin on the palms of my hands where I hold it so tightly.

Who the hell are these people?

* * *

Dad told Lily how special the necklace was, how unique. A colleague from Bali had brought it over for Mum as a gift, only our parents both agreed how much Lily would love it and gave it to her instead on her thirteenth birthday.

After months of searching, when I had given up on the idea of ever getting Lily's necklace back, I looked for a replacement, but I never found anything remotely similar.

Now so many questions skewer my brain. Did Erin see the photo? Did she describe Lily's necklace to me on purpose?

Or is it worse than that? *Did* she actually see it in Will's car?

* * *

Erin keeps telling me she's frightened, but I am too now. Is that, for some twisted reason, her plan? Did they choose me to be their therapist on purpose? I don't really know how they found me, I think, as I remember the answer she gave on her original form to the question *Where did you hear about me?*

Her answer was a vague *word of mouth*.

I inhale a tight breath as I look at the picture of the chain around Lily's neck, then hold my finger to touch the glass of the frame against my sister's skin. It was strange, I think, how Erin told me she thought she was in danger. She didn't talk of her husband having an affair; that wasn't where her head was when she spoke about the necklace. So what *was* she trying to tell me?

Will thinks she needs to see a doctor. He assumes his wife is going mad.

Is she?

On paper I would agree. But I'm no longer so certain.

* * *

"Whoa, they're going to break, Maggie," Richard says that evening when he finds me washing up, slamming dishes into the sink. "What's up?"

I look at my husband and reach out to touch his beard, stroking my thumb down his cheek. Richard and I don't have secrets. On a day-to-day basis we tell each other everything. I don't disclose anything about my clients, of course, but anything that involves me, I tell him. Only I haven't told him this—the story of the necklace Erin described to me, how I can't shake the thought from my head that it *has* to be Lily's.

Richard's skin is crinkled under his eyes, and I move my thumb up, tracing it over his face. I adore every part of him. I love him for all his imperfections that make him perfect.

So why won't I tell him? Is it simply because I don't share my work with him? I tell myself it is, but I know it's not. It's more than that now. It's that I don't trust the Hardings. Or is it really that I don't trust myself: that I don't know what I'll do next?

Because what if Erin did see Lily's necklace in Will's car? And what if Kieran Blake was telling me the truth when I saw him, and he isn't guilty?

It would mean Lily's killer is still out there.

And so, for now, I tell Richard, "I've just got some work stuff going on in my head." I smile and add, "Nothing I can't handle."

Richard kisses me and picks up a tea towel. "That new couple still?" he says.

"Hmm," I agree.

"Well, I think these dishes would survive better if you put them in the dishwasher," he jokes, but he starts drying them anyway. "I know you'll handle it, Mags, but you look stressed. Don't let it overload you. Have you spoken to Elise?"

"I will do," I promise him, though it's the furthest thing from my mind. I can't tell Elise either. "Don't worry about me."

I don't want Richard knowing I've been drawn into Erin and Will's tangled marriage with its layers of secrets. That now I have become a part of it. I don't want him knowing, because already I understand that if I want the truth, I'm the only one who will find it. Whatever it takes.

"I love you," I say, and I mean it. I really do love him, so much.

"I love you too," he tells me, and I know he does. He leans forward and presses his lips against my forehead, and I feel his bristles against my skin and want him to stay there forever.

*   *   *

I lie in bed that night, awake, listening for Lily, going over what I know: Kieran Blake told me he didn't kill her; the only thing we've never found is her necklace; Erin told me she saw the exact replica of it in her husband's car; Erin told me she's in danger; one of them is lying.

When I eventually find sleep, it's restless. Lily's face flashes in my dreams, along with the argument we had the night she died. My last words to my sister. My mother standing in the doorway from her return from holiday. "What have you done, Maggie?" she said.

Erin knows more is my first thought when I wake, and I can't wait until their session next Monday to find out what. I slip out of bed, make myself a coffee downstairs, and take Rocky out for a walk before Richard gets up. He's already in his office when I return at quarter to nine. "Just making a call," I say to him from his doorway.

"You sleep okay?" he asks. "You seemed fidgety last night."

"I was just hot," I tell him. "I'll make more coffee in a moment."

My fingers linger over my phone as I deliberate last minute, but then I tap out the numbers and wait for her to pick up. I've pondered over which one of them I trust enough to talk to. I still don't feel sure of the answer, but my instinct tells me it's Erin I should speak to.

"Erin? It's Maggie Day," I say when she answers. "Listen, I just wondered if you wanted to talk to me on your own?"

"Really?" she says, sounding eager. "I thought you didn't do that."

"Oh, I sometimes make exceptions," I lie, brushing her off. I've never once made an exception, but then I've never needed to before now. Yet when it comes to Lily, it turns out that breaking my rules is a frighteningly easy thing to do. "I just worried about you yesterday," I go on. "I thought it might help."

"I'd love to." She jumps at the chance. "Thank you."

"When?" I say, with a blur of relief and anxiety over the fact that I've made the first step towards going against everything I ever said I would.

"How about Thursday afternoon?"

"Okay, yes that's fine." Two days from now. I would have preferred to see her sooner, but I can wait.

"Then I can see if Will's mum can have Sadie for an hour or so."

"Okay, great," I say. "You tell me where."

"How about the White Hart? Do you know it?" she asks. "It's the pub by the beach. I could get there for two o'clock?"

"I know it," I say. It isn't far from where I live. "I'll see you there."

"Thank you, Maggie," she says, like I'm doing her the favour I want her to think I am, and I hang up the phone as a sinking feeling of apprehension runs through me, because I really shouldn't be doing this and I've already gone too far.

Erin might be scared, but I am too. I'm scared that at least one of the Hardings knows something about my sister's death. I'm scared I have no choice but to put my trust in Erin.

NOW—AUGUST

DC MARGATE STUDIES Richard Day's face. The man is clearly beside himself with worry over his wife, and so Margate is pretty certain he has no idea where she is. Margate attempts to smile, but it's probably coming out more like a frown, and he doubts it's doing the trick of reassuring Richard that there's nothing to worry about.

Fact is, maybe they should be worrying. Two women who know each other—in quite intriguing circumstances. One in hospital in a coma, the other missing.

"We think that maybe Maggie has been seeing Erin Harding as a friend too," Margate says, when he realises he's getting nowhere and Richard really does seem to have no clue about any of his wife's clients. But he sees the way Richard cocks his head at this.

"What do you mean, as a friend?"

An interesting reaction, Margate notes. "We believe when Will Harding, Erin's husband, stopped going to therapy sessions, your wife carried on seeing Erin on her own."

Richard frowns.

"This doesn't sound right to you?" Margate asks.

"I just don't think it's something Maggie would ever do."

"They met up, and not just in her office at"—he pauses and checks his notes—"the Cliff House. But at the harbour two weeks ago."

"I doubt that's true," Richard says.

"A friend of Erin Harding saw them together. Why don't you think it would be true?"

"Like I say, it's not something Maggie would do. If she was with this Erin, she must have bumped into her. It's one of her rules—she only sees her clients as a couple—and she's strict about that."

"Will tells us his wife carried on seeing her."

Richard slumps. Like he's defeated. The man is realising there's a strong possibility it has to be true. And now he's likely wondering how his wife could have done something so out of character. Richard's one of those guys who shows everything on his face, and right now he looks totally crestfallen.

"I don't know anything about Erin Harding," Richard says with a sigh. "And I'm sorry she's been in an accident, but . . ." He drifts off. "I know you're thinking it's linked," he states. "Maggie not being here. Please. Just tell me, what do you actually think has happened?"

"I'm sure there isn't anything to worry about," Margate says. He doesn't actually believe this, and he hopes his own face isn't as transparent as Richard's. "People pop out all the time and don't take their phones with them."

"But it's early on a Sunday morning. And she hasn't taken our dog. And besides, you must think it's something to worry about or you wouldn't be here, questioning me, trying to find her," Richard points out with more than a hint of panic in his voice.

"We just want to talk to her. We think she might be the one person Erin has been confiding in."

"Only she's not here, and—" Richard stops abruptly. "Do you think she's in danger?"

"There's no reason to suggest she is."

"But you said this woman was in a hit-and-run. And my wife is missing, and if they were friends, then Maggie is the kind of person you would ask to help you." He glances at Maggie's phone, the thought clearly going through his head that if he'd been able to get into it, he could have checked his wife's messages. And he's likely also wondering if this is precisely why she changed her lock code.

"I'd like to take her phone," Margate says. "So we can see if Erin Harding has been in touch."

"Oh God." Richard sinks deeper into his chair, hands cradling his face. "Where the hell is she?"

15

Two months earlier
ERIN

I T'S HOT, BUT then it is the first day of June. The longest day of the year is less than a month away, and so it shouldn't be a surprise, but somehow summer has come from nowhere this year. The idea of us celebrating New Year's Eve as two families with Zoe and Dave feels like something from a different lifetime, when in reality it's only five months since the start of the year. I think back to the aspirations we shared that night for the year ahead. The holiday we were going to go on. The summer house Will planned to build for Sadie. And then I wonder: How did it all go so wrong?

Maybe Will never had any intention of following through on the summer house. Or possibly things have just changed so much that it's no longer his priority. *We* are no longer his priority, or at least I'm not anymore.

* * *

I drop Sadie off at Pauline's at one thirty PM on Thursday. I told my mother-in-law I needed to do some food shopping, the lie burning into my tongue. I started explaining it was easier on my own, but she wasn't listening. She was already telling me that of course she would love to have Sadie over, that her girl could stay as long as she wanted. I hate the way she calls her *my girl*. I said as much to Will once, but he brushed me off, as he always does when it comes to his mother. "It's a saying, Erin," he said.

Now I stand on Pauline's doorstep, and she tells me, "I'll give her tea."

"Oh, that's not necessary. I won't be that long."

"Nonsense. You want to stay for tea at Gran's, don't you?" she says, and Sadie replies that she does, and so the arrangement is made without me having a say in it. It's no use arguing when Pauline has taken the decision out of my hands, offering it up like she's doing me a favour.

"I'll see you later, then," I say as the door is already closing on me.

I'm not blind to Pauline's ways, but when it suits me, as it does today, I go along with her, because now at least it means I'll be able to go food shopping after I've seen Maggie.

It's ten to two when I pull into the car park of the White Hart pub, a building almost nestled into the base of the cliffs, a white-stone-walled old-fashioned pub slightly off the beaten track. It has always been one of Will's favourites, not just because it's so near the beach but because they do the best pies around.

I find a spot in front of the pub and get out to wait at one of the outdoor tables, fanning my T-shirt to cool myself down in the heat. Five minutes later and Maggie is pulling up too. There are no more spaces at the front, and so I watch her drive around to the rear, but as I get up to walk over and meet her, I suddenly spot Will's car.

My breath catches in my throat like a hard ball. As Maggie gets out of her Land Rover, I see the way she clocks it and then looks at me in surprise.

I carry on walking towards her. "Will's coming today too?" she says, seemingly agitated at the idea. "I thought this was just going to be the two of us."

"Will *isn't* coming," I say. "Or at least, he isn't supposed to be." I look back over to where he's parked. The car is just under one of the trees, almost tucked in, as if it's trying to hide.

My immediate thought is that he's found out I'm meeting Maggie this afternoon, though I can't imagine how. He should be at school, even if Thursday afternoon is sports for Keyport Secondary and sometimes he doesn't have to be involved. But there's certainly no reason he would be in the pub.

"But his car . . ." Maggie is gesturing towards it.

"I don't know why it's here," I say, and then I gauge the way she's looking at me, frowning, and it dawns on me, slowly, that of course Will doesn't know I'm here with Maggie. If anything, he's likely thought this is the very last place I'd be, and so there's a very different reason as to why my husband's car is here, nestled out of sight. "He's here with someone else," I say plainly.

"No, no." She shakes her head. "That's probably not it."

She's lying, of course.

"Erin, what do you want to do?" Maggie asks kindly.

The question makes me feel sick. Do I want to go inside and confront my husband and finally find out what he's up to? Or do I walk away?

"What do you think I should do?" I say, already knowing what my answer needs to be.

"I can't tell you that."

"What would you do?"

Maggie takes a deep breath and looks over at the pub too, as if by looking in its direction we can see through the walls. "If it were me, I'd go in and see what he's up to, because it's likely nothing," she says. "He could be meeting a friend, couldn't he?" She pauses. "So that's what I would do. But I'm not you. You need to make your own decision."

"I don't think he's meeting a friend," I mutter. "Not when he should be at school. But anyway, you're right; we should go in."

"No, Erin. You need to go in on your own. I don't think Will should see us together." Maggie looks more awkward than she did when she noticed his car.

I nod. Will was never supposed to know I was meeting our couples therapist. This is her doing me a favour, wanting to make sure I'm okay. This was going to be my chance to persuade her that Will is lying to me, to get at least one person on my side who can help me forge a way forward.

"I just assumed you wouldn't be telling Will," she says.

"I wasn't going to," I say quickly, because I wasn't. This meeting was for me, and so Maggie is right. If I go inside to see whether my husband is in the pub with another woman when he should be at work, then I have to face him on my own.

"I'll wait here," she says, and eventually I nod and walk away from her and towards the entrance to the pub.

I stop outside the closed doors and think about what she said. Of course he might be in here with a colleague; it's totally feasible. And if he is, then he's going to wonder why I'm here. I can't tell him I'm meeting Maggie, so I must come up with another reason. I was going for a walk, I'll say, and I saw his car. Will he believe that?

Does it matter anyway, when deep down I already know he won't be with a colleague? When for the last week I've been carrying the idea that my husband is cheating on me? Only with this thought comes a surge of nausea, because my marriage might have been challenging lately, but if I see him with a woman, it becomes unsalvageable. What if I find them holding hands over the table? Him looking at her the way he always looked at me until recently?

My breaths are short and rapid as I consider that this isn't what I want. I might have suggested I didn't want him in the house anymore, but that was when I felt I still had things to play with. To be one hundred percent confronted with an affair is a whole other ball game. I close my eyes, thinking how easy it would be to turn around. I can see why some people choose to turn a blind eye, how the thought of pretending you don't know is preferable if it means you don't have to be the one to rip your family apart.

Inhaling a deep breath does nothing to settle the churning inside my stomach. I feel like I'm going to be physically sick as I finally open my eyes again and push open the door.

A cold blast of air conditioning hits me in the face. I can't believe how nervous I am, and yet somehow I manage to step forward, glancing surreptitiously around the bar.

I can't see him. And the farther I walk in, and the more tables I can see, I realise Will isn't on any of them. With the churning settling slightly, I linger a few minutes, waiting for him to come out of the toilet, if that's where he is, but eventually I give up and go back outside to Maggie.

"He isn't in there," I say with a breath of relief. She's waiting by her car and comes quickly over when she sees me.

"Okay, well, that's good."

"Is it?"

"I don't know," she admits. "All you can do is ask him when you get home."

I glance over my shoulder towards the pub again. "But he's not going to tell me the truth. Not when he's lying about everything else."

She gives me a weak smile. "What do you want to do?"

"I don't want to stay here."

"Perhaps we could go for a walk on the beach. That way we could say we bumped into each other if we see him."

I agree, and we take the narrow path that winds through the trees down to the pebbly beach.

"You know I always trusted Will," I start. "Though now I'm starting to question everything."

"Like what?"

"Something happened last year at his school. He was accused of being inappropriate in the way he spoke to a teenage girl. But it was dropped; she withdrew the complaint." I shake my head. "I didn't for one minute think he'd done what the girl said."

"But you do now?"

I sigh. "I don't know. It's not the Will I know at all, but then I don't think I know that Will anymore."

We walk for a bit before Maggie says, "I was worried about you when you said you thought you were in danger. Do you still feel that way?"

I nod. "Yes. But—" I hesitate. "It's not there all the time. Some days feel like normal. Or at least not as bad." My mind isn't really on any of this right now; I'm more concerned by the idea of bumping into Will and what I might see. My gaze trails the beach ahead as we walk, looking for my husband and his potential mistress.

But Maggie is persistent. "Have you told anyone else you feel like this?"

"No," I tell her. "My best friend doesn't believe a word I say against Will. And there isn't anyone else. Not anyone I ever trusted as much as Will and Zoe, anyway."

"Why won't Zoe believe you?"

"She thinks I've got it all wrong. When Coco disappeared and I told her I thought Will had something to do with it, she laughed it off. When I told her I thought he was having an affair, she just told me Will would never do that." I shrug. "Every time she's taken his side, and so I stopped telling her, and now I think she just gets it all from Will instead."

"That's hard to take."

"Yeah, well, I suppose I must have sounded mad. Do you think I sound mad?" I ask her.

There's a beat before Maggie says, "No. I don't."

"So you believe me?" I test her.

"I believe what you're saying," she says.

"Ah, but that's what Zoe said. She believed that *I* believed what I was saying, just not that it was the truth. So I don't think you do either, then?" I stop short on the pebbles, grinding the heel of my trainer into them.

"I've only known you and Will a couple of months, and I only know either of you as well as the other. But I believe what you tell me, Erin."

"I suppose that will have to be enough for now."

"When you told me about the necklace," she says, as we start walking again, "it didn't sound like you suspected Will was having an affair."

I look up at the sky above me, the fluffy white clouds sweeping across it. "Why do you say that?" I ask, because it is what I'd been thinking. But there was also more to it. I couldn't explain the fear or the feeling that I'd seen the necklace before, but now, having seen Will's car today and having expected to be confronted by an affair, I wonder if this is what I've been afraid of all this time: the idea that my husband is cheating on me.

"When I asked you about it, you said you felt like you were in danger," she reminds me again. "And I just think my head would immediately go to another woman. But you said you were scared by finding the necklace. So what was it that scared you, Erin?" Maggie steps round so she's in front of me, her eyes boring into me like she expects something more from me. It's the first time I wonder why she has offered to meet me, when it was apparent from the outset that this is not something she would ever do. There's something different in the way she speaks to me today. She is so much more direct in her questioning.

"Erin?" she insists. "What were you scared of?"

I think back to the moment I saw the necklace, only now I see a different image. I see myself in the passenger seat and Will climbing into the driver's seat beside me, and I feel the way I froze in fear with the absolute knowledge that he was going to hurt me. Only that wasn't how it happened.

"I thought he was going to hurt me," I say quietly, as I try to make sense of it.

"Why would you think that?" she grills.

I try to think back. I'm no longer entirely sure about any of it.

"Tell me about it again," Maggie demands.

I sigh. "What do you mean? What I did?"

"No. Describe the necklace."

I frown, but I tell her anyway. "It was just this gold leaf, like I said, really delicate. It looked like it could break. It was unusual." I can recall the necklace with absolute clarity.

Maggie is looking at me really oddly. "And you saw it in his car?"

"Yes," I tell her again.

"Nowhere else?"

"No, not anywhere else." I'm getting exasperated. "Why are you questioning me about it? This isn't what I thought we'd be talking about. I thought you wanted to help me, but this—" I wave my hand in the air. "This feels odd."

We've turned around now and started ambling down the beach again, back towards the pub.

"You're right," she's saying, "there's something I need to ask you." But her words are fading, and I'm no longer hearing them. My mind has snapped away from Maggie and is focused on what's ahead of me. *Who's* ahead of me.

I grab her arm and pull her over to the edge of the beach, where there's a wall and trees the other side of it that hang over. We see Will coming towards us, though he likely doesn't see us as he turns off to his left to make his way up the path to the car park. Not when he's too engrossed with the conversation he's having with the woman walking with him.

"Do you know who that is?" Maggie says.

I'm shaking, I realise, my hands fluttering.

"Do you know who that was?" she asks again. "Erin? Are you okay?" She holds on to my arm, gently running her hand over it.

"It's someone he works with," I say. "I met her at a school night I went to. Her name's Rebekah Hasler." There was something about her I didn't like—maybe the way she laughed at everything Will said, or how I caught her watching him from the other side of the room. But now it makes sense. The jigsaw pieces are loudly slotting into place.

I can't help but notice once more how attractive she is. In her late twenties, she has blond hair that falls just past her shoulders and long legs that are wrapped in skintight white jeans despite the warm weather. "Maybe now you believe he's lying to me," I say to Maggie, while all I'm thinking is that despite everything, I don't think I ever truly believed my husband could do *this* to me.

16

ERIN

I DON'T SAY ANYTHING to Will when he comes home from school. Possibly this is because I want to give him the chance to tell me about Rebekah without me having to ask. More likely it's that I don't want to confront what he's up to, because as soon as I do, there's no turning back for us.

As we mill about each other in the kitchen, preparing tea for Sadie and a salad for us to eat quickly before Will meets Dave to play squash, I ask him how his day was.

"It was fine," he tells me. Nothing more. He doesn't mention that he was in the pub this afternoon instead of supervising games at school.

How have we come to this? I think as I watch him leave the house. A couple that don't talk to each other but dance around secrets and lies instead. It's unnerving how quickly we have become unravelled.

I go to bed before I hear him come home. I want to ask Zoe if Dave is really at squash, and yet I can't bring myself to do it. After I walked out on her at the coffee shop, we have barely had contact.

I don't want to give any of them the satisfaction of knowing what's going on in my head right now. If I texted her, she would probably tell Dave, who in turn would tell Will, and then all of them would agree it's just another problem I'm causing.

Instead I lie in the bed in the spare room and decide that if Will is seeing Rebekah and looking for a way out of our marriage, I won't let him drag me down whilst doing it. If his plan is to convince everyone I've driven him away with my accusations, I won't let him get away with it. I won't ever let him hurt me or Sadie. I will confront him the next morning before he leaves for work.

*   *   *

My night is restless, disturbed by frantic dreams and overriding thoughts of what I'm going to say. I want him to walk into school this morning and face Rebekah knowing his wife has caught them.

Despite my exhaustion, I get up with a bravado that makes me think he can do whatever he wants. If he wants to leave me for her, then so be it, but I will not let him take my sanity.

When Will is sitting at the breakfast table, crunching into a piece of toast, I say, "I went for a walk yesterday afternoon by the White Hart." I notice the way some butter sticks to his top lip, making it shiny, and recoil at the sight of it. I wonder if I'm beginning to hate this man I've always loved. Is this how it starts, with the little things? Maybe it will be Rebekah's place soon to tell him he's got butter over his mouth and I won't have to look at it.

I'm busy convincing myself of this, and noticing the way Will's eyes are flickering anxiously, when Sadie wanders in from the living room, holding up a piece of paper she's been crayoning all over. "Oh, what's that, darling?" I say, reaching out to take it from her. I crouch down so I'm at eye level with her and let her talk me through her picture. I want her to know her creation is the most important thing to me right now. She doesn't need to hear the thud of my heart, the quickening of my breath, or feel the anticipation hanging over me in a blanket of heavy dread.

"That's you there," she points out, "and that's me next to you. And that's Daddy over there." She prods a finger onto the paper. My eyes well up with unexpected tears at her poor timing. I don't move for a moment, and then when I do, I pull her into me, squeezing her and telling her what a wonderful drawing it is and how much I love her.

"Can I see too?" Will asks, and Sadie pulls away and proudly passes it to him, and I do realise I hate him then. I hate him because I love him and because Sadie loves him, and I can't bear the idea that he could even consider walking away from us.

He is intense as he studies her drawing, a frown creasing his face. He doesn't say anything for a while, and I doubt he's concentrating on the paper in front of him; I imagine he's rehearsing what he's going to say to me when our daughter walks out of the room again. Eventually he looks at his watch and tells Sadie it's a very clever picture.

"Can you draw us another?" I ask her, before Will has the chance to tell me he has to leave for work.

Sadie nods and runs out the room again. "As I was saying . . ." I begin.

"You went for a walk?" Will replies, omitting the part about it being near the White Hart.

"I saw your car there."

He stuffs the last piece of toast into his mouth, a deliberate play for time. "Hmm," he says through his mouthful. "I wasn't needed for sports yesterday afternoon."

"I saw you, Will," I go on.

"Why didn't you say anything?" he asks, like this is the surprise. That I didn't go up to my husband and his other woman and say hello.

"Who were you with?"

"I was with Rebekah," he tells me. "You've met her before." He finishes his toast and wipes the crumbs off his hands and onto his plate, his eyes never leaving mine. "Erin, whatever you're thinking, it isn't right," he says, cocking his head to one side.

"What am I thinking?"

"I don't know, that I'm having an affair or something?"

"Are you?"

"No!" he lets out with a laugh. "God, no. You must know that. I would never do that." His eyes are screwed up intensely, as if he can't believe I'd even consider it, even though I've caught him red-handed. "We're friends—colleagues." He corrects himself quickly. "That's all. It's no different to me going for a drink with Guy or Lewis," he says, mentioning two other people he works with.

Only it wasn't Guy or Lewis he chose to go for a drink with. It was Rebekah.

"Then why didn't you tell me you were at the pub with her yesterday afternoon when I asked about your day, instead of letting me assume you were at school like you usually are?"

"Because—" He flaps a hand frustratedly in the air. "Because we barely talk to each other anymore, Erin. When you aren't accusing me of something I haven't done, we make small talk or don't even speak. I had a free afternoon and I went for a walk and half a pint with a work colleague, who happens to be a woman, and to be honest, I just didn't want to tell you when we don't have normal conversations anymore."

"But you always would have done," I insist.

"Yes, you're absolutely right. I *always* would have done. Right up to the start of this year, I would have told you, but that's not where we are anymore is it?" he says. "Is it, Erin?"

"You think this is all my fault."

Will shakes his head lightly and lets out a sigh. "I'm not doing this now," he says. "Not when you know I have to leave the house." He checks his watch again, pushes his chair back, and takes his plate to the sink. "I'll see you tonight."

He hesitates over kissing me on the cheek but leaves the room without doing so, and I listen to him calling goodbye to Sadie. I can no longer remember when he last kissed me; it could have been any point within the last three and a half months.

I'm leaning back against the counter, feeling more confused than I did fifteen minutes ago, when Will surprises me by appearing in the kitchen doorway again. "I would never do that to you, Erin," he says.

NOW—AUGUST

Zoe Sawyer isn't sure how long she should hang around the hospital. She's been here for a few hours now, waiting for news, and she doesn't want to go. When Erin wakes up, she wants to be here. She wants to tell her best friend she's sorry for her part in what has happened, that she should have been there for her. Zoe doesn't know what she would do if anything happened to Erin.

After speaking to the detective, Lynsey Clayton, Zoe has been trying to piece together what her best friend could have been doing back near Harberry, walking away from Harberry Woods and the estate.

The woods were a big part of their teenage years, though Zoe had been banned from going in them after dark. Her mother had told her, "You never know what goes on in those woods when the light has been sucked out of them."

They went anyway. It was where they used to spy on Will Harding and his mates.

But Zoe knows how much Erin hated Harberry. How the day she left home she swore she would never go back again.

So what the hell was she doing back there in the middle of last night?

Zoe has been unsettled ever since DI Clayton left her in the cafeteria. By now she's walked back to ITU, where she's been watching the other visitors and trying to fathom what her best friend has been going through recently. What made her return to the one place she said she would never go to again.

There's Will, who's been pacing back and forth, stopping every nurse or doctor he passes to ask what's happening to his wife.

Somewhere is Corinne Pashley, Erin's mother, even though Erin told her sixteen years ago she didn't ever want to see her again.

And then there's Pauline Harding, who keeps popping up from nowhere like a mole, checking on her son, bringing him coffees he isn't drinking.

When Erin wakes up, there will be—if Zoe includes herself—at least four people she won't want to see.

Oh. Strike that. Make it five. Someone else turns the corner at the far end, and Zoe watches Will's face go beetroot red. Zoe's hackles are up as she paces forward. "What's she doing here?" she hisses at him.

"I don't know," he growls quietly, and scurries forward. "Rebekah?" Will attempts to usher her away, and they finally both disappear around the corner.

A surge of heat courses through Zoe's body. An anger ripples through her veins. Has he duped them all?

Suddenly she sees a glimpse of another side to this man whom she has always stood stoically by, whom she has defended over the last few months at the cost of losing her best friend.

17

Seven weeks earlier
MAGGIE

A S FAR AS I see it, there are three possibilities:

> One: Erin is lying about the necklace. She knows
> about Lily. She's out for her husband, and for
> some reason she's targeting me too.
>
> Two: There's an innocent explanation. The necklace
> isn't Lily's, just one that looks uncannily similar.
>
> Three: Erin Harding isn't mistaken at all, and the
> man who's parking up on the gravel outside the
> Cliff House has done something dreadful.

* * *

I suppose I expected a call from Erin to cancel this session,
or at the least to update me on what's happened since we saw
Will at the White Hart last Thursday, but there has been radio
silence. In the days since we saw him with another woman, I've
been wondering what this means—if he's having an affair, and
whether it has any bearing on what Will might know about
my sister. With every question I come up with blanks. I don't

even know if I'm right to trust Erin, but her shock at seeing her husband was palpable.

I deliberated over texting her, just starting with a simple *Is everything okay?* Even though what I really wanted to say was *Can we talk again?*

But then I chose not to put any contact into writing. I have no idea if Will knows I was with her. I don't even know if she's brought this Rebekah woman up with him at all, if it ball-rolled into some huge argument. In short, I have no clue what's going on with the Hardings, and while my focus isn't particularly on the state of their marriage as it should be anymore, I desperately need to speak to Erin again. But I need to be careful.

Their car doors open, and they both climb out at the same time. *Can I trust you, Erin?* I wonder as she stares at my shuttered windows, where I'm peeking through pinched slats. *Is it you I should be looking out for, Will?* I think as he strides purposefully towards the front door.

I gulp down a breath, feeling the tingle in the tips of my fingers. What if Will starts to question *me?* What if he asks me why I spoke to his wife without him, when it's the one thing I determined I would never do? Would he consider making a complaint about me?

The doorbell buzzes, and I don't move. It rings again, a shrill sound that goes right through me, and I shake myself, answer the door, and eventually let them in, plastering on a smile like everything is fine as they sit on the sofa and I go to my armchair.

"So how has your week been?" My gaze is drawn towards Erin, and I hold my breath, unable to anticipate what her answer will be.

"Up and down," she says, watching me carefully in return. I notice the way Will's hand moves closer to hers on the sofa, as if he's about to hold it, but he must see my gaze drifting towards it, for he moves it slightly farther away again.

"We've been talking more," he tells me.

"Oh? That's good," I reply.

"Erin saw me with a female colleague and jumped to the wrong conclusions." He looks at his wife, his hand edging closer again. "There's no way I would do that to her."

I feel my breathing slowing as he talks. I don't believe he knows I was with Erin, and the more I study her expression, I get the impression she's trying to tell me as much. In fact, there's a lightness in her face that I didn't notice when she first walked in.

"Erin, how do you feel about this?"

"I don't believe he would," she replies, giving a small smile that disappears quickly, but it's enough for me to know that whatever he's said to her over the last week, she's chosen to believe him.

"That's good to hear," I tell her. I smile myself, nodding in the hope of conveying I'm happy for her, though I'm not sure I am. "It sounds as if this means a small breakthrough in your communication?"

"I think so," Will replies.

I carry on smiling, trying to figure out what I would usually do or say next if my head wasn't filled with questions about Lily's necklace and what this couple knows about me and my sister.

"Maggie?" Will says, and as I snap my head towards him, I realise I haven't heard whatever he's been saying.

"Yes? Sorry." I shake my head. "I'm sorry. I felt a bit light-headed for a second."

"Are you okay?" he says. "Should we go?"

"No," I say sharply, and then more softly, "No. Honestly." I smile. "I'm perfectly fine."

He frowns at me but doesn't say anymore, and I deliberate over what to say to them. If I dive straight back into the necklace like I want to, I'll raise suspicion, and I still don't know who knows what. No. I need to tread more carefully, and so I think maybe I should go back to Erin's childhood, back to the time when Lily died.

"Erin, a couple of weeks back, we began talking about your childhood."

"Oh?" She's clearly surprised. She must have expected me to talk about her week with Will and the aftermath of her seeing him at the White Hart. And in any normal circumstances, I would have done, but this isn't normal.

She gives Will a sideways look. He in turn continues to look at me strangely.

"I don't know what more there is to say," she tells me. "I moved on, I met Will, I had a family. I've come out of it stronger." She says this concisely, like she has nothing more to add on the matter.

"I think you have," I agree. "It's common for children to grow into adults who don't know how to form relationships, and yet you have. You had no one to learn from, nothing to bring forward with you, and yet you did it anyway."

Beside her, Will is nodding. "When we first met, Erin used to put up barriers," he says. "She wanted us to move to London just to get away."

"I would have if we could have afforded it," she says. I recall it was his parents who bought them the house down here. "I didn't want to live so close," Erin says plainly. "I wanted to get away. But instead I had to try and blank it out. Forget what my house used to look like and the way I would listen to my mum's footsteps on the kitchen beneath my bedroom when I was little and wonder whether she was going to come and kiss me goodnight. Sometimes she stood in my doorway and told me to stop reading. Sometimes she didn't bother coming up at all."

"It must have been awful," I say, but what I'm really wondering is *How close? Where was it you used to live?* "Where was it?" I ask.

"Sorry?"

"You said you didn't want to live so close," I say, at the same time Will is saying, "Why was she like that?"

I snap my attention to him as Erin glances, confused, at both of us.

"I mean, isn't that the question?" he asks, giving me a curious look. "*Why* Erin's mum was like that?"

He's right, yes, that should be the question, but it isn't the one I want the answer to.

"I think she often just forgot," Erin says.

"I meant more what made her so detached?" Will goes on, like he's taken on the role of therapist.

"My grandmother was exactly the same. My mother was allowed to hang around the woods like I did when she was young. She used to meet up with older friends down by the lake, and her mother didn't have a clue."

As Erin speaks, I home in on one word. It couldn't be the same lake. *Could it?*

"I assume Grandma never cared that she was there, just like my mum never did either," she's saying. "You know, no one I knew from school was allowed to go there on their own, and not at all after dark, but I could have walked straight through the woods to the other side and not been back till morning, and if my mum asked anything, it would be, 'Nice evening?'"

There's something eerily similar about what our parents told Lily and me about being out after dark. *Don't go through the woods on your own. Stay away from the lake.*

"I know Erin wasn't keen to stay in Dorset," Will pipes up, "but with my parents offering to pay the deposit on our house . . ."

Like I'm interested in what his parents did or didn't do, though I have the fleeting thought that they could have paid a deposit on a house anywhere for their son and daughter-in-law if they'd really wanted to help them out.

"Where were the woods?" I say, ignoring him.

They both look at me quizzically.

"You said you grew up near woods." I can hear the urgency in my own voice, and know I should probably lighten it, but I'm unable to.

"In Harberry," Erin tells me plainly. "I grew up near Harberry Woods. You must know them?"

I feel myself sink into the cushions of my chair, like they're pulling me inside it. Of course I know Harberry Woods. I know them too well: my own parents' warnings; the boyfriend I used to meet there when I was a teenager; my sister's body being dragged out of the lake that sits smack in the middle of them.

"Maggie, are you sure you're okay today?" The question comes from Will again.

"I just—" I stumble, trying to focus on him and Erin as they swim in and out in front of me. He's staring at me strangely. Erin, more cautiously, is frowning.

Jagged pieces of a puzzle fill my mind. Erin seeing Lily's necklace in her husband's car. Erin and Will both come from Harberry, the place we grew up, the place Lily died when she was only fourteen.

"Here," Will is saying. He's holding a glass of water out towards me. I take it with trembling hands. It's dead on ten to ten. "Sorry, your time—" I say.

I might need answers, but for now I just want them both out of here.

18

MAGGIE

MY WHOLE BODY trembles as I watch them leave—this couple who have upturned my world. Who came to me three months ago with issues I still haven't managed to get to the bottom of.

Maybe I never will. Because it's possible that what they've sought me out for has nothing to do with their marriage and everything to do with Lily.

I no longer know what's true. As a couple, they appear to be unravelling in front of me. I've seen this in the way they talk and contradict and defend themselves. In the way they're quick to attack each other's family.

I saw with my own eyes the way Erin cracked apart when we saw Will on the beach. None of that felt like an act.

It would support the assumption that they aren't in this together and that only one of them knows why they're here. Possibly only one of them knows anything about my sister.

Only today, they seemed to be drawing together again.

* * *

I go back to my bookcase and pick up the photo, remembering the way Lily used to play with the leaf charm of her necklace, constantly rubbing her finger and thumb over it until Dad told her to stop before she rubbed it away.

Lily had big plans, much bigger than working on the shop floor like I did. She was going to university. She wanted to be a doctor; she would have been the first in our family. Lily was the sensible one with the brain, while I was the fun-loving older sister, the party girl. My parents pointed it out to us often enough. They told us we couldn't have been more different.

But still I did everything I could to look after my sister. Mum always used to say to me that I was going to make a wonderful mother one day. I believed it too, until the day Lily died.

If Erin and Will came from Harberry, they would know the name Lily Rowe for sure.

I pace my room, getting my head around this. Erin would have been eleven or twelve when my sister died, but Will would have been the same age as Lily. Maybe even in the same year.

I would have already left school, too many years between us for me to know who they were. They wouldn't recognise me; they'd only know me as the sister of the dead girl who was found by the lake.

*   *   *

My other clients come and go in a blur, and by the end of the day, I can't recall how their sessions went apart from the notes I made. I haven't given any of them my all as I usually would.

Lily has taken over every thought, every inch of my brain.

I may have worried about communicating with Erin over text, but with my last session over, I find myself tapping out a message and pressing send. *Erin, can we meet alone? I need to talk to you.*

I wait for her response, but when half an hour passes and she still hasn't read my text, I drive back to Richard.

"I was just about to take Rocky out for a walk," he says when I pull into the drive. "Do you want to come?"

I look at my dog and then at my husband. How I want to tell him everything, but I know I daren't. I shake my head. "I don't feel too good," I say. "I'm just going to have a lie-down."

"What's wrong?" he asks, concerned.

"It's nothing, don't worry. I think I'm just tired." I let myself into the house. All I want to do is wait for Erin to message me back, and I don't want Richard to know. Not yet.

When it comes to my sister, it frightens me how easily I'm able to cast protocol aside. I may not know whom I can trust between Erin and Will Harding, but I will hunt both of them down until they tell me the truth.

CHAPTER

19

ERIN

IN THE WEEK since I saw my husband at the White Hart, he's been making more of an effort with me. I thought Maggie would have wanted to talk about it this morning—I wanted to discuss with her how I felt my marriage was shifting, albeit slightly, for the better—and yet her questions were about something else altogether.

Tonight he comes home early from work. He's been doing this since we had the conversation about my seeing him outside the White Hart.

"I'm going to make dinner tonight," he tells me. "Is there anything you want to do?"

"Like what?"

"I don't know. Have a bath, or work on your book?"

I shake my head. The last time I was in the shed writing, I came out to find Coco gone. I haven't been back in there since, and I don't want to go now.

"Spend some time with Sadie, do something fun together?" he persists.

"I've spent all day with Sadie."

Will doesn't sigh, as I might have expected him to, but says, "Well, I want to cook for you, so go and put your feet up."

Ever since I saw him with Rebekah, it's as if he wants to show me he loves me and urge me to believe him that nothing is going on with her, though all I have is his word.

I do as he says, however, and I take some time for myself, telling him I'm going to have a bath. A luxury for five PM, but he insists Sadie will be fine and there's nothing I need to do. And so I run hot water and tip a good glug of Molton Brown under it, grabbing a new book I bought back in February and still haven't been able to read past the first page of.

I slide into the bubbly water, closing my eyes, my book perched on the side, forgotten for now.

I think about how Will and I are dancing around the root of our problems and also how at times, like now, the "root" of them feels so distant I can hardly hold on to it.

The mistrust I felt on Valentine's Day, the feel of his hands on my neck, my accusation that Will had something to do with Coco—it all sprang from nowhere and I let it spiral, but what if I'd handled it differently? If I'd seen Coco's disappearance for what it likely was—that some arsehole had stolen my baby? And that morning I must have had a panic attack, and somehow I must have been wrong about the taillight, because realistically, how could Will have fixed it in the middle of the night?

And maybe Rebekah Hasler is only a colleague, like he says, and he would have told me he'd been out with her if our relationship hadn't become such a mess.

I can argue it all away, everything except the necklace. Or maybe I saw one of Sadie's and it was some paranoia that replaced the image of it.

Eventually I get out of the bath, my fingertips wrinkled and the water much cooler. I grab a towel and go downstairs. Sadie is eating beans on toast in front of the TV, a line of teddies either side of her, each with their own bowl filled with dry Cheerios. Will is stirring a pot of pasta on the hob, a bowl of salad already prepared on the counter beside him. He's unaware of me watching him from the doorway as he turns off the hob and drains the pasta, tipping it into an oven dish and pouring over the sauce.

His phone beeps to alert him to a new message, but he doesn't pick it up to look. Instead he puts the now assembled pasta bake into the oven and then starts loading the dishwasher. Eventually he notices me. "Hey!" he says. "Nice bath?"

"It was, thank you."

"Dinner's going to be twenty minutes."

I nod.

He stands awkwardly by the counter, his hand twitching at his side until he holds it out to me, and I feel like I have to take it, even though I'm not sure if I want to or not. But I walk over and he meets me halfway, and I reach for his hand. "I've done nothing wrong, Erin," he says to me. "I wish you would believe that."

"I want to," I say, because I really do.

He nods, then smiles. "Well, that's a start," he says.

"I was wondering, maybe we shouldn't go back to counselling anymore," I tell him. I don't think it's getting us anywhere except rooting through our pasts, and more recently I've felt that Maggie's focus hasn't been on us as it should be.

"Okay," he says. "If that's what you want."

"It is. I'll call her in the morning."

*　*　*

We eat dinner and put Sadie to bed, and it isn't until I'm getting something out of the spare room that has become my bedroom that I pick up my phone from the bed and notice a message from Maggie has been waiting for me.

Erin, can we meet alone? I need to talk to you, it says.

Immediately I feel a familiar pang of disquiet. If Maggie wants to speak to me, something must be wrong.

In the mirror my reflection stares back at me. There are dark shadows under my eyes because I haven't been sleeping. I look thinner than I used to.

My fingers hover over the phone. Of course there's a part of me that wants to know what she has to say, but I type back. *I'm sorry. Will and I have decided not to come back to counselling, so please let me know if we owe you anything.* I realise I'm not aware of any notice we're supposed to give her, but I'm prepared to pay if I have to.

I press send, and a reply comes through straightaway. *We really need to speak, Erin*, it says. *This is important.*

"Everything okay?" Will asks from the doorway.

"Yes. Fine." I tuck my phone into the back pocket of my jeans. "I've told Maggie we won't be going to counselling anymore."

"Good," he says. "I think that's the right decision. Do you want to come and watch something downstairs? Have a glass of wine?" he asks.

"Sounds good." I smile and I don't reply to Maggie, and though her words don't leave me, I feel like I need to give my husband a chance. It's odd to think that the best way to do that feels like stopping our therapy.

The next morning, for the first time in a while, Will kisses me on the cheek before he leaves for work. "I love you, Erin," he tells me earnestly as he picks up his bag.

I want to believe him. With all my heart I want to know I was right about the man I married. I want to tell him I love him too, but I just can't bring myself to say it yet.

What I do do is message Maggie back. *I'm sorry. But we don't want to continue and I don't want to speak anymore.*

NOW—AUGUST

Detective Lynsey Clayton still hasn't left the hospital. She's been waiting for the doctor to give an update on Erin Harding. Besides, where else would she be when all the relevant people are gathered in the same place? The husband. The best friend. The mother. The mother-in-law. The father, who has since appeared. And now some woman called Rebekah Hasler, who Lynsey has just learnt appears to be Will's new girlfriend. It's a detective's dream to have them all here. And yet the two women she most wants to speak to, she can't. Because Erin Harding is still unconscious, and no one knows where the hell Maggie Day is.

Lynsey grabs a doctor, who tells her there's little more they can do but monitor Erin for now. She has a one-to-one nurse who's with her all the time. They won't be waking her up until she's stable, and only then will they have any indication of recovery.

Lynsey has positioned an officer, Derek, outside the ward just to check on any other surprise visitors Erin has today. She may be being overly cautious, but if someone did drive into Erin on purpose, she isn't taking any chances on them coming back to finish the job.

And as for Maggie Day, they're all in the dark. According to DC Margate, the husband is frantic. Margate has told her that Richard wants to file a missing-persons report; he feels that whatever they're worried about regarding the hit-and-run, they need to be worried about regarding his wife too.

Lynsey has to concede that she's also wondering whether Maggie Day's safety is in jeopardy. She's made the call to send more officers back to Harberry to look farther afield, expand the search to a wider area. There's every chance Maggie was somehow involved in whatever Erin Harding was up to last night, and right now their priority for both women is preservation of life.

Lynsey finally turns away from ITU, desperate for a packet of the pickled onion Monster Munch that she saw smiling at her from behind the glass of the vending machine. She actually salivates as she heads towards it, thinking about how the two women might be involved.

The thing she has always hated about therapists is their ability to unearth the things you don't want to talk about. They have too much power, she's always believed. Why anyone would want someone interfering in their marriage, she has no idea. Just think of all the chaos that could create.

Lynsey slots her coins into the machine and watches the crisps pop out. She grabs them and carries on towards the hospital lobby, where she sees Will Harding's female friend sitting on a bench, seemingly refusing to leave.

"Rebekah Hasler?" Lynsey says as she approaches her.

"Yes?"

"I'm Detective Clayton."

"Oh, hi." The young woman shuffles up along the bench to make room for her.

"It's good of you to come here," Lynsey says, when actually what she's thinking is that the woman must be mad. What's going through her head to make her turn up at the hospital where her boyfriend's wife is in a coma?

Lynsey now has the chance to get a look at her close up.

She's young, maybe in her late twenties, with highlighted blond hair that's been pulled up into a scruffy knot. She's wearing joggers and an oversized khaki green T-shirt with nine shiny gold hearts on the front of it that glisten as they catch the stark lights of the hospital foyer. She looks glamorous and has even had the time to put makeup on, Lynsey realises, noticing the mascara and perfectly applied foundation.

"I just wanted to be here to support Will," Rebekah says.

"Of course. I take it you two are together."

"Well." She finally looks awkward. "I mean, we've been friends for a long while. I'm here as a friend."

Lynsey nods. "Did his wife know about you?"

"Will and Erin were separated," Rebekah says sharply.

"Mm-hmm. How long has that been?"

"A month."

"Of course. Did Erin know that the two of you are in a relationship?"

"It's not what you're thinking," Rebekah says.

"What am I thinking?"

"That this accident has anything to do with us."

Lynsey doesn't answer.

"It doesn't. That's ridiculous," Rebekah goes on. "Will says someone must have hit her with a car. What would that have to do with me?"

"I don't know what any of it has to do with anyone at the moment," Lynsey tells her. "That's what I'm trying to piece together."

Rebekah looks at her cautiously. "I shouldn't have come," she says eventually. Lynsey stifles a laugh. The woman isn't the brightest. Of course she should never have come. Even if this weren't an investigation. Even if Will and Erin had been separated for months, it was never her place to come.

"What did Will tell you about his marriage?" Lynsey asks her.

"That's private."

"Not when we're investigating a potential murder attempt, it isn't," Lynsey points out.

Rebekah stares back at her in horror. A short shudder visibly ripples through her body. "I'm not comfortable answering this," she says.

"Rebekah, you're not under any suspicion," Lynsey tells her.

"I know, but Will—"

"Will what?" she prompts.

"Well, you're suggesting Will might be."

"I don't think I am." Lynsey smiles at the young woman, trying to get her on her side.

Rebekah blows out a puff of air. "He just told me the way his wife was accusing him of things he hadn't done. He said it started when she made out he'd killed their dog. Which is ridiculous, because the dog was found. You know that, right?"

Lynsey nods. "I do know that."

"Well, exactly."

"Did he tell you they went to counselling?"

"Yes. He was late in for work every Monday, so Will was honest about it. He told people they were having problems they were trying to sort out."

"So you knew he was trying to save his marriage?" Lynsey says.

"Well," Rebekah says sheepishly, not answering the question.

"But it didn't work out?"

"No. I suppose it didn't."

"And did he say why the marriage counselling wasn't working?"

"He told me they just stopped going. I know when it was, because he was there for my Monday assembly. It was six or seven weeks ago, the second week of June. I said to him I didn't expect him to make it, even though I really wanted him to, and then he was just there. He said Erin had stopped the sessions."

"Erin had?"

Rebekah nods. "Will was relieved. He said they hadn't been helping."

"And he never went back?"

"No. But his wife did. Will saw her car one day pulling into the Cliff House, where the therapist was. He followed her up there, apparently, and saw them talking on the cliff. He said they were arguing about something."

"Who was arguing? Erin and their therapist?"

"Apparently."

"Funny thing for a therapist to be doing, isn't it?" Lynsey says. "Arguing with her client on a cliff top?"

"I suppose."

Lynsey sucks in a breath. Maggie Day. Who is this woman?

She walks away from Rebekah and makes a call to one of her officers. "Find me everything you can on Maggie Day," she says. She has a feeling this woman is holding all the answers.

20

Seven weeks earlier
MAGGIE

I'M SITTING IN Richard's car on the corner of Lexington Close, waiting for Will to leave for work. When I recognise his car pulling out of a driveway farther down the road, I sink a little deeper into my seat. He doesn't come past me but instead drives off in the other direction. It's eight forty five AM. He has gone to work. Erin should be home alone.

This seemed like a good idea when I left my own house fifteen minutes ago, but now I'm not so sure. Erin told me she didn't want to speak to me and that they were no longer coming to therapy.

It's not always easy when couples leave; sometimes you have to let them go before you think they're ready. You don't know how their lives are going to pan out, whether they'll stay together or go their separate ways. Often you've grown to really like them, but always you know there's nothing you can do but sit back and let them go. No more contact.

But I can't do that with the Hardings. I can't let them walk away from me when they've come into my life and turned it upside down. I remind myself of this as I start the engine again and pull forward, parking opposite their driveway. They're the

ones who sought me out. They're the ones who know something about my sister.

Do I follow Will, or do I ring on their doorbell and talk to
Erin? It's an easy choice, really, I think, getting out and walking up their driveway.

Erin is clearly surprised when she opens the door to find
me standing the other side of it. She glances over my shoulder
and then back to me, like she's checking to make sure Will
has left.

"I'm sorry, but I need to see you," I say.

She frowns, a puzzled expression on her face.

"I know I shouldn't turn up like this, but it's important."

"We don't want to continue counselling anymore," she
tells me, her guard up. "I said that on my text."

"I know. And that's fine. But I need to ask you something."

She frowns. "What is it?"

"Can I come in?"

Erin stands aside begrudgingly, holding the door wider
for me to walk through to her hallway. "Lovely house," I say,
looking around at the cream-coloured walls and wooden floor-
boards. The staircase is carpeted in a dark cream, and a little
wicker basket sits on the bottom step, filled with toys. There
are photos on the walls in chunky white frames that have been
taken in a studio—the three of them in various poses when
Sadie must have been about a year old.

"Come through to the kitchen," she says. "Sadie's still eating her breakfast." She pauses by her daughter, who is sitting
up to the table with a plate of Marmite on toast cut into strips
in front of her. "Is this about Rebekah?"

"No." I shake my head emphatically. "No. It's nothing like
that."

"Okay." She seems to relax a little, but still she watches
me carefully.

"Hello, Sadie," I say to the little girl, who's staring at me.
"That looks very yummy."

Sadie frowns and regards me as cautiously as her mother is.

"Well, if you don't want it, I might have to have it." I smile.

She looks at me thoughtfully and then down at her toast before eventually picking a piece up and pushing it into her mouth.

Erin raises her eyes. "Can I get you a coffee or tea?"

"Tea would be lovely. Thank you."

"Take a seat, if you don't mind sitting next to Sadie."

"Of course I don't."

Erin fills the kettle with water, then turns back to me. She must know I won't say anything in front of her daughter, because she tells Sadie, "Have that, and then why don't you go and watch some *PAW Patrol* as a treat?" She turns back to the kettle, and when it boils, she makes a cup of tea, which she passes to me, and turns her attention back to Sadie, encouraging her to finish her toast. When the little girl eventually does, she gets down from the table.

Erin takes her through to the living room, which I can see from here is decorated similarly to the hallway, with its neutral colours and tidy shelves. She turns on the TV, and when she comes back into the kitchen, she says, "What is it you want to speak to me about?"

I take a deep breath. "Why did you come to see me in the first place?" I ask.

I can see the question has taken her by the surprise. "I don't understand what you mean."

"What did you know about me before?"

Erin's forehead creases as she slides into the chair opposite me. "I didn't know anything about you. Well, I read a bit, I suppose. A few of your articles."

"Why did you choose me?"

"I didn't. I—what's all this about?"

"Please. Just tell me. Why did you and Will come to see *me*?"

"I don't know… Will found your number." Erin breaks off and shrugs. "Why?"

"Did you know I grew up in Harberry too?"

"No." Erin shakes her head.

"Did you know my sister, Lily Rowe?"

"Lily Rowe?" she repeats. "No, I don't think . . . should I?"

"The necklace you found in Will's car. You described perfectly a necklace that belonged to my sister."

"Did I?"

"So you don't know that?" I ask her, watching for any signs of deceit, although as far as I can make out, either Erin doesn't have a clue what I'm talking about or she's hiding it very well.

"No," she says, beginning to sound irritated, and then after a beat, she adds, "Are you trying to suggest Will knows her? Is that was this is about?"

Not in the way you think, Erin.

She glances past me as Sadie pads back into the kitchen, sucking intently on her thumb. "Has your programme finished?" Erin crouches on the floor so they're at the same height, and Sadie walks into her outstretched arms, flopping against her mum's chest. "Are you okay?" Erin asks.

"Want you to come and sit with me."

"I will do, darling, when my friend has left."

Sadie eyes me over Erin's shoulder.

"And I will be going very soon." I smile at her.

"Do you want to watch one more programme, and then I'll be in?" Erin pulls back and runs her fingers through her daughter's fine blond hair, then kisses her on the head and releases her. It hits me just how much love she has for her child. How it doesn't matter what else is going on; the moment Sadie needs her, Erin's attention is on her.

When Sadie is gone, Erin stands and says to me, "You said it was important. So please just tell me what it is you're here for."

"I need to speak to you about the necklace."

"The one you think is like your sister's?"

"Yes."

"Go on, then," she says. "Just tell me what you're thinking. That Will is having an affair with her too?"

"No. My sister is dead," I tell her. "She was murdered twenty-three years ago in Harberry Woods. You must have heard the name Lily Rowe?" I ask her again.

"Oh." She stops, appearing to mull over the name. "She was the teenager who . . . Was she the one who was found by the lake?"

I nod.

Erin holds a hand over her mouth. "She was your sister?" She shakes her head. "I'm so sorry. I was only eleven, but I remember it happening. I'd just finished primary school that summer."

"Lily had a necklace exactly like the one you described to me," I go on. "She wore it every day, and I know she was wearing it the night she was killed. Only it's never been found since."

Erin stares at me. I have no idea what's going through her head.

"And I get that it might be a coincidence and it may just be one that looks the same, but I don't think it is. I've never been able to find one that looks similar. My father was given it by a colleague from Bali." I reach down into my bag and pull out a photo of my sister. I look at it for a moment before passing it across the table to Erin. "See for yourself what it looks like," I tell her.

Erin gapes at the picture, her eyes trailing the photo. I see the way she inhales and holds her breath, then looks up at me and passes the photo back.

"Is it the one you saw?"

Erin nods. "Yes."

"You said you were frightened when you saw it," I go on. "Remember? I asked you at the White Hart why you said that rather than anything else."

Erin holds a hand up to her throat, her eyes glazing over as if she's trying to recall a memory, or rather as if she has one sitting there that she doesn't want to recall.

"Why were you frightened?" I go on, as Sadie calls her mum from the living room, a high-pitched shriek that makes Erin's head jolt towards the room. "Erin." I grab her arm as she goes to get up. "Why?"

"I can't do this," she says, her gaze flicking towards the living room.

"Then come to my office," I tell her. "Please."

She shakes her head. "My husband didn't have anything to do with your sister's death. Surely that's not what you're thinking?"

"I hope not," I say, as Sadie lets out another yell. "But you said you were frightened. And if you can't tell me why or you don't know, then let me help you work it out."

She stares at me and then at her daughter, who's running into the room, demanding her mum's attention.

"Just a moment, Sadie bear," she says, holding a shaking hand on her daughter's head.

"Erin, I need to know what's going on," I say.

*   *   *

I trust Erin. This is the conclusion I come to.

Over the weeks she's told me many things she believes her husband has done, but none of them make sense to her. They're like fragments of a story that she can't piece together. Flashes of memories out of order, like she's opened the lid on a box and found a jumbled mess of images.

I mull over what I'm thinking. Exactly like triggering a memory—something buried long ago but that lies beneath the conscious.

Is this what it means? Has Erin repressed a memory? Because this is how it appears. But if she has then it has been to protect herself.

I looked into this phenomenon after Elise first mentioned it to me when I started my counselling training. I responded at the time that my problem was I remembered too much. But I've been intrigued by the idea that our minds are so powerful that when something happens that's so traumatic we can't function with the memory, we can forget it ever happened.

The more I think about it, the more it feels like this is what happened. And what I also learnt back then is that, in cases where this happens, it's possible to retrieve the memory again.

I play with the idea, unable to let go of the thought that is what happened until I reach the decision that I have to persuade Erin to let me try retrieving her repressed memories. Even though it isn't something I should be doing. Not least because I'm not trained to. But moreso because it's so far against my ethics.

But I know just enough about it, and I'll do anything that helps me find out anything she might know about my sister. It hits me that I trust Erin, but I'm no longer sure she can trust me.

At that moment my phone rings, and the number flashing on my screen isn't one I recognise. I pick it up and say, "Hello?"

"Maggie Day? This is Detective Jack Lawson. You might remember we spoke—"

"I remember," I say. "You called me about Kieran Blake." Which means there's more news, I think, as I sit down on the edge of the bed, my fingers wrapping tighter around my phone.

"I just wanted you to know that a date has been set for his parole hearing. July thirty-first."

"The end of July. But that's less than two months away," I cry, as Richard appears in the room. I grab my diary and flick to the date. It's a Friday in seven weeks' time. "Please just be honest with me: What are the chances of him getting out?"

"Honestly? I don't know. I'd say fifty-fifty. With good behaviour, and the fact he admitted his crime . . ." The detective pauses. "It could happen," he adds.

I put down the phone and turn to Richard.

"It's not happened yet, Mags," he says, catching on to the conversation. "Try and not worry about it before you know what's happened."

"Do you know what I remember?" I say to him, as he sits beside me and takes my hand in his. "It was right back at the beginning, maybe just after the trial had begun. Mum and Dad were talking in the kitchen. Dad was saying how well he thought the trial was going, that there was no way Kieran would get away with what he did, and my mum said to him, 'But what if he's innocent?'

"My dad was so cross," I go on. "He asked her what she meant by that when the police told us they had the right man. Everyone knew what he was like. But my mum said she wasn't so sure. She said there was just something that niggled her, that didn't feel right. Then she never mentioned it again. So—" I stop.

"Don't think like this, Mags," he says. "They have the right man. He won't be let out on parole."

Up until now I've been thinking that the worst thing that could happen would be Kieran Blake getting released from prison, but now I know there's something even worse. Because if Kieran is telling me the truth, then Lily's killer has been walking free for the last twenty-three years. He's still out there.

CHAPTER

21

Six weeks earlier
ERIN

I T HITS ME, in the days following Maggie appearing at my
house, how much she knows about me while I know barely
anything about her. I don't know where she lives, if she's married, if she has children, though I assume she might not.

Such is the role of a therapist, but I haven't really considered before now how unbalanced our relationship is.

Maggie knows the innermost parts of my past that I didn't
even want to talk about. She knows where I live; she's seen
inside my house. She knows the intimate details of my marriage that I no longer even share with my best friend. I have
shown Maggie my core, but I don't know who she is other than
the sister of Lily Rowe.

I've been looking up the murder of the teenager and
remembering snippets that I absorbed at the time, trying to
recall what I saw in the news or the gossip that circulated
around school or even what my parents told me.

The name isn't one I particularly remembered until
Maggie told me she was the girl who had been killed in the
woods. Like I said to Maggie, I was only eleven. I wasn't
going into the woods myself that summer, and my parents

barely mentioned her. We had a school assembly to talk about stranger danger and the importance of staying safe, but the name didn't stick with me.

I've read that a man called Kieran Blake was arrested for her murder, a name I now recall. I remember reading something on the news about him not that long ago, a piece about local murderers, but I didn't put two and two together at the time and didn't have any reason to.

This week it's been reported that, after twenty-three years in prison, he's up for parole at the end of July. He admitted to killing Lily Rowe five years ago.

So what the hell can any of this possibly have to do with Will?

I feel sick at the thought of how our relationship with Maggie started. How I sat in front of her and accused my husband of killing Coco. I wish I could take it back. I wish we hadn't gone to see her in the first place. We aren't talking about a dog anymore; we're talking about a fourteen-year-old girl. And my husband cannot have been involved in her death.

*   *   *

I believe this, so why do I find myself withdrawing from my husband again as the days pass? Any feelings I had of reconciliation and belief that we could put everything behind us feel like nothing more than fleeting relief.

"What's going on now, Erin?" he says to me on Friday. "I thought things were getting better, but you aren't acting that way." I sense his irritation with me in the way he snaps.

I regard him cautiously, finding myself wondering what he knows and yet unable to ask him outright for fear he will shut me down like he has every other time, telling me again I'm going mad.

Instead I say, "How did you find Maggie?"

"What?"

"I just wondered," I say.

He shakes his head, baffled. "Mum gave me the number," he eventually admits, embarrassed. But I don't have the energy to address that she dictated this too.

Maggie has been messaging me, asking me to come and see her at the Cliff House in our usual slot on Monday at nine AM, only this time without my husband. I don't want to go. *I don't.* Only I do want to know what the hell is going on, and if Maggie can help me, shouldn't I go?

And so Monday morning I arrive just before nine, having dropped Sadie at Pauline's house, telling my mother-in-law I have a doctor's appointment. In return she nodded at me and smiled conspiratorially, making me think Will had told her plenty about our spiralling marriage and that she's pleased I've finally made this doctor's appointment to work out what's wrong with me.

I am left angry as I ring the bell to Maggie's door and she buzzes me in. I feel exposed, and even more so because Will isn't by my side.

Maggie pours me a glass of water and pushes it across the coffee table. "Thank you for coming. I appreciate it."

Am I here for her or for myself? I no longer know; the lines are too blurred. I shrug, and she walks over to her bookshelf and picks up a photo frame. She looks at it for a moment before coming back and passing it to me.

"This is me and Lily together," she says.

I take it from her and look at the two girls in the picture. Maggie is recognisable, though she must be in her late teens. Her sister is the same age as in the photo she showed me last week at my house. "She meant everything to me," she says. "She was my world. She still is."

She takes the photo and puts it back on her bookcase. "Like I told you, everyone looked for the necklace after she was killed. Me, the police, my parents, Lily's friends. It was the only thing of hers we couldn't find." She sits down in the armchair opposite.

"It still doesn't mean it's the same one," I say.

"No. And I've thought of that. But there are too many coincidences for my liking. Your showing up to see me, the fact you and Will both lived in Harberry. Where exactly was your house?" she asks.

"On the edge of the town," I tell her.

"We were just outside it."

"I don't remember you."

"You wouldn't. I'm eight years older than you. I'd left school before you even started secondary."

"I didn't really remember your sister until I read up about her after you told me. I'm sorry," I add. "It must have been horrific to lose her in that way."

"It was."

"I don't know what you want from me, though," I say. "There's nothing more I can tell you. I can't help you."

"I think you can. You've found the one link to my sister's death that we've been looking for all these years."

I feel sick at the idea. If I have, then what was it doing in Will's car? "Even if I did find Lily's necklace, I don't know where it is now. I saw it once, but—" I look away from her. "It's gone."

"It must be somewhere." She presses forward in her chair. "You have to look for it. I can help. I can come round, and we can search the house."

"No!" I say. "I'm not doing that."

"Why not?"

"Because!" I don't know what else to give her. I don't want her rooting through our home, searching for some piece of evidence to try and prove my husband knows something about her sister's death.

"Because you're scared? I get that," she says. "But you have to see how important this is."

"No." I shake my head. "I'm not scared. But you're suggesting Will is involved somehow, and he isn't. He wouldn't be. I don't know what's going on here," I say. "But we don't know anything about Lily. I'm sorry. I shouldn't have come."

"Then why did you?" she says. "Why did you come? I think it's because you want to know if Will *does* know anything. You don't know for sure he isn't involved. You've told me yourself you don't trust him."

"I can't—" I shake my head and go to stand up. "I can't do this."

"Please." Maggie gets up too and reaches out for my arm. "Please don't go. I can help you," she says.

"I don't want any help. I made a mistake coming." I shake her hand off me. I don't want to be here anymore, with her making me question whether my husband could either have knowledge of or had involvement in something too awful to accept.

"Then I'll go to the police," she says defiantly. "I'll have no choice; you must know that. The necklace is evidence."

I stare at her, thoughts of the police trawling our house instead of Maggie now running through my mind, of what they might find.

Sensing my reticence, she jumps in. "Or we can help each other."

"How?"

"We find the answers together. Look, you think this all started back in February, when Coco went missing, and you said yourself you didn't trust what Will was telling you, but you could never explain why."

"So how does this help?"

"I think you know more than you believe you do," she says. "I've been thinking about this a lot. Erin. You don't just get feelings like that out of the blue. I believe for some reason your brain has shut out memories. Ones you have hidden and can't quite reach right now."

I gawp back at her.

"It's possible to repress memories. But it's also *very* possible to retrieve them again. I think something has happened, and while right now you don't remember what, you've been experiencing flashbacks that have been triggered by something.

And they feel like these shards of an image that might not fit together."

I feel a tightness inside me as she speaks, how she's describing exactly what it's felt like over the last few months.

"None of your feelings make any sense to you, but I can help you," she promises. "We can work through it and get the memory back again."

I consider what she's asking of me, and that I actually don't know if I want the memory back.

"Please," she goes on. "I don't need to involve the police or anyone else. Not until we both know what we're dealing with. Then we can make a decision about what we do. Together," she urges. "But until then we just take this one step at a time."

"I don't feel I have any choice," I admit reluctantly.

Maggie's face lights up. "Thank you, Erin," she says, her hand gripping around my arm again and giving it a squeeze.

"It'll have to be when Sadie is in nursey," I tell her. I'm not asking Pauline to have my daughter again.

"That's fine. Whenever it suits you," Maggie says. "But Erin," she adds, as I'm walking out the door. "You need to keep this to yourself for now. You mustn't tell Will. Not yet."

22

Five weeks earlier
ERIN

"I'M STILL NOT sure how ready I am for this," I say to Maggie when we meet for our first session. I've looked into the concept of repressed memories since our last meeting. It's a theory based on the idea that you can put unwanted memories into an unconscious zone that you don't think about.

"I Googled it," I go on. "Apparently repressed memories often come from a traumatic experience. If that's the case, then I've forgotten them for a reason."

Maggie nods slowly. "That's true. And we'll be careful," she says, though she can't hide her eagerness to start as she bustles me onto the sofa and closes the blinds so that only thin slits of light escape into the room. It's suddenly much darker than it normally is.

"What are you going to do?"

"I want to take you back to the time Will told you Coco had gone," she says. "That's where we'll start."

"You're going to hypnotise me?"

"No. Not hypnotise. Just get you to picture it. You'll be conscious all the time. You'll know what's going on," she says. "There's nothing to worry about."

"There's plenty to worry about," I mutter.

"You're scared, I get that," Maggie says. "But you need the truth too, Erin. That's one of the first things you said to me at the start. You said you wanted to know what was happening because you didn't understand it."

"I didn't know what was at stake," I reply.

"You knew you didn't trust your husband," she points out. "So what else is at stake?"

With the dead body of a fourteen-year-old girl, there's a lot more now than there was when we started, but all I say is "And I can stop at any time?"

"Of course." Maggie brushes me off as she shuffles in her seat, opening a notepad and placing it on the arm of her chair as she presses forward towards me. We both must know that she has a lot more to gain from this than me. "Shall we start?" she says.

I don't know. I don't want to. I'm reluctant when she tells me to close my eyes; the feeling of how much power she has over me is unsettling. The imbalance in our relationship is shifting even more in her favour. But more than anything, I fear what I might remember.

"Erin?" she says. "Are you ready?"

Eventually I nod and I do as she says, closing my eyes and letting her begin talking to me about the day Coco disappeared. I find myself drawn back to it. There are so many things that are as clear as if they happened only yesterday. "What do you see?" she asks me.

"Will is giving me a necklace with a charm of Sadie's fingerprint," I begin. I love my necklace, though it still sits on the dressing table where I put it that morning.

"And how does that make you feel?"

"Happy. And loved," I tell her. "But then Will goes to put it round my neck." I hold up my hand again, touching my skin as I feel my breaths shorten. "And I pull away from him."

"Why did you do that?"

"I felt a flash of something, like I thought he was trying to hurt me. Only I didn't know why." I frown at the memory.

"And did he hurt you?"

"No. He never has," I say, although even as I'm telling her this, I'm wondering, *Has he?*

"What happened next?"

"I ran into the bathroom, and he followed me, but he looked worried. And then I didn't know why I'd felt scared. It was like the moment had gone and everything was back to normal."

I go on to tell Maggie about the rest of the day, how Sadie felt poorly and lay on the sofa, not wanting to eat her lunch, and how Will's mother, Pauline, turned up. My insides tighten as I picture my mother-in-law's shadow behind the stained-glass tulip on our front door. I didn't want her there, but there was nothing I could do about it.

"What happened next?" Maggie asks.

"Pauline sat on the floor with Sadie, playing with her tea set." I was annoyed with Pauline and her constant need to fuss over my daughter and make me feel like an outsider. At the time I knew there was no point in mentioning any of this to Will, because he always took her side.

"Then what, Erin?" Maggie says.

"Will came home early with flowers. He asked if I wanted to do any writing. I think I was excited at the thought of being in my shed on my own; I hadn't done it in a while. Then—" I break off. The images start to swim in and out of focus. I see Will standing in the doorway to the house as I come out of the shed, but it's his words that are screaming at me now. "He said, 'The dog has disappeared.'"

Now other things flit into my head. Broken pieces that I can't quite fit together, because they're not how I remember them.

"What is it?" Maggie urges me. "Erin, what is it you see?"

"He's asking me to help him look for her," I say, as though I'm taken back to the moment. But that's not how I remember it. Wasn't it me who said we had to search the roads? Wasn't Will more complacent as he told me she'd be nearby and that he was sorry he didn't end up taking her out?

In my lap I feel my hands twitching, my fingers fluttering against each other.

"Stay with it, Erin." Maggie's words are firm, and yet they make me squeeze my eyes tighter. "What do you see?"

I don't know. I can't think.

"His car," I say eventually. "I think it's his car."

"Will's car?"

"The taillight's been smashed in."

I shake my head. None of it makes sense, and all the while my heart is picking up pace rapidly.

"Erin, what's happening now?" Maggie persists. "You've seen his car. Do you look for the dog?"

"I don't know, I . . . I don't know."

"Okay. How are you feeling?"

"Something isn't right," I say. "I know something isn't right."

"How do you know that?"

"The necklace." I uncurl my hands, then bunch them up again into fists. Suddenly my eyes ping open. Heat is ravaging my body; my breaths are shallow. I reach for the glass of water on the table in front of me, gulping it down as my other hand touches my throat.

"What is it?" she says.

I shake my head. "Nothing."

"Yes it was. It was definitely something. Did he hurt you?" she asks me again.

"No." I let my hand drop. I don't want to tell Maggie the pressure I felt, like he had his hands on my throat, because it doesn't make any sense. I don't remember it.

But Maggie is determined. "Erin, what happened?" she says, her gaze flicking to my throat, which feels warm from my own touch.

"I want to go," I say. "I don't want to do this."

"You did well, Erin." Maggie jumps up as I stand. "This was such a good start." Whatever her words are telling me, the truth of them doesn't reach her eyes. I can see how she's trying to put together what I've told her today and what it means for her.

"It doesn't make sense," I say. "All those things—they didn't happen at the same time."

Maggie nods, all the while looking at me carefully. In the end she says, "But what if they did?"

I stare at her quizzically.

"If you've been having flashbacks and remembering fragments, then they could be part of a bigger picture. Coco disappearing was a trigger, or possibly earlier, when Will gave you the necklace. But what you've done today is start to put it all together. Like I say, you've done really well, Erin."

"You're suggesting this didn't start when Coco went missing?" I say. "That whatever I'm remembering, it might have happened before that day?"

"Yes. Probably. So next time we'll pick up where we left off," she adds with a smile.

I stare at Maggie blankly. She's figured we'll just carry on like I don't have to go home tonight and face my husband. Like it doesn't matter that I have to live with the consequences of whatever comes out of this, while she acts like it's all wonderful progress we're making.

I can't switch off. Now my mind won't allow me to stop wondering when it was that I might have lost this memory. Is it something I've consciously forgotten for years? Did Will once hurt me so badly, and yet I can't recall it? Did I marry him and stay with him regardless?

And how can Maggie not realise that these thoughts will haunt me now, and that there's no way I can do anything but hold my husband at arm's length until I find the truth? Or does she just not care?

"And Erin. Please still don't say anything to Will," she reminds me. "It's better this remains between you and me for now, until we know more. We need to work through your memories, and then you can speak to him when we know what happened."

"I don't know if I can do that," I say.

"You have to." She blocks her doorway as I walk towards it. "Erin, you have to understand how important this is. All Will is going to do is tell you what he wants you to hear. He could try and manipulate what's hidden in here." She taps herself on the side of her head.

When I don't answer, she says, "Promise me, Erin. Promise you won't say anything."

"Okay." I hold up my hands. "But you're asking a lot of me."

"I know. And I'm grateful," she says as she eventually steps to one side, satisfied I'm going to keep my mouth shut.

My husband is the man I've always trusted more than anyone, and yet right now I'm putting my trust in a woman I met only four months ago. And I know that Maggie isn't doing this for me. She's doing this for herself. And I don't know if remembering is a good idea.

NOW—AUGUST

CATHERINE ROWE HASN'T been down to the flower group at church for weeks. She doesn't actually give a toss about arranging flowers for the Sunday service. She was cajoled into joining by her neighbour, who was constantly telling her she needed to get out more and see people other than the ones on her television. "Otherwise you're going to end up an old woman on your own with nothing to do but stare out of your window," she said to her.

What was that supposed to mean, anyway? Firstly, she is an old woman, or rather she feels it. She isn't really old, she's seventy-two next birthday, although her neighbour is seventy-nine, and to be fair, Catherine does recognise she's living the life of a woman in her eighties at the very least.

She is fit and healthy, as far as she knows. She just doesn't have any inclination to socialise. But her neighbour dragged her down to her church one Friday afternoon and shoved a bunch of peonies in her hand and told her to arrange them, saying that when she had finished they would have tea and cake with a bunch of other woman the same age who were there to be as helpful as she was.

That was three years ago, and she didn't stop going until right after her daughter called her out of the blue. Catherine made an excuse not to go the next day and hasn't been back since.

Her neighbour was right about the other thing, though. Without flower arranging, Catherine really has nothing else. She's on her own, and right now she's sitting in her armchair in the bay window and looking out at the front, watching a mother with her two little girls walking down the pavement.

They take her back to thirty-plus years ago, which is a frightening thought and one she will never be able to get her head around. How could it be that long since her own two daughters used to skip along the pavement next to her?

Catherine's eyes fill with tears. She would like to wave at the family outside her house, but she knows she'd look odd. Once they're out of sight, she draws herself away and picks up her crossword from the table beside her, on which are three silver frames. In each of them is a photo. A single headshot.

In the first is her dear, late husband, Arthur, who would have something to say if he were able to. "I don't want you wasting your life anymore, Catherine."

They spoke about it when he was still alive and before his heart gave out for good. How she was to get on and live, do something for herself. Arthur always told her Lily wouldn't want her mother grieving. But it was all right for him. He went and selfishly died of his heart attack and left her alone. He didn't have to face life.

In the second frame is her gorgeous Lily. Her youngest. Her brightest star, if that's not too awful for a mother of two daughters to say. If Lily were here now, she would absolutely agree with her father and say, "Mum, please can you go and be happy and bake cakes again like you used to, and sing at the top of your voice when you're in the shower and meet people with grandchildren who you can buy presents for at Christmas?"

If Lily were still here, Catherine might very likely have grandchildren of her own. She always expected she would one day, when her girls were little; Catherine was thankful that having two daughters meant a future of grandchildren who would hopefully be around every week for their Sunday lunch. She painted herself a picture that never materialised. A picture of hope. The day Lily died, she stopped hoping.

In her third frame is a photo of Maggie, taken the day she turned sixteen, all smiles and a train track of late braces. Maggie was of course the reason she didn't do the flower arranging at church that Friday. The call from her daughter was a surprise. It left her remembering and wallowing in the past again. Not just thinking about Kieran Blake and what he said, how she saw the man in court and deep down in her bones felt she might *not* be looking in the face of a killer, but also wondering about all the other things that could have been so different. How has she gone from a family of four to no one but herself?

Catherine wasn't allowed to grieve for Lily properly, as she had another daughter whose guilt overrode everything else. And then when Arthur died, he left her to carry on worrying about Maggie—that she might be next in line for a heart attack if she wasn't careful. Not that Maggie ever let her close again after the day she and Arthur got back from the Algarve.

It was supposed to be a week's long-awaited holiday for just her and Arthur in their friends' time-share. Lily was only just fourteen, Maggie not even twenty. They should never have gone. Maggie was supposed to be looking after her younger sister; it was the only reason they eventually said yes.

Then they got the call. Catherine had been sipping her coffee at the breakfast buffet, and someone came in from reception and said she and Arthur had an urgent phone call. They both followed her through. Catherine's thoughts leapt to a fire in the house; Arthur later admitted he thought the girls had thrown a party that had got out of control. One thing was certain: neither expected to be told that their youngest daughter had been found dead.

Every time it seems to be a phone call that shakes her life, and little does Catherine realise she's about to get another one.

* * *

Back in the Algarve, they packed up immediately and left via Faro Airport that afternoon, flying back to Gatwick and racing home. Maggie was beside herself. Catherine remembers seeing her in that moment as if it were yesterday. She has replayed it so many times in the years since. She took one look at her daughter's face and knew there was something Maggie wasn't telling her.

"What is it?" she asked her. "What do you need to tell me?"

"Nothing," Maggie said. "It's . . . nothing."

"Was it an accident?" There, the words were out now. She wasn't accusing her daughter. As such. She just needed to know.

"What?"

"I just want you to tell me the truth."

"You asked me if it was an accident! You mean you think I'm responsible?" Maggie cried.

They never did finish that conversation.

* * *

Right now her phone starts ringing, and she picks it up to hear her son-in-law, Richard, on the phone. "Catherine, I didn't want to tell you this," he starts, "but I don't have a choice." He pauses. "Have you heard from Maggie?"

"Yes," she tells him.

"Really?" He sounds excited. "When?"

"Eight weeks ago. She called me out the blue."

"Eight weeks?" She hears his voice deflate. "I meant this weekend. In the last day or so?"

"Oh. No, then. Why, what's happened?"

"I can't get hold of her."

"Since when?"

"Last night."

"Oh." Catherine is thinking, *Is that all?* It seems very soon to be worrying, but then what very little she knows of the man her oldest daughter married is that he's a kind soul.

"Only there's a woman—a client of hers—who has been in an accident," he continues to tell her. "A hit-and-run." Richard pauses, and a silence fills the line before he says, "And it happened at Harberry Woods. And the police, well, they need to speak to Maggie about it."

"Harberry Woods?" Catherine repeats as her stomach sinks, images of Lily lying by the lake crashing into her head.

"Only no one knows where Maggie is," he goes on.

Catherine thinks he sounds like he's about to cry, and all she can see is the face of her daughter Maggie again, standing in the doorway as Arthur dragged their suitcases up the path to the house. And she wants to say to Richard, *What has she done?*

But this time she knows better.

23

Four weeks earlier
MAGGIE

W HAT IF KIERAN is telling me the truth? I didn't believe him when I spoke to him. I didn't want to, but as Erin recalls snippets of a memory that involves Lily's necklace, I can't help but ask the question: *Did* they get the right man?

I don't know whether I'm getting anywhere with Erin. Some moments I feel like I am, and like she's slowly building a picture of what she remembers, but at the same time I worry that her resistance will stop her from getting the answers. I don't know how much she wants to know the truth.

So I find myself wondering what else I can do. Who else knows what really happened. And I keep coming back to the fact that the only person who truly holds a key to the night is Kieran.

Could I go back there again? Could I see myself sitting in front of him asking, begging him to tell me if there's anything else, anything that might help? If I do that, then aren't I suggesting I believe him? *Do I believe him?*

I don't know, and yet all these thoughts whip up like a storm inside me until I find myself making a call to Jack Lawson, telling him I want another meeting with Kieran.

He says he'll put in the request, but it might take a couple of weeks to come through. In the end, it takes only one, and the following Friday I find myself back in the one place I never believed I would go again.

I am alone this time. Richard isn't here waiting for me, ready to catch me when I come out. He doesn't even know I'm here. I've kept him in the dark for fear of what he'll tell me: that I should go to the police; that what I'm doing with Erin is not ethical.

It's the idea of Richard not knowing that pains me the most. As I walk into the visitors', room I don't feel the fear I did the first time I saw Kieran. I have looked in his eyes and I know what to expect. I tell myself I'm not frightened, so I don't have to confront whether I am or not.

But Richard? He is another matter entirely. I kissed him goodbye this morning, allowing him to think I was leaving for work. "Have a good day," he told me. He was still in his dressing gown, having just got out the shower, his hair smelling of my coconut shampoo and his face cold from where it was still damp. I pressed myself into him, not wanting to let him go. I'd never been anywhere Richard didn't know about, but if I told him, I would have to explain myself. I haven't even told him about Erin and Will, or Lily's necklace.

I hate lying to my husband, keeping things from him, I dread losing him. That's what scares me most. Only it isn't enough to stop me. Not when it comes to Lily.

Deep down I know what I'm doing is wrong, but I can't stop. Erin is my client, and I'm not delving into her memories for *her*; I'm doing it for *me*. And I still haven't told Erin the whole truth either.

*   *   *

In the visitors' room, Kieran is waiting for me. He raises his eyes and gives a short nod as I sit down.

"Was there anything else that you didn't tell the police?" I ask him outright.

"What do you mean?"

"About that night, when you saw Lily coming out of Tony's home. What else was going on?"

Kieran cocks his head.

"I want you to tell me everything. Go through it all again, every moment."

"I saw her turn up at his house," he tells me. I picture the mobile home that belonged to Tony's dad that sat at the edge of the Harberry estate, on the other side of the woods to where we lived just outside the main town of Harberry. Lily would have run through the woods in the middle of the night, angry and upset. I know this already because I pieced together what happened in the aftermath of her death from talking to Lily's friend Cassie.

She told me how she'd seen Lily climbing out her bedroom window and onto the flat roof. She was watching from the window of her own house, which was opposite ours. The story the prosecution put together during Kieran's trial verified what Cassie said. But I want to hear the details again, just to see if there's anything I've missed. By now I'm certain Erin knows more than she realises, and if there's anything I can use, I'll do it.

"She was upset. She was banging on their door, calling Tony's name," Kieran tells me. "But eventually it was his dad who answered. He must have told her Tony wasn't in, and she started crying harder. It wasn't a place for a girl her age to be that time of night. It wasn't a place for her to be anytime."

"Did you see anyone else around?"

"There were always people coming and going from that place. There were two or three men there that night, playing poker or whatever they were doing, and another lad who was a friend of Tony's hanging about. I told the police all this, though. Nothing came of it."

"Who were they? The men who were there? Tony's friend?"

"I didn't know them by name. But like I say, I pointed the police in their direction, only they weren't looking for anyone else. They had me." Kieran shrugs, and I lean back in my seat.

Is he telling the truth? Was someone else there that night who followed Lily home, or is Kieran Blake lying to me? It's four weeks today until his parole, and it scares me that the truth may not make any difference to the outcome. But one way or another, I have to get to it.

CHAPTER

24

ERIN

W ILL COMES HOME late the evening after my last session
with Maggie. He's had parents' evening, and it's eight
o'clock by the time he walks in the door.

Sadie has been asleep for an hour, and I'm holding a large
glass of wine, my back to the sink, watching my husband saun-
ter in and drop his briefcase on the floor in the hallway.

"Glad that's all over for another term," he says. "Ooh, glass
of wine. Perfect. I'll join you."

If he expects me to get him a glass, I don't move. I watch
him from a distance, my husband whom I loved beyond words,
asking myself if it's possible that this man has ever hurt me.

He goes about the kitchen, fetching his own glass, chatting to me as he has been lately, as if we're moving ahead and
forging a path forward in our marriage again. He has no idea
what I'm remembering. I want to scream at him, *What have
you done to me, Will?*

He comes towards me as he goes to the fridge, and I automatically step away. I'm frightened of my own husband. I don't
know what he's done, and maybe it's this that scares me most.

He doesn't seem to notice, and so I carry on watching him,
but the more I do, the less I can see. Does he know anything

about Lily Rowe? Has he stopped me from finding the truth out before? Or is none of that true—is he still the same man I married, who adores me and our daughter and will always keep us safe?

"Are you okay?" he says as he opens the fridge and finds the near-empty bottle, which he surveys with interest.

"Yes, fine," I say. Maggie was right. She has her own interests at heart, but I can't risk my husband muddying my memory. We're making progress; she told me as much earlier. All I have to do right now is pretend everything's okay.

"What is it?" Will says. I realise I'm staring at him, and so I blink and look away as he takes hold of my elbow.

By reflex, I pull away from him, recoiling from his touch. "Don't," I utter. I don't want him near me.

He drops his hand sharply. The look of worry leaving his face is palpable. It's rapidly replaced by a flash of fury, and I can feel my heart pounding as he stares at me. "What is it now?" he says, his jaw jutting forward tensely.

"Just—I don't want—" I stop abruptly, unsure what to say. *I don't want you touching me.*

"Erin." A sigh. "When is this going to end?" He says it through gritted teeth as he turns and walks away from me, then stops in the doorway, one hand resting on its frame, his back still to me. "I thought it was getting better. I thought we were getting back on track." When he finally looks back at me, his expression is now plastered with something else. Anger? Sadness? I'm not sure which. "You've been treating me like shit for the last four months, and you haven't given me one good reason why."

Will leaves the room, and still I don't move. I'm relieved he's gone, but I know we can't go on like this. My heart is beating so fast it aches. I don't want to have to face Will. It would be better if he weren't here. That way I could figure out what I do and don't remember so that I can move on.

I need to confront the truth, whatever it is. Once I know what I'm dealing with, I can find a way forward. Just Sadie and me, if that's how it has to be. At the end of the day, all that's important to me now is my daughter.

Everything else is lost. My best friend, Zoe, who chose to side with my husband. Will, who I once fell in love with and allowed myself to trust with every piece of my heart. They have both torn me apart and broken me down, but I will not let them keep me here. I will do whatever it takes for me and Sadie to be safe.

* * *

It all means that by the time I see Maggie again, I'm not so reticent. By the following week, the only thing on my mind is that I will not lose my daughter too. If this is what it takes to keep Sadie and me safe, then I'll do whatever Maggie tells me.

"Are you ready, Erin?" Maggie asks me when we're seated in our normal places, and when I nod, she says, "Then close your eyes. I want you to go back to the moment you found the necklace," she says. "Tell me what you see."

"I'm in the passenger seat," I start. "I'm looking out the window." I furrow my brow as I try to gauge what's going on. There is no Sadie tugging on my skirt, no bags of shopping. "And it's dark outside. Pitch-black. I can hardly see anything." I screw my eyes up tighter at the memory.

"Are you driving anywhere? Where are you going?"

"The car's stationary, but it's not in our driveway." I shake my head. I don't know where we are. "I want to get something from my bag," I go on. "It's by my feet." Now the memory is flooding back. "I look down and see the necklace." My pulse is beginning to race again, and I fight the urge to open my eyes and make it all stop.

"What do you do?" Maggie is asking.

"I reach for it," I say, feeling my hands gripping for something now. I can feel the weight of it as my fingers graze it, and then the way it's yanked away from me, and a swipe to my face.

I'm gasping for air as I open my eyes. Maggie is startled, and I reach out my hand to touch my cheekbone, expecting to feel the soreness. It seems so real.

"He hit me," I tell her this time, because I'm certain of it now. "He hit me when I went to pick up the necklace," I say. "He didn't want me to see it, but—"

"But what?" she says.

"I don't know." I shake my head. "I think we got in an argument, and he hurt me." When I saw the necklace, I recognised it; I'd seen it before somewhere. I know that for sure now. And in that moment, I knew that finding it meant something awful.

"It's okay," Maggie is saying, plucking a tissue out of a box and handing it to me. Only now do I realise tears are trickling down my face, my hand still pressed against my cheek, absorbing the dampness. I pull it away and take the tissue. No, I think. It's anything but okay.

*   *   *

That night I can't bring myself to be near Will. In the last week we have diverted so radically off course that we barely speak.

I am scared of my husband. Terrified of what he might have done and what he could be capable of, and yet still I know nothing for sure.

Will eyes me suspiciously, his mind clearly also somewhere else entirely. And then, after he has told me he's saying good-night to Sadie, he comes downstairs half an hour later, dropping a bag by his feet.

"We can't go on like this," he tells me.

I look up at him but don't speak.

"Neither of us is happy. This isn't a healthy way to live. I'm giving you some time to think."

I pull in a breath and try to keep my composure. It's for the best that Will leaves—of course it is. At the same time, my mind wanders to Sadie and how she's going to wake tomorrow morning and wonder where her daddy is. I'm going to have to tell her a version of the truth without breaking her world apart, and with this thought, tears prick at the backs of my eyes.

"You've got nothing to say?" he persists.

"Where are you going?"

Will laughs, shaking his head, as if he's incredulous I'm not begging him to stay. "Mum and Dad's."

"Okay."

"Okay? That's really it? Jesus, you're unbelievable, Erin. You're not even going to stop me?"

This is what he wants me to do. He's trying to shock me into a reaction I cannot give.

I feel sick at the thought of Will leaving us, but I feel sick at the idea of him being here too. All I want to do is cry and scream, because everything is folding in on me and I can't do anything to stop it coming apart.

"Fine," he snaps. "So this is how it will be. I'll come home in the evenings to see my daughter, because I care that she doesn't realise whatever the hell is going on with her mother is affecting her life. Then when she's in bed, I'll go. And it's up to you, Erin, to put a stop to this madness, because that's what it is. It's bloody madness. *You* are mad."

"I'm not mad," I tell him quietly. I am not. Though I feel myself slowly getting there.

"You know what you're throwing away right now, don't you?" he says. "Only *you* can stop it."

I don't answer him. *I don't know anything, Will, I think. That's what I'm trying to figure out. I don't know who you are. I don't know what you're capable of. All I know is that right now, it is probably better you go. Leave me and Sadie here so I can keep her safe.*

I don't say any of this as he picks up his bag and walks out the door, and I drop my glass into the sink behind me, listening to the shatter of it as it breaks into pieces. Then I double over and sink onto the floor as if I've been punched in the gut.

The idea that I have to keep my daughter safe from her father taunts me. Because what if Will did have something to do with that young girl's death? What if he's been hiding it from me for all these years? What if he once hurt me so badly I chose not to remember it? I don't know how Sadie and I would ever move on from that.

NOW—AUGUST

Lynsey Clayton picks up the call from one of the officers at Harberry Woods. "Yes?" she says. "What have you got?"

"We've got Erin Harding's car," he tells her. "Parked quite a distance from where she was found. I'll send the location through to you."

"Hold on." Lynsey puts her phone on voice mail and opens her messages, waiting for the alert to ping through. When it comes, she opens up the map and enlarges it. She swears her eyesight is getting worse. Don't they say when you hit your early forties, it starts to deteriorate?

"The other side of the woods?" she says. "What's it doing there?" She stretches the map open further still. "How would she have got to where she was found?"

"Chances are she either got taken there by car or she walked through the woods," the officer adds.

"They're the only possibilities?" she asks, studying the shape and size of the area.

"I think so. It's highly unlikely she'd have walked round them. It's quite a way."

"So she drives to Harberry itself. Leaves her car at the edge of a residential area, right?"

"Correct. Wilton Close, to be precise."

"Not far from where she used to live," Lynsey muses. "And then what? Potentially walks through the woods to get to the other side? What the hell for?"

"We're doing house-to-house to see who might have seen her arriving," he tells her. He can't, of course, tell her why Erin did whatever she did.

"No other sighting?" she says. "Nothing on Maggie Day's Land Rover?"

"Not yet. And it's not been picked up by any cameras."

"Hmm." Lynsey has since learnt a bit about Maggie Day. Or Maggie Rowe, as she used to be. Family came from just outside Harberry; sister Lily was killed in the woods twenty-three years ago. Lynsey doesn't recall the case—she moved to Dorset when she was in her midtwenties—but it's one more link between the two women.

And yet, while they still haven't got anything concrete placing Maggie near the woods last night, Lynsey has no doubt in her mind that Maggie must have been there at some point. Otherwise, it all comes back to too many coincidences again.

"How long would it have taken Erin?" she asks. "To get from one side to the other?"

"Without stopping, and going the most direct route, I'd say about half an hour," he says.

Lynsey tries to fathom what Erin was doing there—looking for someone? Running from them? Whatever the case, it looks like she went to Harberry first, potentially to meet someone or see where she used to live. If she met someone, did she then cross through the woods to get away from them? Or did she go through them to meet someone on the Harberry estate? Lynsey hates that she's still left with far more questions than answers.

25

Three weeks earlier
MAGGIE

RICHARD KNOWS HOW I loved Lily with all my heart. When
we met, the grief was still eating me up. It wasn't hard to
see how much her death had stolen my twenties from me.

In our early days I told him the story of the night it happened, but it was the bones of what took place in the house
that evening. I told him how the police showed up at the door
the following morning, the words they used to tell me my sister was dead when I thought she was still sleeping upstairs in
her bed.

But he wasn't there to hear the accusations and the gossip.
When Richard and I met, Lily had been dead eleven years and
I hadn't seen my mum for three, the last time being when we
buried my dad.

"It sounds to me like you're a good person with a big heart
who's just had very bad things happen to them," he said at
the end of our first date, the night after we'd met in the coffee shop. We were sitting on the beach, the discomfort of the
pebbles under me not even registering as we looked out to the
sea, which was black except for the slither of moonlight that
sliced across it. I smiled sadly, letting him believe that because

I wanted to believe it too. I *was* a good person. I just hadn't always done the right thing.

It was months later when Richard asked me the one thing I had been anticipating he would since we met. It said so much about him that it took him that long to dig into my past.

"Maggie, they questioned you about your sister. They thought you did it?"

My heart sank into the pit of my stomach when he said the words. I stopped peeling carrots over the big farmhouse sink Richard had lovingly installed in the house he used to live in, dropping the one I was holding. He came up behind me, took hold of me, and turned me around to look at him. I waited for him to question me too, ask why they had, and also why I had never thought to mention it to him before.

But instead he just wrapped me in his arms and pulled me in tight and whispered into my hair, "How could they have thought that?" It was a rhetorical question, and so I never answered him.

I never told anyone, including my first counsellor, or Elise, how it felt to have my mother return from the Algarve and stand in the doorway to our living room while I was curled up on the sofa. Her eyes were already lifeless. As soon as I looked into them, I could see she had lost everything. I would never be enough for her anymore.

"Was it an accident?" She said the words so quietly that at first I didn't hear them properly. I certainly didn't think I could have understood their meaning, but it was the way she was looking at me that made me realise I did know what she meant.

"What?" I replied, pushing myself to sit up.

"Was it an accident?"

"You think I'm responsible?"

There was a small glimmer of a shake of her head, but not enough. "I just need the truth," my mum told me.

I got up and walked out of the room.

Detectives were in and out of our house, asking us questions, while my mother pondered whether I was responsible for

Lily's death. She had no idea how I would carry that weight forevermore.

* · *   *

Lily had always been the studious daughter. She was the one set for great things. I didn't mind that my parents thought so, but I didn't so much like the way they would often say it. I knew they believed in Lily more than they did me, that they thought she showed more promise than I did, with her straight-A grades compared to my B minuses.

None of us was paying close enough attention to notice those As were slipping, or that Lily was doing as good a job at hiding it as she did at hiding everything else. Later I argued it wasn't my place to, though it never stopped me drowning in guilt anyway.

After leaving home, I begun clubbing at night with my new boyfriend, Joey, and became too wrapped up in my own life and my own problems to notice what I might once have done. My parents didn't notice either. Lily had fallen into a new crowd.

I wonder what she thought when our parents were offered a week's holiday in their friend's time-share in the Algarve. If she was secretly overjoyed at the prospect of her big sister, with her mind elsewhere, being in charge of her.

Mum fretted about going. I saw the way she eyed me as I made my promises. I assured her there was nothing to worry about, that nothing would go wrong. Lily would be fine. "What's going to happen?" I said. "She goes to school every day, comes home. It's nothing I can't deal with."

Four days into our parents' holiday, Lily died on Thursday night.

At nine thirty that evening, she'd stormed off to her bedroom, furious with me for telling her she couldn't see her friend, Cassie, so late on a school night. "Why does Cassie want you to go over now?" I'd said.

"She wants help with homework."

"She should have thought of that earlier. No. I'm sorry, Lily, you're not going." I might have opened the living room curtains a crack and peered down the road to Cassie's house. It wasn't far, and maybe I was being tight, but Lily's reaction was over-the-top angry, which was what made me adamant that I wouldn't back down.

We ended up having a huge fight, and she stormed upstairs and didn't come out of her room again. I heard her stomping to the bathroom, back across the landing. How lucky Mum was that her youngest's only demands to go out at night were to help her best friend with homework, I'd thought at the time.

At eleven PM I had a call from my friend, Amira, telling me that Joey was in a club called Fifth Avenue with another girl. "You should come and confront him," she told me, fuelled with alcohol and angst on my behalf.

My cheeks had burned with fury and my heart with betrayal. "I can't," I told her. "I'm looking after Lily."

"She's fourteen! And you can be here in fifteen minutes. You'll be back home within the hour."

I hung up the phone, unable to get the thought of Joey and someone else out of my head. Amira was right; I had to see him. I had to speak him. I hoped he'd be able to persuade me my friend was mistaken.

By eleven fifteen, I was picking up my car keys. I didn't do what I knew my mum did every night and check on Lily before she went to bed. She'd always done it with both of us, just to make sure everything was okay. I didn't even tell Lily where I was going as I left the house, driving into town to Fifth and then begging the doorman—who knew me well enough by then—to let me in for half an hour without paying.

I didn't get back until one AM, distraught, Joey having been unable to convince me of anything other than my own stupidity for staying with him as long as I had. I fell asleep, splayed on my bed in my clothes, and woke up with mascara smeared down my face to the sound of the doorbell ringing.

I opened the door to a policeman, whose face was grave as he asked if he could come in, and when I'd let him inside, he told me a body had been found at the edge of the lake in the woods. A body they believed to be my sister. A sister who had escaped through her window at 10:40 PM, before I had even gone to the club, and run through the woods in the middle of the night, angry and upset with me.

Before the night she was killed, she'd never climbed out of her bedroom window at night. Of this my mother made sure, I knew, because like I say, she checked on her daughters every night.

*   *   *

I look at my husband over the dinner table now, and I know without doubt that if I ever lost Richard, my life really would not be worth living.

I have no choice but to continue to dig into Erin's repressed memories, even when she's likely done this to protect herself. As her therapist, I know I shouldn't be seeing her on her own, and I certainly shouldn't be using her in this way. But I need to know the truth. And Erin is the key to it.

I find myself wondering if Richard would understand. If he could see that this is a need so raw, it has driven me to throw aside my ethics. I think he would implore me to stop, because my integrity is what he loves about me. He'd remind me how important my work is to me.

But it's not as important as Lily.

I live for my dead sister still, though I've done a good job of existing without her memory haunting me so much for the last twelve years. But she's back, and I owe it to her to get to the truth.

After dinner I message Erin again and ask her when we can next meet. Then I change the passcode on my phone, just in case.

The thing is, there's something I've been keeping from her too. I know how memory repression works. And while the memories Erin is experiencing are most likely from a traumatic event that happened in her past, it's unlikely it happened recently—during this last year, or even the one before, or probably anytime during her marriage to Will. We're most likely to repress memories when we're young. Which means that whatever happened to Erin, it probably happened when she was a child.

Only I haven't told Erin this, because what if she walks away? I can't afford to lose her, and in doing so lose my only hope of discovering what really happened to my sister.

As far as we ever knew, Kieran Blake was the last person to see Lily that night. For twenty-three years he's been locked away for murdering my sister, but what if he *didn't* do it?

His parole hearing is July thirty-first, only three weeks away. His words continue to fill my head. "I didn't kill your sister, Maggie."

Did they get the wrong man?

I don't know the answer. All I know is that with Erin, we could be digging up a memory from her teenage years. Anytime after she was eleven, the year my sister was killed. And her family, Will's family, Kieran Blake . . . every one of them was living in Harberry.

NOW—AUGUST

Pauline Harding wonders whether there's much point in her still hanging about the hospital. If she went home, she could pick Sadie up on her way through, and they could make cakes together this afternoon. She remembers when Will and Jenna were young and they used to help her bake cupcakes. Jenna was never as fussed as her brother, but then she's always been a little more distant. She never needed Pauline like Will did.

It'll be fun to do it again with Sadie. Pauline misses those times when the kids were small and they wanted to do everything with her. She misses feeling needed. Clive shows her no interest and hasn't done in years. Up until recently her children had their own lives and partners and families to think about. It's nice having her house full of people and chatter again.

Besides, there isn't anything more she can do here. At home she can keep an eye on Sadie, where she knows she's safe. It's not that she doesn't trust Jenna to take care of her, but Pauline needs to prioritise her little girl.

As soon as the opportunity strikes, she grabs her son and pulls him to one side. "I'm in the way," she says. "I don't think there's any need for me here."

He's been distracted, speaking to doctors for updates that don't bring any news. She wants to tell him to come home too; there's nothing he can do while they wait. She wishes he would get some rest.

"Okay," he says. "Fine." He isn't even concentrating on her as he answers.

"I'll see you back there soon?" she says.

Will nods, but he isn't looking at her.

Pauline sighs and shakes her head. "Don't be long, Will. You need rest."

She has a call first thing tomorrow morning with the solicitor she's been speaking to, a very polished man who knows his stuff and assures her they won't have any problems getting custody of Sadie. If she were to tell Will this, he would probably demand she cancel it now, and so she won't say anything. By the time they've woken Erin up, the wheels will already be very much in motion, which is the best thing all round.

She kisses her son on the cheek and turns to walk down the corridor. The thing is, she'd already started the process even before two nights ago, when Erin turned up screaming on their doorstep.

Will had been more reticent before then, but after Friday evening, he agreed with Pauline they couldn't continue this way. Erin needed help. And while she was getting it, Sadie needed to be kept safe.

Pauline can't quite believe all that happened only two nights ago. Erin was in such a state, demanding things from Will that Pauline couldn't even fathom. Wasn't it enough that she'd accused Will of killing their dog months back? A dog, lest everyone forget, that had just turned up again?

Now there she was, accusing him of killing a fourteen-year-old girl twenty-three years ago. Lily Rowe. A name Pauline hadn't heard in a while.

She shudders, walking quickly. Of course she would never have wished this accident on Erin, but right now there's some comfort in knowing her daughter-in-law can't hurt any of them any more than she already has.

CHAPTER

26

Two days earlier
ERIN

It's Friday, the thirty-first of July. I stare at my calendar, flicking up the page to August, looking at the blank spaces that are usually filled with fun summer breaks and activities. It seems impossible another month has passed and soon it will be autumn, then Christmas, and then the year will be over.

Sadie's nursery is about to close for a month. It's her last day today, and I have nothing planned for the two of us to do.

For the first time in over three weeks Will didn't return home yesterday evening to say good-night to Sadie, as he's been doing in a pretence to our daughter that everything is fine. Instead, he asked me to say he had to work late but that he'd pick Sadie up from her nursery tonight and then come by the house to collect her things. He'd be taking her for the weekend.

"No!" I exclaimed. "You aren't taking her anywhere." Panic rose inside me. The idea that my husband—a man who has potentially tried to harm me—would be looking after her was too much to bear.

"I am, Erin," he replied, his voice bored by the exchange. He sounded exhausted. He couldn't be bothered to have this conversation that he knew would go his way. "I want to spend more than two hours an evening with my daughter."

"Where will you take her?"

A sigh, and then, "My parents', of course. She'll love it. You know Mum will make it fun."

I let out a choked laugh. Of course his mum would make it fun. Pauline would revel in having Sadie and Will to herself.

"I'm not doing any of this to make it harder on Sadie. I'm doing everything I can to make it easy for her."

If he were making it easy on her, he wouldn't be putting any of us in this position in the first place, but then what was the alternative? I ask him to come home?

The thing is, since Will has been staying at his mother's and it's just been Sadie and me in the house, I've felt like I can breathe again. Every night, the moment he walks out the door after Sadie's in bed and I lock it behind him, I feel safe.

"You aren't to take her anywhere but your parents' house," I said, adding, "No one else can see her."

"For God's sake, Erin," he muttered. "You do not get to control what I do."

He hung up, leaving me shaking as I dropped my phone, staring at Sadie, who was moulding a clump of Play-Doh at the kitchen table. My precious daughter, oblivious to what was happening to her family.

I wanted to pick her up and run away with her, just the two of us, somewhere Will couldn't find us and where I didn't have to dig up my memories with Maggie. All I wanted was to keep her safe. *That's all I'm doing, Sadie,* I wanted to tell her. *You just have to trust me.*

The thought that I have to trust Will tonight fills me with a different type of anxiety. I can't bear the idea of not having Sadie with me, even though it's her dad who's looking after her. But this is the problem. I no longer know who her dad is.

* * *

This afternoon I see Maggie again. She ushers me into her room and onto the sofa.

"He's left me," I tell her. "And now he's taking Sadie for the weekend." I wipe away tears that pool in my eyes. "My life has fallen apart. I don't know how much more I can take."

In return, Maggie looks at me dolefully.

"I don't know how much use I'll be today," I say. Or how much I actually want to remember. I don't know what the point is when we haven't got any further in the last couple of sessions anyway.

I think she's about to tell me not to worry and that we don't need to do anything I don't want to, but instead she says, "Let's pick up where we left off," and I realise her expression is not one of pity; it's much more urgent.

Does she not feel any responsibility for how broken my world has become? I'm of two minds as to whether to get up and walk out.

"I read on the news that Kieran Blake's parole hearing is today," I say.

"Yes," she says blankly. "It is."

"What do you think will happen?"

She stares back at me. "I don't know."

"I know the name," I admit. "It's so clear." I screw my eyes up, frowning, as I try to think why I recall Kieran's name so much more than I ever have Lily's.

"Did you know him?" she asks me.

"No. I don't think I did."

"Could you have met him?"

"I don't think so." I shrug. "Why?"

Maggie is chewing on the corner of her lip, thinking, though all she eventually says is, "Close your eyes, Erin."

I do as she says, and even though my heart isn't in it, I feel myself back there again, in the car.

"You went to the pick up the necklace," Maggie says to me, "and you felt a hand slap you."

"Yes. He swiped the necklace off me and slapped me away, and then . . ." I try to bring up the memory, but I don't see much more. "I don't know," I say.

"Come on," she says, and then softer, "Try and see it, Erin."

I focus on the moment. I think I might have opened the car door and tried to run, and that he stopped me. And then I feel it again, his hands round my neck.

I open my eyes. "I can't do this. I don't have it in me."

"What is it? What do you remember?"

I reach for my bag and get up to leave. "I'm sorry," I tell her. "I don't remember any more and besides this—it scares me."

"I know it does," she says. "I know it's frightening, but we have to do it. You have to remember, so you can move forward."

"So *you* can move forward, you mean."

Maggie looks awkward as she leans to one side. She doesn't know what to say, because she knows I'm right.

"I didn't want to do this in the first place. It was you who pushed me into it."

"You wanted the truth. That's why you and Will came to me in the first place. And we're getting to it."

"And I'm finding out my husband is violent," I cry. "And that he may have had something to do with your sister's death. And now he's taking my daughter for the weekend, and I can't trust him. So right now, this"—I wave my hand in the air—"is not my priority. I have to go. I need to collect Sadie from the nursery before he gets to her. I can't let him have her."

"Will isn't—" Maggie calls, but she stops abruptly mid-sentence as I open her door and step out into the reception hall of the house.

"Will isn't what?" I spin around to face her.

She's breathing deeply, the rest of her body rigid. "Nothing," she says. "It doesn't matter. Can we meet tomorrow? I think we should go to Harberry Woods," she suggests. "Where my sister—" She doesn't finish.

I stare at her, appalled. Nothing would get me back to the woods; doesn't she know that? I can hear her desperation, but I'm desperate too. I am exhausted. Drained. And right now all I want is my daughter back home.

*   *   *

I don't remember to switch my phone off silent as soon as I get into the car. All the way home I'm thinking about how much time I have, that as long as I walk round to pick Sadie up in half an hour, I'll be there before Will leaves school. I have plenty of time to get to the nursery ahead of him.

It isn't until I reach Lexington Close and pull onto the driveway, stopping the car, that I remember to check my phone, and it pings and pings with message alerts of missed calls from the nursery and Will.

"Oh God," I mutter, feeling sick as I press voice mail, thoughts of what could have happened to Sadie haunting me. Will suddenly looms in my rearview mirror, making me jump. I watch him walking around the car.

A woman's voice talks to me on my voice mail as Will opens my door. "Hi, Mrs. Harding, this is Tanya from Grange Nursery School."

"Where have you been?" he demands.

I ignore him, straining to hear Tanya tell me Sadie has had a fall.

"You had your phone off," he's saying. "Sadie fell over at nursery."

I glance up at him. He already knows this. "What happened? Is she okay?" I push him out the way so I can climb out of the car.

"Yes. Yes, she's all right. She's bruised her arm, but she's okay. Mum picked her up."

I click the message off. "Your mum has her? Why does she have her?"

"Because I couldn't leave work any earlier and no one could get hold of you. Where were you? Why didn't you answer your phone?"

"I'm going to get her," I say.

"No you're not." He laughs unkindly. "She's fine. And she's staying at Mum's anyway tonight, so I'm here to collect her things."

"She isn't coming with you," I say. "I want her back. I don't want you anywhere near her."

"You don't get to make that call," Will says. "She's my daughter too."

"I do when her father is violent," I blurt out.

"What?" Will laughs again, his face tight with anger this time. "What the hell are you on about, Erin? When have you ever known me to be violent? You are out of control." He shakes his head. "You need help. And *actually* I came with good news."

He walks away and heads round to the porch at the side of the house, opening the door to let himself in. I need to change the locks. I don't want him walking in and out whenever he feels like it.

But when Will reappears, he's pulling the dog lead behind him, and attached to the end of it is Coco.

"Oh my God." I sink onto my knees as he lets her come running up to me. "What?" I shake my head. "I don't understand. Where has she been?"

"Someone found her and took her to a vet. My number's still registered with them. They said she'd been tied up to a lamppost outside a shop for a few hours, and eventually the shop owner realised no one was coming back for her . . ."

Will stands there for a moment watching us as Coco leaps excitedly around, her tail wagging as she tries to lick my face. I can feel how skinny she is under her coat and can see she has lost weight.

"I was going to take her to Mum's, but I brought her here. I was being nice, Erin. Because that's what I am. I am actually a nice guy."

But I'm not listening to him; I'm burying my head in my dog's fur, tears escaping onto her, making her damp. "Coco, where have you been, girl?" I say. "I love you so much. I've missed you." The words choke out of me. "I thought I'd never see you again."

When I eventually look up, Will has disappeared into the house, and so I follow him in, carrying Coco with me like a baby in my arms.

"Will?" I call out, when there's no sign of him in the kitchen. I hear him walking about upstairs, and so I go to the bottom and call up again. "What are you doing?"

He appears at the top and starts walking down, carrying Sadie's pink Trunki. "No!" I put Coco down and try to take it from him.

"You can't stop me," Will snaps. "So please don't try."

"This is all very convenient," I say, as I follow him back to the door.

"What is?"

"Coco coming back."

He turns to me, incredulous. "What's that supposed to mean?"

"Your timing's spot on," I say. "I know what you're trying to do, Will. You want to make out I'm mad. This all started when Coco went missing, and now miraculously she's back, and you're trying to take Sadie away from me instead."

"I'm not trying to take her away from you," he says coldly. "But I promise you, Erin, I will not ever let you stop me from seeing my daughter."

* * *

My husband walks out of the house with Sadie's bag and a promise he won't let me stop him. I never wanted to before now. It was always the last thing I'd want for Sadie, not having a father in her life. I should know, having experienced that firsthand.

My dad chose my mother over my half brother, Sam, and me. What he did changed us and made us both into two people who were hardened to what life threw at us.

I saw Sam again but only the once. I bumped into him one day four years ago, in a fishing shop where I was picking up a gift for Dave, on the outskirts of Keyport. He didn't recognise me as he slipped past and out the door, a cap on his head and not looking up at me. I barely recognised him either. He was scrawny, like his muscles had wasted away and left him with nothing but bone and a thin layer of skin to hang over them.

"Sam?" I said, walking back out the door after him. He stopped, looked up, and stared straight through me. Where was the boy I knew? The one who always looked out for me and who had spent at least a year of his teenage life caring for his ailing mother?

"It's me. It's Erin." I laughed, but Sam just turned and walked away.

"Hey, wait up," I called after him, and I went to catch his arm, but he'd moved away too quick. "Sam?" I called again, but he just held up his hand to show me he didn't want to talk. I stood there, watching him walk away, knowing only in that moment how he must have felt so betrayed by our dad and by my mother, and in turn by me too.

I hated my dad for turning his back on us and turning Sam into a shell of the man he could have been. As I think about him now, I see how right Maggie is and how we're all shaped by what happens in our past. Sam's life could have been so different if my father had stood up to my mum.

I've thought a lot about my dad over the years. About how weak he was, how obsessed with making money for my mother through his so-called deals and how he was always striving for a future he never got, which meant he never realised what he already had.

My father could have been a man who loved his children more, if only he'd put us before her.

CHAPTER

27

ERIN

In the end I run out onto the driveway, but I'm too late. Will is already gone. All I can do is drive after him, but then what? Cause a scene at his mother's? Pauline would love that.

As the hours of Friday evening pass, I curl up on the sofa, Coco on my lap, and I sip a glass of wine that tastes like acid in my mouth. I don't want to drink. I can't talk to my best friend. I don't know that I trust my therapist, as she's just using me for her own gain. I literally have no one to turn to.

By nine thirty I've spent six hours sitting, then pacing, making myself two slices of toast because I can't bear the idea of cooking for one. I've called Will, who hasn't answered, and left messages asking how Sadie is. Eventually he texts me back, telling me not to worry about her. He says that after some Calpol, she is totally fine and isn't in pain from her fall.

I have Coco back, but I'm losing my daughter. Is this some sick twist in Will's plan? As the evening starts to blur into night, the idea that he might have had something to do with Lily's death makes me more and more anxious. The thought that Sadie is with him even more so.

I pick up my keys and lock the house behind me, climbing into my car as I drive towards my in-laws' house, a journey of less than ten minutes. So close. Too close.

I don't know what I plan to do when I'm there. Maybe just seeing the house from the outside and knowing my daughter is in there will be enough to calm me.

I turn into their road, a quiet cul-de-sac. Their house is at the end of it. It's a four-bed semi that sits on the right-hand side of the curve along with a neighbouring house that is a mirror image of it, both with their little in-and-out driveways, lined with pots filled with plants.

In Pauline's house, Sadie will be sleeping in the top bedroom on the right. Her curtains are drawn, and the only lights on are in the living room beneath her, but even that window is shuttered out by curtains so that I can't see in.

I pull over and park on the left-hand side of the road so I have a good view of the front and then sit in my car, my hands resting on the steering wheel, not knowing what I'm going to do.

How did it come to this? Me sitting outside Pauline's, a place I know so well, that I've spent countless Christmases in and that I've always been welcomed into. Now I'm a stranger while my husband and daughter are the other side of the walls. I wipe my hand across my eyes, soaking up the wetness that has pooled in them. My heart has never felt so heavy for what I had and what is still so near and yet out of my reach. I want my daughter back. And in this moment I hate Will for taking her; I hate his mother for the fact that she has what is mine. But I feel so powerless.

In the end, I turn my key in the ignition to start the engine and put my foot on the brake and the gear in drive. I'm about to leave when the front door opens and a figure appears, and so I switch the engine off again, automatically dimming my lights to nothing, and peer forward as they leave, the door finally closing.

Rebekah. Swishing a handbag over her shoulder, her ponytail swinging as she walks. The realisation that she has been at

Will's parents' house with my daughter makes me feel sick. My hands tremble as they tap against the steering wheel. I watch her walk to her car, which is parked on the other side just in front of mine. She's oblivious to me sitting here. She climbs in and starts her own engine, then does a three-point turn to get out of the curve of the street, passing me as she leaves.

Rebekah. My husband is setting up a new life, supported by his mother. *This* I will not accept. This I will not walk away from.

I get out of the car without even properly checking that I've locked it. My heart is thumping but my head is straight as I stride across the road and over their driveway to the front door, ring the bell, and wait for them to answer.

It's Will who opens it, with a smile that rapidly drops when he sees it's me and not Rebekah standing on the doorstep.

"I don't believe you," I say. The words come out in a hushed, shaking whisper. "I don't believe you could do this, Will."

"It's not what you think," he hisses back at me, trying to keep his voice low. His gaze darts to the neighbour's house, like his worst fear is that I'm going to make a scene.

"No? Of course. It never is, is it?"

"It isn't," he says. His hand tightly grips the doorframe. "I promise you, Erin."

"I don't believe you, Will," I say. "When did it start?"

"It didn't—it hasn't. Nothing has started."

"Before?" I ask, my voice rising now. "Was it before Coco went missing?"

"No. God, no. Please, Erin, don't do this. I'm telling you, you've got it all wrong."

I laugh, incredulous. To my right, the curtain in the living room window flickers and Pauline's face appears, eyes screwed up as she looks out and finds me on her doorstep. She drops the curtain. She will be here in a second. And then, sure enough, there she is behind her son.

"What are you doing here, Erin?" she says. "This is Will's time with Sadie."

"This has nothing to do with you."

"Oh yes it has. When it involves my son and my grand-daughter, it has everything to do with me."

"Mum, I can handle this." Will turns to her. "Please."

But Pauline isn't going anywhere. Surely he must know that. "All these things you have been suggesting and accusing him of. Do you realise how much you're hurting him?"

"Are you serious?" I say, louder again. Is his father going to appear any minute too? But no, I don't think he will. When it comes to their children and grandchild, it's Pauline who takes control.

"Mum!" he says again. "This is between me and Erin."

"You need to leave us alone, Erin," she's saying to me. "You keep shouting and you'll wake Sadie."

"She's my daughter," I shout. "Don't you dare tell me what to do when it comes to her."

Pauline takes a step forward, almost knocking Will out of the way as she presses herself into the gap beside him. "The moment you started making accusations about my son, you gave me the right to step in."

I laugh at her then, and at Will, who is now simply closing his eyes and shaking his head.

"You have no idea what you're talking about," I say.

"Oh yes I do. Will has told me everything."

"Has he?" I ask. "Has he really? Because that will be inter-esting, if you do know everything. When the police become involved. Because if you know everything, Pauline, then you will have to tell them what you know."

"What *are* you talking about?" she says, and I know that right now I will do anything to wipe that look of indignation off her face.

"Lily Rowe," I shout out. "Does that name mean anything to you?" I glance from her—noticing the look of recognition, which suggests that it does—to Will, who's staring at me blankly. "Do you know what your son did to her? Did he have anything to do with her death?"

Pauline's mouth opens and closes, her eyes wide, her pupils enlarged. Then she takes another step forward, her finger reaching out to me, prodding forward until it's almost touching my chest. "You stop right there." She flashes me a warning. "You stop whatever game it is you're playing, do you hear me? You utter one more word against my son, and I will be calling the police. I will get an injunction against you. I will make sure you don't get to see your daughter again. She isn't safe with you," Pauline is saying. "She needs to be with us."

My heart is hammering as I look back at Will, waiting for him to pull his mother back, but he's still just staring at me, his brows furrowed, and then eventually Pauline turns, splaying her hands against his chest to push him back into the house before slamming the door shut behind me with her foot.

I stand there, stunned, unsure whether to ring their doorbell again. Without Sadie I have nothing. I am nothing. But I can't give up now—my only option is to keep fighting.

NOW—AUGUST

RICHARD DAY SITS up to the kitchen table, his hands curled around a mug of tea that has since turned cold, Rocky sleeping soundly in his bed, which the dog has dragged to Richard's feet. It's like he knows, somehow, that something terrible has happened. Like he wants to know Richard's there for him, but he's also saying, *I'm here for you too, Dad.*

Richard reaches down and touches Rocky's head, his hand gliding over his soft fur. It's been a while now since DC Margate left him, alone with his thoughts of what's happened to Maggie. He has called her mother, her friends, Elise, but no one has heard from her. He has asked Elise what she knows. She told him that he must know she can't discuss clients with him, but that she does know the Hardings stopped therapy after three months.

Richard is torn between admitting that the police believe Maggie's been seeing Erin on her own since then and keeping his wife's secret. He'd never do anything that might harm her, but finding his wife is paramount, and so he lets it slip, lets the suggestion drop into her lap.

Either way, it's clear Elise can't add much, but she promises she'll call the number DC Margate left him. He supposes that the police wouldn't even be considering Maggie a missing person after less than twenty-four hours in normal circumstances, and so he's glad they're already invested in finding her. Maybe that's one positive he can search out.

He still hasn't moved when twenty minutes later the doorbell rings, and he leaps out of his seat to answer it. There's a woman standing on his doorstep, who introduces herself as DI Lynsey Clayton and asks if she can come in.

"What is it?" Richard says. Rocky is by his feet again, wanting to know as much as he does. "Have you found her?" He is filled with a sickening dread.

"No. My officers are still looking. I just want to ask you some questions," she says.

He lets her in and leads her through to the kitchen at the back.

"Can I?" The DI gestures towards a seat, and Richard nods. He's forgetting all his manners, but he supposes it really isn't important as they both sit up to the round table. "Erin Harding was found by Harberry Woods," she says.

"Oh?" Richard says, inhaling a tight breath. Surely that doesn't mean anything, he thinks, but he has a sinking feeling that it possibly does.

"Erin Harding and her husband both grew up there. I believe your wife did too. And that her sister was murdered there twenty-three years ago."

Richard nods. "But how can that have anything to do with this woman?"

"I don't know that," she tells him, frowning. "Not yet. Only I wonder if it does somehow. There's too many links, don't you think?"

Richard stares at her. He cannot fathom what possible link there could be.

"We've accessed your wife's phone records," she goes on, "and she made a number of calls to Erin Harding yesterday. And then, at twenty-two fifty-nine last night, Erin called Maggie. They had a conversation that lasted four minutes. I'm working on the assumption Maggie might have been the last person who spoke to her."

"Oh God." Richard hangs his head in his hands, all sorts of thoughts tumbling through his head. He wasn't able to accept that Maggie had done something as out of character as continue to see Erin, especially without telling him or Elise why, or that she must have changed the passcode on her phone lately, but then it becomes a whole other story if it has to do with Lily. He knows, deep down, that there are no rules when it concerns her sister.

Since Margate left, he's been questioning his wife, trying to work out what's been going on. She's been distracted lately, he has seen that, but he's put it all down to her seeing Kieran Blake and waiting for the news of his parole.

"She knows something," he says. "This Erin, she must know something about Lily."

"What do you think she might know?" Lynsey asks him, though there's no point when he doesn't have a clue.

"She'd have gone," he continues. "She'd have gone to the woods too. Oh God," he says. "That has to be it, doesn't it? They know what happened, and whoever it was has—" He stops. Has what? Has tried to kill Erin? And done what to his wife? His hands tremble on top of the kitchen table as fear floods through his body. Rocky's nose nuzzles into his leg, and the dog whines as if he feels it too. "Please," he begs the woman sitting opposite him. "You have to find my wife."

28

MAGGIE

I T's THE DAY of Kieran Blake's parole hearing. Earlier, it felt like everything was aligning, with Erin coming back for another session. But I'd hoped we'd get further than we did. I considered that by the end of the day I might know at least something more, and yet it's five PM, and not only has Erin walked out on me, but I've still not heard any news from Jack Lawson.

I pick up my phone and bag and lock up the room behind me. It's a hot day, a nice evening to take Rocky for a long walk on the beach. With Richard away until Sunday night, I planned to pick up a pizza and bottle of red wine on my way home, but I don't care for either any longer. My mind is too full, dragging me down, my stomach twisted in knots with apprehension for the call and about what happened at the end of my session with Erin. Plans for a leisurely weekend and fresh air with my dog no longer give me the joy they did earlier.

I didn't want Erin to leave thinking what she did about her husband. I'd wanted to put her straight. I even started to tell her. "Will isn't—" I said, but I never finished. *Will isn't going to hurt you. He isn't violent like you're thinking he is.*

I should have said it, because I'm almost certain I'm right—that it isn't Will's actions she's remembering but something from a long time ago. Which means that all Erin is doing is transferring her flashbacks onto her husband, convincing herself they are to do with him.

So yes, I should have told her this today. I should have told her before it got to the point where Will walked out on their marriage and took her daughter to stay the weekend at her in-laws. I should have, but I didn't.

Because what if I lose her? As soon as I tell Erin I don't believe Will hurt her and that it wasn't Will's car she found Lily's necklace in, I'm certain she won't want to see me. Without the threat of it being her husband who's responsible, she'll want to leave the past where it is. And if I tell her what I think, she'll blame me for letting her think it was Will. So I can't take that risk. I can't let Erin go when she holds all the answers.

Instead, I asked her if we could meet tomorrow. I thought we could go back to Harberry Woods, because places, smells, and sounds can trigger more memories. I know this is asking a lot of her, when she hasn't been back in eighteen years, but I believe this is the solution. So I have to find a way to get her there and make her understand it could be the way to finish this.

I get into the car and drive home, and I'm pulling onto my short driveway when I finally get the call I've been waiting for from DI Lawson. My heart hammers as I answer, vibrating through my body. "Yes?" I say. "What happened?"

"He didn't get parole," Jack tells me. "He's not getting out, Maggie." A pause. "It's the good news you wanted."

"Oh God," I say breathlessly, sinking down into my seat. "Oh my God."

"I know. You can relax. It's what you wanted."

No, I think. It's not good news. It's not what I wanted. Only the detective doesn't know this. Nor Richard, nor Elise.

Because in my heart, I no longer believe Kieran Blake killed my sister. I think that all the things Erin is remembering happened when she was a child: a dog was missing; she saw the car with its smashed-in taillight; she got in it; she found Lily's necklace in the footwell.

Only Erin barely knows the name Kieran. And the person she describes wasn't a stranger to her; she got into their car happily. Which means it has to be someone she knew.

29

One day earlier
ERIN

I DON'T REALLY KNOW for sure how I've ended up back in Harberry Woods on a Saturday night, when it's the one place I've always said I would never return to. And yet here I am, standing on the edge of it.

It wasn't one moment that changed my mind, but most likely a culmination of them throughout the day.

Maggie put the idea into my head this morning when she called to suggest it, telling me it could be the very thing to help me remember. I told her no and slammed down the phone.

Later this afternoon, I found myself pacing the hallway, Coco weaving in and out between my legs, and I remembered it wasn't so long ago I considered that if Coco did reappear, I would have to admit I was wrong for accusing Will of anything sinister, the way I did last night.

Earlier in the evening, I found myself curled up on Sadie's bed, hugging one of the teddies that Will hadn't packed for her, and I knew I had to do something to change the way our lives were unravelling. That it was in my hands.

Then, just an hour ago, I stood at my living room window, and it smacked me how I had nothing without my family, and that in the last six months I had either lost or was losing all the people who meant anything to me.

So what if I had blocked a memory to protect myself? What use was being frightened of the truth if my life was falling apart regardless?

All I have left to do is fight, and so fight I will.

I got into my car at the time I'm usually checking on my daughter to make sure she's sound asleep, and I drove to the place I grew up. Back to the woods, which hold my unhappiest of memories.

*　　*　　*

I pull into Wilton Close, which leads onto the northwest entrance to the woods and is just around the corner from where I used to live.

Daylight has long gone and the air is deathly still, and so I hesitate at the path at the end of the close, because now I am an adult, I appreciate danger much more than I ever did back then.

I used to run through the trees with Zoe, filled with excitement at the idea of seeing Will. Deeper beneath the surface, I harboured other emotions I tried to ignore. Like the loneliness I felt whenever I was at home, and the hatred towards my mother that burned in the pit of my stomach.

This hits me again now as I walk towards the dense woods. How I was once so angry, and how at times I wished I had never been born or that *she* no longer lived.

But instead of trying to brush the feelings away, I hold on to them tonight, until they become so vivid they make my skin tingle, a numbness spreading to the tips of my toes and fingers as if I'm a child again. And I carry on walking, weaving through the trees, until I come to the clearing that houses the old electricity building, with its DANGER KEEP OUT signs and the colourful graffiti that adorns its walls.

Ahead, to the north, is a dirt track, little used other than for no good. Once it might have been a work access point, but later it became a place for couples to make out or drug deals to take place. You can't drive any farther into the woods, so the road no longer serves a purpose.

I'm not sure why I take this route instead of towards the lakes, where Will and his mates used to hang out and where Zoe and I would hide and watch them. But that was years later, when I was in my mid to late teens. By then the clearing and the dirt track were an alternative path back home to me sometimes, a route I might take if I was in no hurry.

Now I'm here in the woods, I'm unsure what to do. My head is full of thoughts of my past, but there are many to sift through and I'm too aware of the present. Eventually I do what Maggie has always told me to do and close my eyes, allowing myself to go back there. Back to the car and the necklace, the moment in time I keep reliving.

*   *   *

"The dog's disappeared. Will you help me look for him?"

"Where's it gone?" I say.

I wasn't worried. Not like I thought I had been. Maybe because this time it isn't Coco.

A shrug. "Will you help me look or not?"

"Okay."

The ground is muddy, and there's the scent of fresh rain in the air. Twigs crack underfoot, and the leaves are brown. It's autumn. I have a pocket full of conkers that I feel my fingers pressing against. I've always loved their smoothness.

The zipper is halfway down my coat. I tug at it, trying to pull it up, because I'm cold now, but it's stuck. It's my blue Puffa that swallows me up. Dad always laughs at it and says, "What are you wearing that big thing for? You look like the Michelin Man!"

I must have been about eleven, because I stopped wearing the coat that winter when my mother never mended the zipper and the sleeves got too short for me.

"Come on. The car's here. We'll go looking in that."

"Okay."

I open my eyes now and find myself stepping forward. I hadn't seen the car by then, because it wasn't in sight at the end of the dirt track. Now I look around, willing it to come back into focus, though my sharp breaths and the beat of my heart tell me what I already know. I don't need to see it; I don't need to close my eyes again to visualise the rusty red Ford Fiesta Dad had bought three years earlier.

"What do you want this piece of rubbish for?" my mum had said to him when he drove it home the first time. She never did like that car.

"It's not a piece of rubbish," he'd said. "It reminds me of my first car. I'm going to do it up."

He *did* do it up, but still Mum didn't like it.

My fingers tingle, and I flex them to get the blood moving. Part of me wants to turn around and go home and stop myself from remembering the rest, but I already know I won't do that. I don't even think I could stop the memories, even if I wanted to, any longer. And I already know that when Dad's Fiesta comes into sight, I will notice the paint is scratched off at the back and the taillight is smashed in.

"We'll look for the dog up and down the lanes. Jump in." He swings the dog lead in his hand, back and forth like a metronome, but I'm not too worried, because our old dog is always running off.

I climb in the passenger seat and shut the door, then pull at the seat belt that's always getting stuck. I give up in the end, letting it ping back.

"What's that?" I ask.

"What's what?"

"That. On the floor." I can see something shiny and gold, a chain coiled around like a snake. I lean forward for a closer look, tapping it with my foot to dislodge it. "It's a necklace," I say. "Whose is that?"

"Don't! Don't touch it."

I laugh at how angry he suddenly sounds. If there's one thing he never is, it's angry—or at least he wasn't before. Not when I was younger. He's been more so in the last few months, I realise.

I can see how pretty the necklace is. It's gold, with a pock-marked leaf, and it looks fragile enough that it might break if I pick it up.

I bend closer, but as I do so, I realise I recognise it. I've seen it. A picture of it in the paper. I feel the blood drain right out of my body. "It's—" I reach down and grab hold of it.

"Give it to me."

I don't let go. "It's the girl's," I say. It belongs to the dead girl. The police have been looking for it. It's been four months since the girl was killed. A man from the other side of the woods has been arrested. "Why do you have it?" I can hear the thumping of my heart.

"I said give it to me."

My fingers curl tighter around it, and I pull it back. I've become quite adept at not doing what I'm told, but right now I'm more frightened than I've ever been.

He grabs my wrist and leans over me, giving a swipe to my face as I try to move my hand away. His breath smells of stale beer. Lately this has been happening a lot more too.

I'm so scared, scared enough that I try to get away. Not because I think he'll hurt me—he's never laid a finger on me before—but because of his desperation. Because I know it's all so wrong. Because I suddenly realise he might have done something very bad and that I might not know him after all.

I pull at the door handle and try to open it, but he grabs me tighter, still trying to reach for the necklace, which is curled up in my hand. For some reason, I don't want to let go of it.

I sob as his hands grip tighter and his face becomes more con-torted. He lunges for me, taking his hands off my wrist and as quick as a flash gripping both of them around my neck.

"Let go," he screams in my face, his eyes wild and scared, his fingers digging deep enough that I can't breathe. I drop the neck-lace, but he doesn't notice right away as the pressure of his hands intensifies, making me choke.

Eventually he lets go of me, his eyes staring into me, sitting back when he realises I don't have hold of the necklace anymore.

"I didn't mean to hurt you—" He looks even more frightened now.

I open the door of the car and fling it open.

"I would never hurt you. I'm sorry. What happened to the girl—it was an accident. You can't tell anyone. You mustn't tell your mum—"

*   *   *

I'm gasping for air as I open my eyes, my legs giving way beneath me as I fall to the ground.

It was him. He did it. He killed Lily Rowe. And he must have thought I was keeping my promise as I scrambled away from the car that night and through the woods. Not towards home, I don't think, for I'm sure I wouldn't have gone there, although I don't recall what I did next.

But I didn't tell anyone. I unwittingly kept his secret for all these years, even from myself.

"Oh God, no," I cry, because how could I have forgotten?

*   *   *

A chill runs through me from head to toe, pricking my skin as it ripples down. I pull my mobile out of my pocket and punch in Maggie's number.

The memory of that night twenty-three years ago is now as clear as day, as if it happened yesterday, and yet I had hidden it so deep that I stopped myself from ever reaching it. She told me I'd buried memories to protect myself. She was right about that, but what she wasn't right about was that it had anything to do with Will.

"It wasn't my husband," I cry. "I thought it was Will. Did you know there was a chance it might not have been?"

There's a beat before she answers. Just a fraction too long. Then, "Where are you, Erin?" she says instead. Her voice is level, but I can hear something in it. Only small, but it's there. Like she's shuffling forward on her sofa, excited that I've remembered something, while my world is falling apart.

"You already knew," I say in disbelief. "You already knew my husband was innocent. Didn't you?"

"I—" She stumbles over her words. "I didn't know anything for sure."

"But you let me carry on thinking it could be him. Even when I told you he'd left me and that he was having Sadie for the weekend. Even when I told you I feared he might hurt one of us." My own words come out slowly, surely, gaining momentum with the knowledge that she has kept this from me all along. "You never once told me there was a possibility it wasn't Will I was remembering."

Maggie doesn't answer me.

"Why not?" I say. "Because you were afraid I might not help you? Is that what it was? Is that what you thought of me?"

"No, I didn't think that," she says, but I know she's lying. "I was scared. I just wanted the truth, Erin," she begs. "You must understand that. You've remembered it, haven't you? Are you there? Are you in Harberry?"

I don't answer her. Instead I hang up the phone. Yes, I know the truth, and yes, I also believe Maggie has every right to know what it is, but not right now. Not until I'm ready.

*   *   *

I don't know how much time passes before I dial another number. This one I have learnt by heart, and yet I never wanted to put it into my phone again. It rings three times before it's picked up.

"Hello?"

The moment I hear my dad's voice, I feel a sharp intake of breath.

"It's me," I say. "It's Erin."

"Erin?" He muffles the phone. "Are you okay?" I hear him walking, maybe moving away from my mother, maybe towards her.

"I know what happened," I say. "All those years ago."

"Erin—" He's stopped.

"What did you think I'd done, put it to one side? Made the decision I wouldn't say anything because it was family? You think that was important to me? It wasn't. I had forgotten it all." I laugh. "Can you believe that? It can happen, apparently. Children can bury memoires of traumatic experiences, and I mean, it's certainly pretty traumatic, isn't it?" I spit. "The murder of a teenage girl."

"Erin," he says. "Please. Slow down."

"Tell me what happened," I cry. "What happened to her."

"It wasn't murder." His voice is so low that I know for sure he's making certain my mother doesn't hear him. "It was an accident. I promise you. You have to believe that."

"No." I shake my head. "No." It's only in this moment I realise I'd hoped Dad would deny it and that I didn't remember it right.

He keeps talking, but his words fade in and out of my consciousness. "Where are you?" he asks me.

"Harberry."

"Stay there," he says, but I'm only half listening to his words now. In the distance I can see a figure running towards me, calling out my name. ". . . need to talk . . ."

It's Maggie. She's come here.

"I have to go," I say into the phone.

"Go there," Dad is telling me.

"What? Where?" I say, because I haven't heard what he's been telling her.

"To the Harberry estate," he says, before I quickly hang up.

"What are you doing here?" I say to Maggie. I'm furious with her for showing up, for following me here and for not giving me the time to get all the answers from my father.

But now she's yelling at me, her hands on my arms, shaking me, her eyes manic and wide as she pleads with me. "Was that them? Who you were speaking to? Was that who killed my sister?"

"This isn't just about you," I scream back at her, shaking her off. "This is my family too."

"Your family?" She stops short.

Yes. Because first, before Maggie or anyone else found out the truth, I wanted to know everything about the night Lily died. I needed to work through the memory I'd buried all these years and make up my own mind as to whether it was the accident my dad tells me it was.

I wanted to know what was going through his head and the decisions he made thereafter. I needed to understand how he's lived with the lies all these years.

I wanted to know that everything I've believed in up until now hasn't been a lie. That it was one night, a horrific mistake. I had to hear all this before I decided what to do next.

Only Maggie won't let me have the time.

"Leave me alone, Maggie. For tonight; just give me that. You owe me that for making me think this was Will's fault." I shake her hands off me as I turn to walk away from her.

"Owe you?" she's calling behind me. "I don't owe you anything."

I spin around, as determined myself as her face shows me she is. Maggie Day has had it her way up until now. She has controlled me, but I will not let her do that tonight. Not until I have the truth.

"Yes. You do," I shout, and I start running, deeper into the woods, towards the lake where Lily was found, dipping in and out of the trees as quickly as I can until I'm certain she's no longer behind me.

I slow down and catch my breath. I could hear how desperate Maggie was, but I need to know first. I have to hear the whole story.

I realise I have run so far I'm not even sure where I am. It's been too many years since I've been here. I might have gone in a straight line, or I could have gone full circle.

I pat my pockets, searching for my phone, only to find it's not in there. My mind races back to where I was when I last remember having it. I must have dropped it near the clearing instead of sliding it into my pocket when she grabbed me.

Now I'm truly lost in the middle of Harberry Woods, and there's not a thing I can do but keep walking until I make my way out.

I don't know how long I've been going when I spot a light ahead of me. I aim for it, and only when I'm near do I realise I'm walking out of the other side of the woods, near to the Harberry estate, the place where we were always told not to go but where my dad told me to be tonight.

*   *   *

I don't think I can see him. I don't know that I want to, I realise as I step out onto the road. It was one thing to talk on the phone, another altogether to look into his eyes and hear him tell me that he killed a girl. And so I find myself walking away from the estate, along the unlit road that in places isn't wide enough for two cars to pass. And when I see the car headlights coming towards me, too fast for the narrow roads, and I see the face behind the steering wheel, I already know it's too late.

NOW

DEREK ASHBY HAS been keeping post in ITU since DI Clayton positioned him here. He's done exactly what has been asked of him and kept track of everyone coming and going to see Erin. His list is relatively short:

Will Harding (husband)
Zoe Sawyer (friend)
Pauline Harding (mother-in-law)
Corinne Pashley (mother)
Mick Pashley (father)
Rebekah Hasler (?)

He doesn't know what to call her, and she's the only one of note he would question, and yet the DI wasn't particularly interested in her.

"She's not a threat," Clayton told him.

So who is a threat? he wonders. Not any of the visitors he's seen, he doesn't think, but he admires Clayton, looks up to her, and so he's done what she's said and kept his eyes peeled as he stands guard. He knows well enough that if this was a targeted attack, they can't be too cautious. If the DI is worried that someone might come back to "finish the job," as she put it, then there's a good chance she could be right.

The visitors have gone now, though. The husband, who was the last to leave, went home an hour ago to get a bit of rest. He's coming back when they're ready to wake Erin Harding out of her coma.

Derek rubs his lower back where it's aching after yesterday's fall at football. His girlfriend has just sent through another text message, telling him they have to talk and that if he doesn't call her anytime soon, she's taking her stuff out of his flat and spending the night at her mum's.

Derek looks into the room where Erin Harding is. He doesn't want his girlfriend to go anywhere tonight; he knows he's screwed up. With Clayton not around to check in on him, he could slip out for a bit and make a call. He could do with some fresh air and a sit-down.

He texts her back. *Give me five minutes.* And then, for the first time today, Derek leaves his post outside Erin's room.

* * *

Mick Pashley left home an hour and a half ago. He doesn't want to go back tonight. He can't bear to look at Corinne any longer, padding around in that faded purple dressing gown and oversized rabbit slippers, firing questions at him. A woman he once thought he loved. If he did, he fell out of love with her many moons ago now. Before Erin stopped talking to them. Well before then. He knows he should have left Corinne a long time ago, but life got in the way.

He is weak, as Erin once told him he was. Too weak to stand up to his wife, that's for sure. If he had, he might never have lost his children. He hasn't been the father he should have been to either of them. Not the kind he'd always imagined he would be when he first had them.

He knows he has no one to blame but himself, but he can't help thinking that if other things hadn't come into play, it could have been very different. Like meeting Corinne. If he hadn't been drowning his sorrows in a pint in the bar on his own because his first marriage had failed, he wouldn't have given over his life to the bar woman. It started off as a wild infatuation that slowly burned into resentment.

Mick Pashley has made many mistakes. Some very bad choices. Corinne tells him often enough he's a selfish man and that she should have known no good was ever going to come of him.

At 4:40 PM he finds himself back at the hospital, not having paid for a car park ticket this time. He wanders in through the main doors and towards ITU. When he gets there, he sees the police officer is no longer lingering outside Erin's door, and for a moment he wonders if she's still here.

But no, there she is. His daughter. Still lying there.

Mick glances around him and steps into the room and keeps walking forward until he's at his daughter's bedside. "I'm sorry, Erin," he whispers as a single tear rolls down his cheeks. "It was never meant to come to this."

*　*　*

DI Lynsey Clayton is leaving the Days' house at 4:43 PM on Sunday when she gets a call to tell her that Erin Harding's mobile phone had been found, lying on a dirt track at the northern edge of the woods near to an old electricity unit.

"Who's looking at it?" she asks.

They tell her they're onto it.

"How long till you can give me something?"

"Give us ten minutes."

"Call me as soon as you have anything. I want call logs, text messages, emails everything." She hangs up the phone with a buzz of adrenaline. They're getting somewhere at last, she thinks as she turns on her engine and pulls away down the street of bungalows. She's hopeful Erin's messages and phone records give her something, because right now they have nothing. And Maggie Day is still missing, and she can't help but agree with the husband, who is clearly beside himself, that it doesn't look good.

It's only eight minutes later that her phone pings with a message. Lynsey veers over to the side of a road so she can look at the email that has just come through. Bingo. Erin's text messages.

She scrolls through them, working her way backwards. Surprisingly, there are none at all on Saturday, but before that there are messages between Erin and her husband, brief and to the point. No kisses. There's nothing in any of them that raises any questions as far as she can see as she scans through them, eventually closing down her phone just as another email comes through with Erin's call log.

Lynsey goes straight to yesterday and traces her finger down the list:

10:05 Outgoing call to Will
13:16 Incoming call from Maggie Day
14:45 Missed call from Maggie Day
22:59 Outgoing call to Maggie Day

The last three are calls she already knows about from Maggie's phone.

But then she stops. Maggie wasn't the last person Erin spoke to last night. Because at 23:15 she made one more call to a mobile number clearly not listed in her contacts.

Lynsey dials the number, but it rings out and onto an automated answer service. She calls the colleague who sent her the information. "Can you find out who this last number's registered to and get back to me ASAP," she says, reeling off the digits.

The call comes back five minutes later. "We've managed to get an ID on the mobile number," they tell her. "Belongs to a Michael Pashley."

"Michael Pashley?" she repeats, putting the call on loudspeaker so she can pull up the list of Erin's visitors she's made and double-check what she already knows. "Mick Pashley. Erin's father." She drums her fingers on the steering wheel.

The father who, as far as she's been told, Erin Harding has had no contact with since she was eighteen. So why call him, out of the blue, last night?

She restarts the engine and makes a call on loudspeaker to Will Harding. "We've found your wife's phone," she tells him. "Do you have any idea why Erin might have called her father last night?"

"Called her dad?" He sounds shocked.

"At twenty-three fifteen, she made a call to him, and they spoke for three minutes."

"I don't . . . I don't have a clue."

Lynsey sighs, taking the second exit at the roundabout, back in the direction of the hospital.

"This has to mean something," Will says. "Doesn't it?"

"I'm not sure what it means right now."

"I know, but—" Will stops.

"What is it?" she demands. There's something he's holding back from her.

"It's just—" He starts cautiously, unsure if he wants to tell her or not. "Friday night Erin was talking about Lily Rowe and who killed her."

"What do you mean exactly?" Lynsey asks.

"I don't know, but she was just getting herself in a state about it. I thought maybe she'd spoken to Maggie or something. I wasn't sure."

"Did she say anything about her father?" Lynsey asks.

"No. Nothing."

"And you didn't think to mention this to me before?"

A pause. "No. I'm sorry. I just didn't think."

She rolls her eyes. There's clearly some other reason he didn't want to. "And is there anything else you didn't think about that's now come back to you?" she asks.

"No."

"Fine. But Will, please tell me if there is," she says. "You do realise this could be important." She clicks off her phone as the hospital comes into sight ahead of her.

The car park has thinned out now. It's easy enough to get a space not far from the double doors. She gets out and locks her car with her beeper. She's started walking towards the main doors when she catches sight of a familiar figure pacing across the pedestrian crossing in the other direction.

"Mick Pashley!" she calls out, but he either doesn't hear her or is doing a good job of ignoring her as he scurries across the car park and disappears behind a Luton van. She goes to follow him, stopping quickly as a car spins round the corner and fails to stop at the crossing. By the time she's crossed back over it, she's lost sight of him.

She makes another call, this time to Derek, the officer she's had stationed in ITU. "Mick Pashley, did he say anything to you?" she asks. "How long was he just there?"

"Mick Pashley?" he repeats as she hears him fumbling around, most likely for some notes, which he really shouldn't need when the man's only just been in. Eventually he answers. "The dad? He was here earlier, he didn't stay long, came in at eight AM and was gone by eight fifteen."

"No, Derek. Just now. The man must have just been back. I've seen him in the car park. He's just come out the hospital doors."

"Oh, I—"

"Derek? Where the hell are you?" she asks as the sound of what appears to be a car horn blares down the line. "Are you outside?"

"Erm, I . . . I just popped out. I had to make a call. My girlfriend—"

"Derek! You're supposed to be watching our victim," she yells. Her heart starts to thump, and she scans the car park, eventually spotting what she believes to be Mick Pashley reappearing at the far side of it.

"Yes. Sorry. I'm going back now," he puffs. "I'm sorry, but no one had been here since the husband left half an hour ago."

"Christ," she mutters as she runs across the car park, calling out. "Mick Pashley!"

The man turns and looks around himself as the car next to him flashes its lights to signal it's been unlocked. "Wait!" she shouts, and then back into the phone, "Call me as soon as you're there, Derek, and hope to God for your sake that she's okay."

*   *   *

"Mick Pashley?" Lynsey says as she approaches him. He's still standing by his car, watching her approach, his expression blank. "Can I have a word? DI Lynsey Clayton," she reminds him. "We spoke earlier."

"Oh. Yes. Of course."

"Is there a reason you came back to see your daughter just now?" she asks. She really is out of breath, just from that short run.

"I—" He shakes his head. "She's my daughter. Can't I visit her?"

"She called you last night. Just before midnight," Lynsey goes on, hand still clutched to her phone, willing Derek to call her with news of Erin. She really hopes Mick Pashley hasn't done anything stupid. There's little chance with the nurses in and out, but sadly, she's seen it happen once before. It only takes a minute.

Mick's face has dropped, the air billowing out of his body as he looks up at the sky.

"Mick? Can you tell me why she called you after sixteen years? Isn't that what your wife told me earlier? That you haven't spoken to your daughter since she was eighteen?"

Mick nods. "We hadn't. Not until last night."

"Why did she call you?" Lynsey persists.

He shakes his head, closing his eyes.

"Mick, do you know where Maggie Day might be right now?"

"Who?" he asks.

"Maggie Day. We believe she was with Erin last night in Harberry Woods. Do you know where she is?"

"I don't know any Maggie Day."

"She's the sister of Lily Rowe," Lynsey says. "Do you know that name?"

"Oh God," he replies, and his face goes so pale that she think he's about to pass out.

"Where were you at one AM this morning, Mick?"

"I was at home. With my wife."

"Are you sure about that?" she asks.

"Are you arresting me?" he says, as her phone starts ringing. Derek's name flashes on her screen. "Do I need a solicitor?"

30

MAGGIE

I START TO FOLLOW Mick Pashley as he steps outside the hospital and towards the car park. I go to yell out his name, but just as I open my mouth to stop him, someone else calls him from the left. I look over and see the detective woman who was hanging around the hospital all morning, so I turn away quickly, my heart racing at the possibility she might have seen me as I veer off to my right, weaving between the cars until I notice Erin's father has stopped.

Here I dip behind a camper van and pretend I'm looking for my keys as I watch her running over to him. I'm not close enough to hear their conversation, but I daren't move. I can't risk her seeing me and questioning why I'm at the hospital when I have no idea if by now they're looking for me or not.

My chest feels tight as I watch them. What is she saying to him? Is she arresting him for what he did to my sister? It takes everything I have not to run over there and pound my fists against him, this man who murdered Lily. Not to demand of him why he took my sister's young life all those years ago.

* * *

Last night I had the call from Erin telling me she knew it wasn't Will. She was in Harberry Woods, the memory had come back to her, and yet instead of telling me what she knew, she was angry with me for letting her believe it could have been her husband.

All I could think was, how dare she keep this from me a moment longer? For twenty-three years, I'd just needed to know what had happened to Lily before she died, and here was a woman who had come into my life five months ago, needing my help to save her spiralling marriage, and she had the answers. It was inconceivable that her anger could outweigh my grief, and yet she was playing that card. And so I didn't need to think twice before grabbing my keys and driving to the woods to find her.

My starting point was where she used to live, and as I drove around the neighbourhood, it wasn't long before I spotted her car on Wilton Close and knew she must have gone into the woods, as I'd earlier suggested to her. I didn't expect to find her so easily, but she was standing in the clearing that led from the path at the end of the close.

It wasn't until I'd called her name and she spun around to see me that I realised she was on the phone. Her expression told me everything. I knew in that moment that whoever Erin was speaking to was the person who'd killed my sister. "Was that them?" I cried. "Who were you speaking to? Was that who killed my sister?"

"This isn't just about you," she yelled back at me. "This is my family too."

I reeled back, sure I couldn't have heard her right. *Her family?* Was she kidding me? As if her family, who killed my sister, deserved any time or importance. It was too impossible to believe she could think that, and yet there she was, telling me to leave her alone for tonight, as if she thought for one moment I could walk away and tell her, *Oh yeah, sure, Erin, you just take all the time you need.*

"You owe me that, for making me think this was Will's fault," she said.

I was so stunned that it took me a moment to realise she had taken off and was running through the woods to get away from me. A moment too long, because by the time I started after her, I'd already lost her within the black canopy of the trees.

Rage coursed through me, burning my body with an anger deeper than any I'd felt in years. *No, Erin Harding, I will not let you do this to me.*

I raced back to my car and started the engine, blinded by fury. If she kept running, I knew exactly where she would come out on the other side. Right by the Harberry estate. And so I drove around the woods until I saw her, walking towards me on the unlit road.

*   *   *

Now I see the detective hold up a hand to Mick Pashley as she takes a call and turns back to stare at the hospital. Even from here I can see he's as white as a sheet.

I haven't been home since I ran out the house last night, though time is running out, because Richard is due to land any moment. If I'm not back soon, he'll worry where I am. I drove over that way this morning because I needed to check on Rocky, but Hattie stopped me on her way back from yoga at the end of our road. I rolled down my window, and she peered in. "Everything okay?" she said. "You had someone asking after you this morning at seven AM. Looked a bit serious."

They must have wanted to speak to me about Erin, and so I asked her to do me a favour and feed Rocky. I'd given her a spare key a while ago. Then I drove back to the hospital where I waited. I needed to know if Erin was going to be okay. I needed to know I hadn't killed her. I needed to know she wasn't going to die without me knowing the truth, but I also needed to know if she saw me driving towards her.

*   *   *

I had just wanted to talk to her last night. I wanted her to tell me what she'd remembered. I had wanted to hurt her too. I was so engulfed with rage, I wanted to pull up alongside her and grab and shake her and make her tell me. I wouldn't let her get away from me this time.

It was all over in a flash. One moment Erin was holding her hand up to her face, blinded by the full beam of my lights. The next—

I swerved towards her and I meant to brake, and I must have slammed my foot on the accelerator. It all happened so quickly. I tried to turn away, but it was too late.

I hit her. It was an accident, but regardless, I had done something horrendous. I got out of the car, and Erin was just lying there, and I panicked. Because how could I say it was an accident when I'd been following her around the woods like someone who'd lost the plot?

There was enough sanity left in my head to know I needed to call an ambulance, but I didn't have my phone on me, and so I drove off, towards the Harberry estate, looking for a pay phone. When I couldn't immediately find one, I U-turned in the middle of the road and set off, driving back in the direction I'd just come. Past Erin.

But I could see someone was with her. Where they had come from so quickly, I didn't know, and I didn't stop to find out. I just kept on driving, the sound of distant sirens beginning to blare.

*　*　*

There have been many what-ifs.

What if Erin dies? Then I am no better than the person who killed my sister. I didn't mean to kill her, but what does that matter if she ends up dead? I know better than anyone it doesn't.

What if she dies and I never know the truth?

What if she doesn't and she saw me coming for her?

There isn't one good outcome. All I've been able to do is stay at the hospital all day, creep into the ITU when there's no one around who will recognise me, and wait.

Eventually, when Will Harding left an hour ago, I realised it was time for me to go home too. I had to face what I'd done. I had to tell Richard all of it. Between us, we could work out what to do next.

Only I was about to go when I saw Erin's father coming back onto the ward, just as the policeman had left. I waited, unseen, just outside the door, as he went into his daughter's room and leant over her bed and told her he was sorry and that he'd never meant it to come to this.

A nurse appeared, and he asked her if his daughter was going to be okay, and she placed a hand on his arm as they both looked at Erin. She told him they'd know more very soon when they woke Erin up.

And then Mick Pashley turned, a tear rolling down his cheek as he left the room and walked straight towards me, glancing at my face but not registering who I was, of course, and I knew in that moment that I had to be looking into the eyes of my sister's killer and that I was not going to let him get away with what he'd done for one moment longer.

NOW—AUGUST

Will Harding pushes the sandwich away that his mother has put in front of him. He's had a shower and just wants to get back to the hospital. He doesn't want to lie down for a bit like she tells him to, or have the food she insists will make him feel better. If it weren't for spending half an hour with Sadie, he'd have been back there already. He wishes his mum would just leave him alone.

Will's phone buzzes with an unknown number, and he immediately freezes before grabbing it. "Yes?" He expects it to be news from the hospital, but it's DI Clayton.

"You should know we've arrested Erin's father," she tells him. "He's at the station answering questions."

"Her dad?" He looks up as his mum hovers closer.

"For the murder of Lily Rowe," the inspector tells him. "I believe Erin might have found out last night."

"Oh God." He can't believe it. "So was he the one who hit her?"

"I don't know," the DI admits. "But I'm working on the assumption he might have been."

Will wants to know more, but there's another call coming through, and so he puts the detective on hold to hear a doctor telling him they're happy that Erin is stable enough to be woken. "I'll be right there," he says, and he leaps up and grabs his keys, finishing the call and accidently cutting off the DI at the same time.

The news about Mick has blown his mind, but right now his thoughts are on Erin. He needs to get to the hospital for when they wake her up.

When he's in the car and making the fifteen-minute drive, he tries to stay positive and not think too much about what could go wrong, because some of those possibilities are unbearable. Instead he imagines his first words to his wife and how he'll tell her how much he loves her. Because even after everything that has happened, this is his truth.

Everything has gotten too far out of control in the last six months, but he's starting to understand why now. And hopefully he has a chance to put it back on track. He needs to make some changes too. He pretends to Erin that he doesn't see what his mum is like, but he does. He sees it clearly. He's always defended her when it comes to his wife, to keep the peace, because it's easier to make out Erin is overthinking how involved she is than to confront the alternative. That she's a little controlling of his life still.

He loves his mum, but she hasn't made the last few months any easier. She sought out Maggie Day because she "specialises in people's pasts," as she told him. He recalls how she raised her eyes knowingly, convinced that all the issues in their marriage stemmed from the fact that Erin's parents didn't want her. His mother believes when anything goes wrong, it's because of this, and with the recent news, he supposes she has a point.

But she took it too far when she started out with the idea of him applying for custody of Sadie. He should have told her no outright, but on Friday night his head was all over the place and he wasn't thinking straight. Now he's just angry with her for putting her own wants first and for not thinking of him and Erin. He knows what his mum is like, but he's seen a whole other side to her lately.

Two nights ago, as she spouted off about how crazy Erin was being, all Will could think of was how desperate his wife had sounded. Yes, Erin was accusing him of killing a girl he had never even heard of, but for whatever reason she was convinced of her story.

If the whole thing hadn't been so screwed up, he would have reached out to help her. As it was, he decided it best not to contact her for the rest of the weekend. He asked Zoe to instead, but now he knows she didn't, and he hates that in Erin's darkest hour, none of them were there for her.

Instead, the last time Erin saw him she'd watched Rebekah walk out of his parents' house. The woman whose friendship he had appreciated at first, when he hadn't been aware she was mistaking it for more.

He can't shake the memory of opening the door to Erin on Friday night, thinking Rebekah was back again with another excuse to see him. How had he missed her growing infatuation? He should never have confided in her about his marriage all those months back, but at the time he was grateful to talk to someone so willing to listen, who wasn't as intrinsically linked to Erin as Zoe and Dave were.

But sadly, he now doesn't think his own mother has Erin's interests at heart either, and it's this that breaks him more.

Now at least he can start to piece together what Erin was talking about on Friday night, although he still has a long way to go in understanding how Maggie Day and Lily Rowe and Erin's father all fit together.

He pulls into the hospital car park and races back towards ITU, where the doctors are waiting for him as promised. On the drive, he's tried to quieten his brain from plaguing him with questions that haunt him, but they come back at him with a vengeance now: *Will my wife die? If she lives, will she be the same person she was before?*

31

ERIN

THE DRUGS MAKE everything hazy. People come and go, in and out of my room. In soft voices they tell me it's good to see me, to take it easy and, as one nurse words it, that I've been through the mill a bit.

Pain streams through my body, and there isn't one part of me that doesn't hurt. I feel bruised, like I've been beaten up. I see Will's face staring at me, with a palpable look of relief, like he can't believe what's in front of him.

"Don't try and talk too much," he's saying to me, although he must have plenty of questions. "I love you," he adds. "I love you so much," he says again, before I close my eyes again.

* * *

Later, when I wake, he's still here. He's sitting on a chair by the window. Zoe is standing next to him, leaning against the wall, tapping out a message on her phone. When she looks up, she gasps. "You're awake." She drops her phone on the windowsill and comes to my side. "Oh, Erin." She leans forward, tears filling her eyes and plopping onto my cheek. "I thought—" She stops herself. "Erin, you don't know how good it is to see you."

I smile at her.

She crouches down beside me. "I'm so sorry," she says.

"Don't." I try to shake my head, and she just nods in return, biting her lip. It's not important what happened between us.

Will is next to her too now, smiling at me. "How are you doing?" he asks, which I assume is a rhetorical question. Zoe says she's going to leave us alone for a bit, but she promises me she isn't going far. She hesitates by my bed, wanting to say more, but then she finally leaves.

Will pulls the chair over so he can sit next to me. He doesn't take his eyes off mine. They trawl my face like he's searching for answers, but at the same time he looks like he just wants to take all of me in. "I thought we lost you," he says.

"No," I say. "You didn't."

He takes hold of my hand and squeezes it. "I don't ever want to," he tells me. "I couldn't bear it."

"What happened with us—" I start, but my throat feels sore, and I need to stop.

"I know, I get it," he says. "Well, not all of it, not yet. But I will do."

I look at him quizzically, but Will just frowns and squeezes my hand tighter. "Nothing matters other than you're okay."

I smirk at him jokingly. Plenty of it matters, but maybe he's right. When it all comes down to the bare bones of life, isn't it the mere fact we're alive that matters the most?

"I'm sorry," I say eventually. "What I put you through."

"You don't need to talk about this right now," he reminds me.

Will must want to hear what I have to tell him, but he's right. It's too much to tell him everything; that can come later. So instead we fall into silence, and I watch my husband looking back at me, and there's an expression on his face that makes me think there's something he isn't telling me.

I feel the air leaving my body. Is there something I don't know? Have the doctors kept it from me? Have I lost a leg? Do they think I have some kind of brain damage I haven't realised? Am I imagining all this, and am I actually dead?

"What?" I say urgently. "What is it?"

He pulls back, ever so slightly, but enough for me to know I'm right. And then it dawns on me that it might have nothing to do with me and my body, and that despite his relief I'm awake and alive, Will doesn't love me the same way anymore, because there's someone else. Rebekah.

"Her?" I say.

"What?" He frowns.

"Rebekah."

"Oh. God, no, Erin. No, nothing happened between us. That's honestly one big misunderstanding. I was just talking to her when you saw us at the pub. She listened to me, and I thought she was a friend and I wanted someone to confide in who didn't know you and she was just there. I didn't know how bloody besotted she was with me, and if I had, I'd never have encouraged it. And then at my mum's, she'd come by making out I'd left something at school, and Mum let her in. There's nothing going on," he tells me. "Although before you hear it from someone else, she turned up here today as well."

"Here?"

Will nods. "I got rid of her. I think she got the message."

"Sadie?"

"She's at mum's, and Coco is too. They're both fine, and Sadie doesn't know anything—we didn't tell her."

"Good," I say, a flash of relief. I don't want my daughter worrying.

"I know Mum overstepped the mark." Will looks down, not wanting to meet my eyes. "She means well, but I know how she can be. I do know that," he says.

Then he changes the subject. "I'll take Sadie home tomorrow. She wants to be back in her own bed with her things. I mean, if . . ." He trails off, looking at me apprehensively.

"Yes," I say. I want him there. I don't want to lose my family now, not after everything that's happened.

I watch my husband as he watches me back. Can we move on from this so easily? I search his eyes for what I'm missing, because I'm still sure there's something.

"What aren't you telling me?" I ask.

He glances away, biting his lip.

"Will?" I persist.

"Your dad's been arrested," he says eventually, and I feel my stomach sink. "I didn't want to tell you, but . . ." He drifts off. But I'd have found our sooner or later.

"Arrested?"

"For Lily Rowe's murder," he says. "Maggie's sister, who you were"—he hesitates—"talking to me about on Friday." He doesn't say *accusing*. "Your dad's admitted it. He's told them what he's done, Erin. I'm so sorry. I can't even begin to . . ."

But Will's words fade out of my consciousness. My dad has admitted killing Lily.

There's a tap on the door, and I turn my head to see a woman walking in. "Erin, it's good to see you," she says. She comes over to stand at my bedside. "I'm DI Lynsey Clayton. How are you feeling?"

I shrug. "Been better," I croak.

She smiles wanly. "I don't know how much you're aware of regarding what happened to you."

My mind flashes back to last night, to me in the woods, the conversation I had with my dad on the phone and how Maggie turned up before I'd had the chance to ask him the truth about what had happened all those years ago. How I'd run through the woods in the middle of night, and then how I saw the car coming straight for me.

"You were a victim of a hit-and-run," she tells me, and I nod in return. After a beat she says to me, "Did you see anything, Erin? Do you know what happened?"

"It's blurry," I tell her. "I'm sorry."

She nods and smiles again. "Of course," she says, as a nurse enters the room and bustles past her, telling both her and Will that I really do need to be resting right now. "Well, we can talk again soon, Erin," she says.

When she leaves, Will continues to regard me. "*Did* you see anything?" he asks.

I shake my head.

"Could it have been your dad—" He doesn't finish the sentence, because he doesn't want to say it outright. *Could it have been my dad who hit me with his car?*

"No," I say adamantly. "No, he wouldn't have done that." I turn my head. "I need to sleep," I say, and he leans over and kisses me on the head. I don't want to talk to the detective or Will anymore right now. There are too many things I have to deal with in my own head first.

CHAPTER

32

MAGGIE

I AM SURPRISINGLY CALM as I reach our driveway, although to my surprise, Richard's car is already in it. I left the hospital car park after the detective showed Erin's father to her car, knowing there was nothing else I could do right now but come home before my husband arrived, although it seems he already has.

He appears in the doorway with a mixture of shock and relief on his face, and I immediately wonder what he must already know, because it's not the expression of someone who's just got back from Heathrow to find his wife has popped out. It's the look of someone who's been waiting and worrying.

"I didn't think you'd be back," I say as I climb out the car, like this is the extent of our problems, when in reality there is something so huge looming above us that I can't even envisage what comes next.

"Maggie, where have you been?" Richard's voice cracks in panic as I reach him, and he lets go of the door to pull me into him. His arms shake as they wrap around me, but his head is pulled back as he studies me, searching for an answer he has clearly been waiting for. "I've been worrying all day. I've had the police here, and—" He breaks off. "Where the hell have you been? I thought you might have been kidnapped, or you were dead."

"Dead?" I say, noticing how his eyes are red rimmed and bloodshot and that he must have been crying. "Why would I be—"

"Because of your client who's in hospital, and they think you were with her last night, Mags."

"You weren't supposed to have landed till this afternoon," is all I say. It wasn't supposed to be like this. Richard wasn't due home; he wasn't meant to be worrying about me.

He pulls me into the house and kicks the front door shut behind us. "What's happened? Where have you been?"

I glance at Rocky, who appears at my feet, nuzzling into my legs like a long-lost friend. I don't know where to start when I don't know how much Richard knows. Bending down to stroke Rocky, I say, "I asked Hattie to feed her."

"Hattie?" Richard shakes his head. She can't have come by; she must have seen Richard's car in the drive.

"How long have you been here?" I ask him.

"Maggie, will you just tell me what's been going on? I've been going out of my mind."

"I will. Just—can we sit down? Can I get a cup of tea?"

"Fine." We go through to the kitchen. Richard gestures to the small two-seater by the back door, and while he fills the kettle, I sit down, pulling the throw over me. "So were you with her? In the woods?" he asks.

"Yes."

He stops what he's doing, two mugs in hand, which he lays carefully on the side.

"A few weeks back, Erin mentioned she'd found a necklace in her husband's car, and when she described it, it was Lily's."

"Her husband?"

"It wasn't him," I say. "But at the very start, I thought it could be."

"Why didn't you tell me any of this?" he asks.

"I wanted to," I admit. "But things spiralled. I thought you'd say I should go to the police, but I knew Erin had triggered a memory and that I could help her get it back."

Slowly Richard goes back to making the tea, and then he hands me one of the mugs, dragging a kitchen stool in front of me and perching on it so that he's right in front of me.

"Erin thought her memory was about her husband," I say. "And I let her think it was."

"Why would you do that?"

I turn away to look out onto the garden. "I was scared that if she knew the truth, she wouldn't help me. That's why I didn't say anything to you," I tell him. "I didn't want you telling me it was wrong. But she knew things about my sister," I cry, turning back to him. "What was I supposed to do when I began to realise she might have known who killed Lily?"

He doesn't answer as he continues to stare at me. There must be plenty of thoughts flicking through his head as he tries to take in what I'm telling him. "And does she? Does she know?" he asks me. "Do *you* know?"

"Yes. She does. She called me last night from Harberry Woods. She remembered something, but she wouldn't tell me. That's why I went to find her. And she was there, talking to them on the phone, and when she saw me, she hung up and started shouting at me to leave her alone."

Now, as memories of last night come to the surface, I feel the anger rising through me again. I put the mug of tea down on the table beside me, clenching my hands together into fists in my lap.

Richard puts his mug down too and takes hold of my hands. "What happened, Mags?" There's panic in his eyes.

"I begged her to tell me, but she wouldn't. She ran off through the woods. Just like that"—I click my fingers—"and she was gone."

"She was in a hit-and-run," he tells me slowly. "Did you know that?"

I nod. Just once. Richard must know what's coming, but he doesn't want to ask. He doesn't want to believe I could

possibly be capable of such a thing, and so I don't want to tell
him as much I also want to confide everything in him.

"It felt like it did the day they told me Lily was dead." I
look up at him. "This rage," I say, pulling a hand away and
tapping it against my stomach. "It just *grew*. Because she knew
who killed her and she wouldn't tell me."

I can almost feel the way Richard is holding his breath.
The air is so close around us, even Rocky is sitting bolt upright,
eyes on me.

"I didn't mean to do it," I say in a whisper. "I didn't mean to."

He doesn't move. I will him to ask me what happened
next, but he doesn't. I want him to pry the truth out of me,
because I need to tell him. I have to tell someone this secret
that is so impossibly huge I can't manage it alone, and there's
no one else on earth I would trust with this. But he doesn't ask,
he just waits for me, and this is so much harder.

"I drove round the woods, and she was walking down the
side of the road, and I just . . . I just wanted to talk to her. I
swerved towards her," I say, "and then it all happened so fast.
But I know I didn't mean to hit her."

"Oh no," Richard says. "No, Maggie, you didn't."

"I didn't mean to." I look at my husband's face, the man
I've chosen to trust with the truth. I can feel the dampness as
tears fall down my cheeks.

My heart hammers at the prospect of what might come
next. Could he ever love me the same way again? "Please, you
have to believe me, I never wanted to hurt her like *that*."

"Was it you who called the ambulance? They said whoever
called didn't leave a name."

I shake my head and tell him how I tried to look for a
phone box, but someone else had already found her. "I didn't
have my mobile," I say, as I realise that what he's told me means
the person I saw with her can't have hung around for the ambulance to arrive, which seems like a strange thing to do.

"The police took it," he tells me.

"Why?"

"For evidence. They didn't know where you were, and they already believed you were with her last night. You were missing, Maggie. No one knew what was happening."

"Oh God." I reach out to grasp his arm. "What do I do?"

"I don't know," he says. "I don't know what we do, Mags, but someone might have seen you. Whoever called the ambulance, they must have turned up right after you. How do we know they didn't see your number plate?" He stops. "I don't think we have any choice but to tell the truth."

"I can't—" I beg. "I'll go to prison."

Richard's phone starts to ring, and he grabs it from behind him, looking at the screen. "It's DC Margate," he says. "What am I supposed to tell him?"

"Nothing. Not yet, please."

"I can't let them keep looking for you, Maggie. I can't lie and say I haven't heard from you when you're sitting right in front of me." I can see his anguish is as deep as mine, but I don't know the answer.

"Don't answer it," I say, holding my hand over his and pushing it down. "Just—not yet. Not until we know what we're doing."

He sighs as the call rings out. A moment later his phone beeps with a voice mail alert, and so he puts it on speaker and plays the message.

"Richard, this is DC Margate," a man's voice says. "I just wanted to tell you that we've arrested someone in connection with your wife's sister's murder. Michael Pashley. We have reason to believe . . . but anyway. Can you call me back please as soon as you get this?"

"He must have confessed," I say, as Richard puts the phone down.

"I guess he must have. I'm so sorry, Mags. You're living through this all again, but we have to talk about you right now, and I'm going to need to call Margate back sooner or later. You have to tell them the truth."

"How can I? I hit her with my car, and I didn't stop."

"And that's hopefully all you'd be accused of, not stopping."

"But they'd make out it was intentional. Now her father's been arrested for Lily's murder, they'd say it was revenge."

"So what are you suggesting? That you try and get away with it? That you live the rest of your life in fear that the truth might come out?"

"I don't know. I don't know, Richard, but what if she doesn't wake up? If she doesn't, then there might not be a need to say anything."

He seems to consider this possibility for a moment, and even in this short time, as I consider what he might say, I find myself wondering if I do really want him to agree with me or not.

"And if she does wake up?" he says. "If you haven't said anything, it could look like attempted murder, Maggie," he starts, as his phone begins ringing again. He checks the screen and shows me it's DC Margate. "The truth is the only option."

Richard is right. I can't hide forever. Sooner or later they're going to know I'm home, and they're going to question me about what happened last night. And so I nod to him, and he picks up the phone, and I recognise the irony: that uncovering the truth of what happened to Lily was supposed to free me, but my freedom may be the one thing I end up losing.

"My wife is home," I hear him say to the officer on the end of the line. "Yes, yes, sure," he says. "Oh? That's good. That's great news. Yes. Okay. We'll be here. We'll see you."

He hangs up. "They've woken Erin up. They think she's going to be okay," he says.

I nod, blowing out a breath of relief. "I *am* going to tell the truth," I tell Richard. "I will do, but not tonight."

"What do you mean?"

"I need to speak to Erin first," I tell him. "I just need to do that."

33

ERIN

OVER THE NEXT two days, my progress is slow but certain.
The doctors are happy with how I'm doing. They tell
me it's my sheer determination and attitude that will ensure
I make a full recovery. I believe that too. I refuse to see any
other outcome.

With nothing much to do, it's no surprise how often I've
been thinking about the past. I try not to blame myself for
burying the memories of that night in the woods and instead
admire the eleven-year-old I once was, who went to great
lengths to protect herself all those years. But it's hard to let go
of the part I played in derailing the lives of so many people.
Like Kieran Blake. And Maggie.

I make promises to myself that it's in my hands now to ensure
I make the right decisions going forward. When Zoe comes in, I
tell her that of course I forgive her. Whatever happened between
us, I don't see a future without my best friend in it.

But when a nurse asks me if I'm up to seeing my mum,
I say no. For now. I will confront her, and my dad, but first
there's someone else I need to see.

"How are you doing?" the same nurse asks me, now I'm
out of bed and slowly walking to the door where she's standing.

"I'm doing okay," I tell her. "I'm meeting my brother this morning. I want to go outside, it's so nice."

"Good idea," she says. "Just take it easy."

I smile and tell her I will, then round the corner to see Sam waiting for me. The sight of him makes me stop in my tracks, and I can tell he's taking me in as much as I am him. The years have changed both of us and made us into two very different people from the children we were when we last knew each other. I may be at my frailest, but it's Sam who looks so broken.

"Come on," I say. "Let's go for a walk."

Sam would have turned forty last March, but he looks older. Where he was once broad shouldered, now his skin seems to hang off him like it's too big for him. He hunches forward as he walks. It isn't until we're outside and we find a bench to sit down on that I study his face and notice that beneath his fragility are the same big blue eyes and long lashes I used to love.

It takes my breath away to see the young man still in there somewhere, under the receding hairline and the patch of grey stubble on his chin that he must have missed shaving.

"How are you doing, you know, after the accident?" He nods to my body, and I find myself looking down at my legs, which feel so limp and thin beneath my jogging bottoms.

"I'm going to be okay," I tell him. "The doctors say I was very lucky. I hadn't been on the road long before the ambulance arrived." I pause. "All those years, Sam, and I didn't know where you were. I hated them for what they did to you, making you leave like that. I didn't understand it."

Sam nods and looks out to the horizon. "I guess you do now," he says simply.

*   *   *

On Saturday night I told my dad that I remembered what had happened when I walked through the woods one night, months after Lily Rowe had been murdered, to find Sam standing by the clearing, swinging a dog lead in his hand. That I had willingly gotten into the red Fiesta my dad had passed on to my half brother six months earlier to look for the dog, but instead I'd found the necklace that I recognised from the papers.

Sam's words echoed in my head, how he'd said to me all those years ago, "You can't tell anyone. You mustn't tell your mum." I knew then that Dad must have already known, and so Saturday night I told my father I needed to hear what happened the night Lily was killed. I screamed at Maggie to leave me alone when she turned up, because I could not comprehend that Sam could have hurt anyone. Not my brother, who'd spent a year caring for his sick mother, who I remembered knocking on my bedroom door at night and poking his head round to check on me when my own mother didn't.

I had to hear it from Sam first, before I told Maggie the truth. I needed him to tell me what had happened.

Dad told me to head to the estate, where Sam was back living again. He told me he'd make sure Sam met me there.

"I always thought you knew," Sam says now. "All this time. I always waited for the moment you told someone."

"What happened?" I ask him. "Dad told me it was an accident, but I need to know the whole story."

And so Sam begins to tell me a story that doesn't start that night but a few months earlier, after he had lost his mother and had moved into our house with a father who was working all hours, a stepmother who hated the sight of him and a half sister who adored him but who he no longer had much capacity to love.

"I missed my mum so much," he tells me. "She was everything to me; she'd always looked out for me. After Dad left, it was the two of us for years. But then suddenly she was gone, and I didn't know how to move forward. Dad used to pat me on the back, and say, 'You doing all right, son?' but he didn't hang around for an answer. You were only eleven," he says to me. "You just wanted me to play with you. You weren't old enough to know how tough it was.

"I got in with people who lived on the estate," he goes on. "I was just looking for people who didn't want anything out of me. Drinking myself into oblivion seemed like a good option so I didn't have to think. Dad didn't notice, and Corinne carried on pointing out I was a failure who didn't deserve to be living in her house, so it just got worse. I drank more and hung out at my mate Tony's place. His dad was always chilled about me being there. I felt more welcome than I did in my own home, and there were always people there, always some kind of party going on.

"Then Tony started seeing this girl called Lily. He told us she was sixteen, but I knew she was younger. I didn't dare say anything to Tony, but I didn't like it, because she was too nice for him. She was too good for any of us, but she was besotted with Tony for some reason. The thing was, I quite liked her too, but I couldn't do anything about it. I thought that if she knew the person I was a few months back, she might have gone out with me, but by the time she met me, she wouldn't have looked twice.

"Anyway, one night I'd been drinking on my own, far more than usual, and I went over to Tony's. I saw her on their doorstep in a right state. I hung back as his dad told her he wasn't in. I thought that I'd walk her home and find out what was wrong, but then Kieran Blake came out of his home and started talking to her. And the next minute she's walking back towards the woods with him and his dog.

"I didn't trust Kieran, because he had a string of records against his name and not much of a nice word to say about anyone, so I followed them. I kept my distance, and all the time I was thinking, what the hell was she doing with him? I think I just started getting annoyed with the both of them.

"But then they stopped by the lake, and she told him to leave her alone and that she could walk the rest of the way on her own. I don't know if he was hassling her or what, but he stood there for a bit with his dog and then just turned round and went back the way he'd come.

"So I caught up with her and tried to talk to her, and because she knew I was a friend of Tony's, she stopped to let me. Only I couldn't help myself from saying all the things I wanted to say. I told her Tony was a waster and that he was using her. I said that if she was with me I would treat her better." Sam stops, and I notice the way his pale face flashes red.

"I thought that if I had a girlfriend like her, I could turn my life around," he tells me now with a laugh. "What a joke. Anyway, she told me to get lost, but I'd had so much to drink, and I had it in my head that I needed her to believe me. I wouldn't let it go. And the more she told me to piss off, the more I went on at her, before she finally flipped out at me. She said it was no wonder my mum died, if all she had was me looking after her. She said she was better off being dead.

"I think she knew she'd gone too far, but it was too late. I lost it," he says. "I gave everything I had to Mum, she was everything to me, and I hated Lily so much in that moment. I remember grabbing her." Sam pauses, dipping his head. "I just held on to her," he says, holding out his hands like he was clasping them round her neck. "And I didn't let go, and she was shouting at me, and I just blanked her out because I wanted her not to have ever said what she had." He shakes his head, a lone tear rolling down his cheek. "I blanked her out," he says again in a whisper. "Until it was too late."

Finally Sam looks up at me. "I never meant to kill her."

His words wash over me in cold waves. It's the truth I've wanted to hear, but it sucks every bit of breath out of me to know for sure that he killed Maggie's sister.

"I did come to meet you Saturday," he says. "When Dad called me. I came, but I was too late. I found you on the road, and I called an ambulance."

"But you didn't stay with me?"

He shakes his head. "As soon as I saw them coming, I hid. I worried that when everything came out, they'd think I was the one that had hit you.

"I'm so sorry about everything," he says, hanging his head in his hands as his whole body shakes beside me.

I want to reach out and hold him. After all these years of not seeing him, it breaks me to think how damaged he was back then. To realise that if my parents had shown him more love, this could have been avoided. Instead he had no one to turn to and his life spiralled out of control—causing pain to him and to others.

After all these years, I also understand why my dad made him leave. He did the one thing I could never have expected of him and protected his son. And now he's prepared to do it again.

"I'm sorry too," I say eventually. "I'm sorry for what happened to you, Sam, but I'm more sorry for what you did and that so many people had to suffer because of it." I turn to him. "You and Dad let Kieran Blake go to prison. Lily's family never knew the truth. That's unforgivable."

"I know," he says. "I know that."

"You know you have to tell the truth now, don't you? You can't let Dad take the blame," I say, and Sam nods. Finally I reach over and take hold of his hand. "I really did love you," I tell him.

*   *   *

The following morning I'm waiting for Will to pick me up and take me home when I look up to find Maggie Day in my room. I sit back down on the bed, and she comes in, sitting on the armchair that's been left at the end of it.

In our silence, the room is heavy with all the words that are unsaid. The knowledge that my half brother killed her sister. And the fact that five nights ago she drove her car into me and left me on the side of the road.

Where do we start? Who apologises to whom first? In the end, it's her who says, "Thank you for doing the right thing."

I nod. "Of course. I was always going to."

"I get that now, but at the time—well, I needed to know who killed Lily."

I try to gulp down a ball of air that has lodged in my throat, but it won't budge. "I'm so sorry my family caused you so much pain. If I'd ever known what they'd done—"

"But you didn't know," she says. "None of it was your fault."

"No. But that doesn't make it any easier."

Maggie inhales deeply, her gaze flitting around the room before it rests on me. I know why she's here. She wants to know what I know. "Saturday night, I was so angry," she says. "I was angry with you for not talking to me. I've lived with my sister's death hanging over me for twenty-three years and then you finally had answers and you weren't telling me. So I wasn't thinking straight. I just wanted you to talk," she says.

"I know that."

Maggie opens her mouth to speak, biting the corner of her lip. "What happened to you, on the road—" She gestures in the air. She doesn't want to say it outright in case I don't know. She can't be sure that I saw her behind the steering wheel, or that I recognised her Land Rover as it sped towards me in the dark.

"Yes?"

"I'm so sorry, Erin—" she starts, but I interrupt her.

"Whoever did it didn't stop," I say. "It could have been anyone. I guess we probably won't ever know."

Maggie stares at me, trying to take in what I'm saying and most likely to work out whether she believes that I really don't know.

"Thank you for coming to see me today," I tell her, "but Will is going to be here soon, and I want to be ready to go home." Back to him, Sadie, and Coco. My family. The only thing I need in my life.

I don't need Maggie to suffer any more. I know in my heart what happened Saturday night was an accident. She didn't mean to hurt me.

I nod at her, just once, to try to let her know it's okay for her to go.

No one else knows this truth. I don't want anyone telling me it's too huge a deal for me to let her get away with, because it's my choice and it's the one I feel happiest with. I owe it to Maggie. For what my family did to her. For what they took from her.

And I can live with this, because over the last six months I have lost everything that's important to me, piece by piece, but today I get it all back again, and that's all that matters.

Two months later
MAGGIE

I NEVER DID TALK to anyone about repainting the Cliff House. The paint continues to chip off the front door, battered by the wind and the salty air. I press a hand against the cool brass of my name plate and hold it there for a moment as I turn my key with the other. Richard follows me in, Rocky behind him, and I close the door behind us.

When I let us into my room, I stand in the doorway, allowing Richard to turn on the light and pull the blinds up to let the October sunshine flood in.

I blow out a breath as tears swell in my eyes. I didn't want to cry, and yet I know I won't be able to help it.

"You okay?" he says as he takes his jacket off and folds it onto the arm of the sofa.

"No. Not really." I didn't ever want it to come to this, but I don't see what choice we have. I can't continue paying for my room in the Cliff House when I'm no longer working out of it. I've tried to find a way around the problem, but I don't see one. I even tried to persuade Richard to work here, but we both know it would be wasted money.

I glance around the room, attempting to accept that this is the last time I'll be in here, trying not to think back to the day I moved in, though I can't keep my thoughts from drifting there. How Richard folded the seats down in the Land Rover to transport my armchair, and how I took so much time filling my bookshelves, choosing my favourite photo of Lily so she would always be in here with me. I can take it all home with me, but it isn't the same.

Eventually I wander over to the window and look out. "I think it's the view I'll miss the most," I say. Richard joins me and puts his arm around me. This isn't strictly true. The view is a big part of it, but it's my clients I will miss more.

A week after Erin's accident, I spoke to Elise and told her the truth, to a point. I admitted that I had helped Erin retrieve memories, and that I had gone about it by letting her believe they involved her husband.

"I can't imagine you doing that, Maggie," Elise said.

"I don't believe I ever would have if it hadn't involved Lily," I admitted.

I knew my life has always been one of layers, each one containing the hidden depths beneath. I would tell my clients to confront their issues and say they couldn't move on without dealing with their problems and delving into their pasts to sift through the obstacles. But for me, Lily has always been there. A thick, black layer that I couldn't move through and that I didn't want to touch, because if I did, I might start feeling less guilty or remembering her less, caring less. And so it meant she was always simmering beneath everything. Beneath my work, beneath Richard.

Only now I know I'm capable of going to terrifying lengths when it comes to my sister.

I am a good person who has done a bad thing. I tell myself this every day. But it isn't enough when it comes to my work. I can't possibly carry on counselling others when I don't live by the rules I hand out.

"I don't know what I am without my job," I say now. I always saw it as a turning point for me, a pivotal time in my life when I reached thirty and realised I needed to move forward instead of living as if I were still nineteen.

Now it's the end of that era, and I'm not sure how I'm going to move on from it. I can't even make any positive plans. I might tell myself that in time I can come back to it, but I don't know if that will be the case. All I know is that for now I need to step away and finally deal with the ghost of my sister, as hard as it will be when there is so much hurt.

But one by one, my husband is helping me address all the things that have been destroyed. Like the broken relationship with my mum that I want to rebuild. When I called her to ask if we could visit, she cried down the phone to me. "I would love that, Maggie," she said, and I felt myself cut deep that we had let it go so far. "I have a spare room that I can make up for you, and there are lots of lovely walks we can go on with the dog." I could hear an excitement in her voice that I hadn't expected. "How long will you come for? Because you're welcome as long as you want to stay. You know that, don't you?"

"I do, Mum," I told her, though I hadn't ever considered it.

"And we don't need to talk about anything. Unless you want to," she added.

"Let's see how it goes," I said. I hadn't told her on the call that I had visited Kieran again since he'd been released from prison. I don't know how she'd feel about it, but it was something I needed to do.

After his release Kieran Blake moved into a small studio on the outskirts of Keyport, and I met him at a café in the harbour. He didn't look much different to how he had been when I saw him a few months ago in prison.

"I don't even know what to say," I said as I placed a mug of tea in front of him and sat down opposite. "I can't begin to tell you how sorry I am for what happened to you." My words didn't mean anything; they didn't stretch anywhere near far enough to make up for the years he had lost. Kieran had told me that he'd been trying to make a better life for himself when he was wrongly convicted. Now he has to start again, and it's going to be so much harder.

"What will you do?" I asked him.

"Oh, I don't really have any plans," he said. "Just one day at a time."

My heart ached for the man who had lived his life suffering for a crime he hadn't committed. If *I* could never comprehend the injustice of it, I had no idea how *he* would be able to.

"I'm sorry no one believed you," I told him.

"Maggie, if you hadn't believed me in the end, then I might still be there," he said with a smile that only just reached his eyes.

I nodded. I didn't think this was true, because I would have pushed Erin as far as I could once she told me about Lily's necklace, but I didn't say anything. I didn't think he needed me to. By now Kieran was gathering his coat and telling me he really had to go.

Nothing could make up for the years he'd been wrongly imprisoned, but at least the right man was now paying for what he'd done to my sister. I know, because I finally have the whole story. Sam Pashley is prepared to tell it to me himself, and one day I might be ready to listen, but for now I have it from Erin. I know what happened to my sister in the moments before she died.

I've seen Erin once since she's been out of hospital. We met at the beach with our dogs for distraction, somewhere we could go where we didn't need to look at each other's faces when the pain between us became too much to bear.

I asked her to tell me the whole story. I needed to hear all of it. When she finished, I said, "Lily never needed to die." Of course I knew that already, but to hear how it happened made it so heartachingly raw.

We walked along the stony beach in silence for a while, both of us most likely grappling with the things we wanted to say.

I wanted to ask her if she ever regretted not saying she knew it was me who'd hit her. Maybe I just wanted to know for sure she was never going to say she'd remembered. Part of me thought that I shouldn't bring it up, in case I was wrong and she really didn't know.

But deep down I felt sure this wasn't the case. And so eventually I asked her, "Do you regret not admitting you knew it was me?"

Erin didn't answer for a moment as she considered the question, and I was grateful for that, because when she spoke, it was with the honesty I wanted. "Some days I do," she admitted. "I don't like having secrets. I feel like there have been far too many of them." No one has been convicted of Erin's hit-and-run. DI Clayton, who was in charge of the case, had to finally concede that it was a random accident and not connected to anything else. It appeared to jar with her that it was a coincidence, but she had no other evidence.

"But," Erin went on, "I then remember why I made the decision. I don't want to cause any more pain to anyone," she said. "I played a part in your family's suffering, even if I couldn't help it. I don't want to create any more."

She said it so simply. She made her decision, and I will be grateful to her forever for that. But it isn't so simple for me. I have it hanging over me again, another cloud that I can't address because I can't talk to anyone but Richard about it. But I also have to accept that it's what I deserve.

Richard. My saviour. I turn around in my room in the Cliff House to find him slowly packing up books around the photo of me and Lily. He's still here with me. He could have walked away after he discovered the truth, but I know he never will. Richard loves me with all his heart, and I know that when you love someone that much, you never let them go.

"Thank you," I say to him as I go over to help.

"Always," he tells me.

ACKNOWLEDGMENTS

T HE IDEA FOR writing about a therapist came from the wonderful Nelle Andrew, my agent of now over seven years. I love the idea of someone having so much power over their couples, and having played with different stories for a couple of months, I finally came up with what I wanted *For the Last Time* to be. So I hope you all love it.

Thank you to everyone who has brought this book to publication in the US. I am very grateful to the whole team behind it at Crooked Lane and in particular to my editor Melissa Rechter, Thaisheemarie Perez, Matt Martz, Stephanie Manova, Mikaela Bender, Madeline Rathle, Rebecca Nelson, Dulce Botello, and Doug White.

In the UK, thank you to my agency team at RML, including Charlotte Bowerman, Alexandra Cliff, and Rachel Mills.

Congratulations and thanks go to Lynsey Clayton for her generous bid for the Ukraine appeal, and for winning the chance to have her name in the book. I hope you like DI Clayton!

Thanks also to those who have helped me with all the medical and policing parts that I would not have a clue about: my cousin, James Read, who gave me sustained injuries in graphic detail—it really was just what I needed for poor Erin to go through. To Lisa Grubb for your insight into

A&E nursing, thank you for helping me hopefully bring it to life. And to Chris Bradford, as always, for your help with everything criminal. You have been there right from the start through every one of my books, and I am truly grateful for your knowledge and time.

I am so grateful to you, my readers, for picking up my books, for recommending them to others, and for sharing your thoughts online. It always makes my day to hear how much you have enjoyed reading a story that has been so close to me for the last year of writing it.

As always, thank you to my family. Mum, for your constant support and love and for always crying whenever you read a first copy, or a second copy or in fact any copy. I know how proud you are.

To my wonderful husband, John. Here it is, your first dedication that you don't have to share with anyone! I hope you know how grateful I am for the time I have always had to write and the constant pride and enthusiasm you give me. One day I promise I will write a book about an evil, gaslighting actuary as you would like me to.

And to Bethany and Joseph. I already said it in another of my books, but you really are my greatest achievements. Being your mum is what I love most in my life.